ashes in the
outhouse

a texas romance by

Joel B Reed

White Turtle Books

Canby, Minnesota

This is an original work of fiction. No character presented here represents any flesh and blood person, living or dead. The events reported never happened except any major historical events mentioned. Yet, these could have been real people living out real events in the real world as I knew it growing up in western Texas, and this is what makes the storyteller's craft.

The quotation at the end of the Epilogue is taken from John Newton's famous hymn, *Amazing Grace,* first published in 1779. It resides in the public domain.

ISBN: 978-1-993482-26-2

Cover design by Joel B. Reed

White Turtle Books
Canby, Minnesota
WhiteTurtleBooks.com

Early unisex toilet. The moon and crescent symbols on outhouse doors are said to have come down from Colonial times. At that time there were many who could not read. The moon was a symbol for women, while the star designated men.

Coincidence is God's way of remaining anonymous.
Albert Einstein

ONE

Miss Milly

June, 1957. I saw the tall, thin woman smile the way she always did when she passed the old men sitting in the shade of the large live-oak trees in the courthouse square. They were always there, four or five of them, sometimes more, sitting around the square, not saying much. Most of them had a scrap of lumber they were reducing into thin shavings and they weren't in any hurry. Their cutting was sure and smooth from years of whittling and what they admired was the longest, thinnest piece they could shave. Later in the day they would head for the hardware store to sharpen the thin, worn blades of their pocket knives. Once in a while one of them would buy a square plug of hard black chewing tobacco and pass it around. Then they would return to the square to make more tightly curled shavings to stain with tobacco juice. Local folk called them the Spit and Whittle Club.

As the tall woman walked by, every one of the men would smile and tip his hat. "Good morning, Miss Milly," each of them would say and she would greet them all by name. They called her that because it was the polite thing to do in the South back then, even if she was married. Then, when she had passed out of earshot, the oldest man among them would say, "It just don't make no sense how the good Lord matched her up with Oliver Bates."

The others would all nod in agreement. And if the former mayor wasn't among them, the next to oldest would say "I guess He give her Oliver for her cross to bear." The other shavers would nod again and go back to their solemn ritual of making tobacco stained shavings.

That morning I was looking through the bars of my office window when Miss Milly came up the walk to the courthouse and I knew she was coming to see me. The courthouse was a big red building four stories high and the windows and portals were trimmed in light colored limestone. They left room for an elevator when they built the place. Years later they put one in, but when I was first elected you had to walk up some broad, wide steps that led to the main floor. Then you had to go up a wide flight of marble steps to get to the court chambers, and on up another set behind a steel door to get to the jail on the top floor.

Yet, Miss Milly rarely had to climb to the forth story when Ollie was a guest of the county. Nor did she have to mount the outside steps to the main floor. Behind these steps was a cove with four steps down to the lowest floor. That's where my office took up a suite of four rooms behind a frosted glass partition. Next to that there was a large room used for public meetings and prisoner visits on Sunday afternoons.

"Good morning, Miss Milly," the clerk greeted her from behind the high counter that divided the foyer from the main office. I was standing next to the clerk and did the same.

"Good morning, Cheryl," Miss Milly said. "And to you, too, Sheriff. I haven't had a chance to congratulate you on your promotion." There seemed to be quite a bit of warmth in her response to me and I saw the clerk trying not to smile. It was none of her business, but I knew I better be careful or there would be talk.

"Thank you, Miss Milly," I told her. "I really do appreciate your support." Even so, I didn't extend a hand. My clerk was the county telegraph and there was no sense giving the gossip mongers more ammunition. I knew why Miss Milly was there but I asked, anyway. "Is there something we can do for you?"

Miss Milly nodded. I hated the way her smile faded just then. "I'm here for Oliver. I need to pay his fine."

I nodded. "May I have a word with you?" I asked, opening the swinging door at the end of the counter and holding it open for her. She passed close by and I liked the way she smelled. She didn't wear any cologne or perfume, but she smelled clean, like soap and water with a hint of wood smoke and something else.

I led her into one of the inner rooms and closed the door. "Please," I asked, pulling out a chair at the long table in the center of the room.

Once she was set, I took a chair at the nearest end of the table. "I hate to have to tell you this, Miss Milly, I said. "I'm afraid it's going to be more than a fine this time. Oliver's going to have serve time. The judge is going to see him this afternoon after we get him cleaned up, but he's really put out with Oliver after the stunt he pulled."

"What did Oliver do?" she asked. I hated the dread I saw in her cool gray eyes. They were the color of a mourning dove with small flecks of gold.

"There was a fight at Randall's and he broke up the place pretty good. He put Morris Acker in the hospital and then he took off and drove over the judge's yard. I'm afraid he tore up the rose bed. I'm sorry to have to tell you all this. The only thing in his favor is that witnesses say Morris started the fight. They were both pretty drunk."

"I'll be happy to pay the damages," Miss Milly answered. "It may take me a while, but I'm good for it."

I couldn't help but smile. "I know you are, Miss Milly. You're better than the bank, but it's not up to me. The judge is madder than a wet hen about his roses. Oliver's been up on charges too many times before this and I think the judge wants to teach him a lesson. I think he's looking at thirty days and maybe ninety."

Milly Bates nodded. "I understand," she said. "When can I see Oliver?" Her eyes didn't show much but I knew she'd sooner grab a rattlesnake. I think any love she may have had for Oliver was long dead by then.

"Not until tomorrow," I said. "Oliver's still passed out and he's pretty filthy, too. We're going to have to hose him down before he sees the judge."

Miss Milly reached in the sack she was carrying. She took out some well worn coveralls and a clean shirt, then clean socks and underwear. "He'll need this," she said. "I'll catch a ride in tomorrow afternoon."

"How are you going to get home?"

Milly Bates smiled. "It's not that far, Sheriff. It's a nice day to walk. It doesn't look like rain."

When she smiled, I saw a bruise on her jaw and I had to push the anger down. "Did Oliver do that to you?" I asked, pointing at the bruise.

"Oh, you know," she answered. "Clumsy me. I must have bumped into something. I'm always doing that. It's nothing."

"If he's mistreating you, Miss Milly...." It's good Oliver Bates wasn't in my gun sights just then. I don't abide raising a hand against a women. I know some folks think it's a husband's right, but they're dead wrong.

"No, Sheriff, please. It's all right. It's nothing. It will be gone tomorrow."

Right, I thought. I might not have noticed the bruise but I was looking for it. Someone had come to me to talk about it a couple of weeks before. She was a friend of Miss Milly who worked as a nurse at the hospital. She pointed out to me how Milly Bates never seemed to have any "accidents" when Ollie was incarcerated.

"All you have to do is file a complaint, Miss Milly." I told her. "We'll take care of the rest of it."

"No, Sheriff. That would just make things worse. It's all right. Oliver doesn't mean anything by it. It's the drink, you know. When he's not drinking he's a different man."

"We can keep him from hurting you, but not if you won't let us." There was no response but a shake of her head. I looked at her for a bit, then let it go. "All right. But I am going to give you a ride home."

Milly Bates tried to object, but I held up a hand and felt myself smile. "You're not the only one who can be stubborn, Miss Milly. I'm going to give you a ride home and I'm going to come and pick you up tomorrow. That's all there is to it. You need to pick up anything while you're in town?"

"You don't want to cause talk, Sheriff," she tried to argue but I could see her heart wasn't in it.

"There's always going to be talk," I said, grinning like a fool. When I did, Miss Milly blushed. "It's all right," I told her. "I need to see a couple of your neighbors, anyway."

Miss Milly looked at me intently. Her face was grave and it felt like those beautiful gray eyes could see right through me. Then she smiled and reached out her hand and put it on mine. I never felt anything that wonderful and I felt a little sad when she squeezed my hand and let go. "You're a good man, John Stone. Don't ever think that I don't appreciate what you do for me." I think she started to say more but changed her mind. "I accept the ride. Let me pick up a few things at the store and meet you back here in an hour."

"I could pick you up there."

That was the first time I ever heard her laugh, and I was surprised how soft and intimate it was. It sounded like sweet music and wasn't any louder than a gentle sneeze. "You really think that's wise?" she asked quietly, looking toward the door to the outer office. "Cheryl goes to fix lunch for Fred, doesn't she?" I nodded. "I'll be back here at ten minutes past twelve," she said.

I walked Miss Milly out and went into my office. I sat there a minute or two, then used the phone to call the jail. The jailer told me Oliver was still passed out and I called the judge. He agreed it would be better to see Oliver the next day and I called Cheryl into my office. I told her what was going on with Ollie. "I think I'll run out to Neville's this afternoon," I said. "I need to talk to him about some missing cattle. If anyone asks, just tell them I'm out on a call. I don't want Neville to know I'm coming."

"You want me to call Buzz to go with you?" she asked. Buzz Wilson was my part-time deputy. He earned most of his living as a parts manager at the local Ford house and probably got paid better than I did. I was lucky to have him. He had served as a military policeman and needed the extra income. He and his wife were saving to build a house and his father-in-law didn't pay that well.

"No, Charlie told me Buzz has missed too much work lately. I'll be all right. If I need help, I'll deputize Neville." I smiled when I said this but Cheryl didn't understand I was joking.

"Neville? That's like hiring the fox to guard the henhouse." Cheryl snorted. Neville Yates was the biggest crook in the county. Most of his income came from bootlegging, and I knew for a fact he was a receiver for stolen goods. He tried to sell me a hot pistol once before I became a deputy. Even his kinfolk didn't trust him.

No, I thought. It would be like using a thief to catch a thief.

While it couldn't hurt for Neville to think I'm a fool, I had no intention of deputizing him. "You're absolutely right, Cheryl," I told her, keeping my voice and face serious. "I was only teasing but I want to talk to him today. I don't think it will come to needing a deputy." It crossed my mind yet again that my clerk didn't have much sense of humor. On the other hand, I knew it wasn't her fault. She was raised that way.

I told Cheryl I needed to finish up some paperwork and not to disturb me unless it was urgent and went into my office and closed the door. Yet, when I sat down at my desk and got out the file I needed, I didn't get started right away. I sat there for a while thinking about when I first met Milly Bates and what I knew about her.

Oddly enough, we met in church. Back then you needed to be something in Texas if you wanted to be accepted in the community and Dan Jenkins, the sheriff who hired me, told me it would be good to find a church. "I don't give a damn which one you choose, Johnny," he told me. "Folks won't trust you until they can hang a label on you, so pick one and join up. It's a damned good source of information about what's going on in the county."

"Which one do you belong to?" I asked. I've always been a free thinker and it really didn't matter to me what the preacher said or what anyone else believed.

"I go to the First Baptist," Dan told me. "It's the biggest church around and a lot of the upper crust go there. They don't believe in drinking, but a lot of them do it, anyway. But God help you if you're caught dancing!"

The sheriff laughed. "You know why Baptists don't make babies standing up?" I shook my head and he said, "Someone might see them and think they're dancing!"

I laughed. It was an old one I hadn't heard in a while. "Then that's where I'll go," I told him. "What do I have to do to join?"

"It might be better if you went to a different church, John. It would give us a wider base of support."

"All right, then, which one is the second biggest?"

The sheriff grinned at that. "You're going to do all right around here, Johnny. The First Methodist is almost as big and the rest of the upper crust go there. One word of advice."

"What's that, sir?"

"When you go fishing, never take just one Baptist with you. Always take two."

I had heard this before but I asked, anyway, "Why's that?"

"One will drink all the beer."

The next Sunday I wound up at the Methodist Church. It was the church where I grew up and I liked it. The people were friendly and the preacher was a young man not long out of seminary. His sermon was well thought out and he didn't read it. He delivered it without notes but with conviction, like he was speaking from the heart about his own spiritual journey. He was also concise and to the point and he only talked for about twelve minutes. As my daddy used to say, the mind can only absorb what the butt can endure.

I also enjoyed the music. They were having a special event that day and the church had a very good choir. One of the ladies caught my attention and it didn't take me long to learn her name. Nor did I have to ask. After the service I heard a couple of ladies talking about a woman in the nursing home that needed something, and one of them said, "Let's ask Miss Milly. She'd know."

Sure enough, she pointed to the lovely tall lady I'd noticed in the choir. For a while I thought she was single or a widow. She didn't wear a wedding band and I was thinking about asking her out. Then I overheard someone talking about something her husband had done. When I asked the sheriff about him, he told me Oliver Bates was the worst drunk in the county.

"Some of the things he's done, I don't know why someone hasn't shot him. Yet," he added. "I think it's mostly because he ain't worth the price of a bullet."

One of the things I noticed early in life is how human beings always seem to want what they can't have. It took me by surprise just how much this applied to me when it came to Milly Bates. When I went back to church the following Sunday and watched the choir sing, I was struck by how beautiful she looked. She was tall and slender, almost my height, with her dark hair pulled back in a French braid, and when she sang a solo, it was like she was pouring out her soul. Her face was radiant, almost like a bride, and I don't think she was singing for the congregation. She was singing like a mockingbird sings, because she had all this wonderful music inside her she needed to let out.

Still, when she sang, I felt a well of sadness building up inside me, even though she sang with obvious joy. It was a terrible sadness that reminded me how empty my life was without someone like her to grace it. I thought what a waste it was for a woman this wonderful to be coupled with a man like Oliver Bates.

I was listening and thinking so deep I wasn't aware of the tears that ran down my cheek. Then the elderly lady next to me handed me a tissue when Miss Milly was done. "It's beautiful, ain't it, Deputy? She sings like an angel. It's such a shame."

I couldn't have agreed more. I left the church feeling both uplifted and terribly sad. Oddly enough, Miss Milly saw me walking out. Years later she told me I looked like I'd lost my very best friend. I told her it was for a best friend I never had. It was a stupid thing to say, but she seemed to understand.

❧

I must have sat there fifteen minutes before I shook myself away from my sad thoughts and plunged into my paperwork. I finished it off and was waiting for Miss Milly when she showed up promptly at nine minutes past twelve. She was carrying a small paper sack. "I'm ready," she told me. "Are you sure about this? We will probably be seen. I don't want to start any talk."

"I guess I could cuff you," I answered. "That would really give them something to talk about."

Miss Milly laughed nervously, as if she thought I was serious. Seeing me unlock the gun rack and take down a shotgun, she asked, "Are you expecting trouble, Sheriff?"

"No, I'm just being a good Scout," I told her. Seeing her confusion, I added, "That's the Boy Scout motto," I explained. "'Be Prepared.'"

"Of course," she answered, laughing. "How silly of me. And giving me a ride home is your good deed for the day."

"No," I said lightly. "It's an honor." Seeing her flush, I wanted to bite my tongue. What was the matter with me? "I beg your pardon," I told her. "That didn't come out right."

Once again, her wonderful grey eyes searched mine. "You must never apologize for being a gentleman, John Stone," she assured me. "Thank you for the compliment. I'm just not used to it. Are we ready to go?"

Neither of us said a word until we were out of town. Once we were over the bridge, Miss Milly turned toward me. "Tell me about yourself, Sheriff. I know you grew up here but you haven't lived here all your life. What did you do before you were a deputy?"

"After graduation, I spent the summer following the grain harvest and spent the next four years at the University. I had to work my way through, so I didn't have much time for anything else. Then I joined the Coast Guard and found out I liked law enforcement more than I did boats. I was lucky they let me serve most of my time on shore. Sea duty always made me sick as a dog. That's about it."

Miss Milly looked at me. "It's a long way from the Coast Guard to Rutherford County, John," she pointed out. "How did you get from there to here?"

I shrugged, wondering what prompted her to use my given name. Yet, I liked it. "Well, I made high grades in college, Miss Milly. I studied anthropology with a minor in Spanish, and that, along with my record in the Coast Guard, got me in the West Virginia State Police Academy. They had a reputation for being the best in the country."

I slowed for a stray cow in the road. "Then I worked with them – West Virginia – for a few years until I got tired of the East Coast. It was way too crowded and things were a little too organized. Then I heard about a deputy's job opening up here and I applied. Dan Jenkins almost didn't hire me. He told me I was too qualified. Said I wouldn't last a year. Someone else would hire me away. I told him that wouldn't happen. I also pointed out I grew up here and knew all the players, and hiring someone as well trained as me at the pay they offered would score him points with the county commissioners. I think you probably know the rest. How about you?"

"Oh, I'm not that interesting," she answered.

"You are to me," I told her. The way she looked at me told me I just stepped in a fresh cow pie. "I apologize, Miss Milly," I told her. "I didn't mean that in any improper way."

She laughed then, the first time I'd ever seen her laugh like that. "You just surprised me, John. Why don't you call me Milly, at least when we're not around other people?" She thought for a minute. "Well, I didn't grow up here. I grew up in Callahan County and you must have been gone by the time we moved here. My mother owned a house in town and my daddy worked road construction. He was a heavy machine operator and sometimes in the summer we'd go to where he was working and stay a while. He did a lot of road work in Colorado and Wyoming, and I just loved it up there."

She smiled when she told me this, but it faded as she went on. "Then my mama died when I was sixteen, and my daddy kind of fell to pieces. I was the oldest so I had to take care of the younger ones. Poor daddy started drinking heavily and we went through some hard times. I stayed on until the youngest was out of school. After that, I got married and ended up here in Rutherford County." As she spoke, she became more and more sad, and when she was done, she sat quietly. Her eyes turned inward on her grief.

I wanted to ask how she got tangled up with Oliver Bates but held my peace. The last thing I wanted to do was bring up painful memory. Then she looked at me and it was like she was read my mind. "I know you want to ask how I met Oliver, John. I don't mind your knowing but that needs to wait for another time."

"Of course, Miss...," I started to say but caught myself. "Of course, Milly. I didn't mean to pry."

"You didn't, John," she smiled. "I started it and turn about is fair play." I really liked the way she said my name. It was very intimate but not improper.

We talked about other things, but I can't remember what. What I do remember is enjoying the conversation. When we arrived at their place, I walked around the car and opened the door for her. "You're such a gentleman, John," she said, offering her hand. I reached out and she took my hand in both of hers, pulling herself out of the car. "Thank you 'til you're better paid," she said, smiling. She seemed reluctant to let go of my hand and I wasn't in any hurry for her to do so. "I enjoyed the company."

"You're more than welcome," I answered. "It was my pleasure. I'll be here to get you about noon tomorrow."

"I'll be waiting," she said, smiling. "I'll have us a nice lunch ready." She reached up and touched my cheek. Her touch was wonderfully soft and it was all I could do not to take her in my arms.

I know she saw this in my eyes, the desire, the struggle, the sad resolve. "You're an honorable man, John Stone. Thank you for your restraint."

"That's by choice, Milly," I answered. "Not by inclination. I beg your pardon if I'm speaking too plainly."

She was still holding my hand and ignored my apology. "Well, how can there be virtue without temptation? Don't put me on a pedestal, John. I'm a sinner just like everyone else. It's good that one of us is strong, isn't it?"

She released my hand, reluctantly, I thought. I tipped my hat and she smiled. Then I got out of there before I did something rash. She was still standing there looking after me when the road curved and I lost sight of her in the dust.

TWO

Arraignment

I was at loose ends after I got back to town that afternoon. When I got back to the office there was a note on my desk from Cheryl. It told me she had left early for a beauty shop appointment and that Tony Schmidt, the owner of Randall's, had called. He had added up the damages Oliver and Morris had done to his place and was ready to make a written statement.

I called to make sure Tony was still at work and he laughed when I asked how late he would be open. "Are you joshing me, Sheriff?" he asked. "It's Wednesday night. We've got a tournament this week followed by a grudge match between old man Carter and Billy Simpson. I'll be lucky to be out of here by midnight."

I knew Tom Carter was the reigning domino champ in the surrounding ten counties and that Billy Simpson was an up and coming contender. There would be men coming in from all over to watch and a good many of them would be going out to their trucks for a nip all evening. This meant I needed to be there to keep order.

People up north don't understand our Southern passion for five-count dominoes. The only thing I know that rivals it is our obsession with friday-night football and hard-shelled religion. A historian once told me Southern domino playing goes back to frontier days when drinking, dancing, and card playing were all associated with saloons. Disputes over card games were often settled with guns and knives, and people often died. So by the time the country became settled and civilized, these things were considered sinful. Preachers spoke out against the evils of such things from the pulpit and laws were passed. Yet, dominoes was considered a respectable form entertainment, of passing time and fending off boredom.

I thanked Tony for reminding me and told him I'd stop by

in the next hour to pick up the damage report and take his statement. I'd need both when Oliver was arraigned the next day. Judge White would be expecting them and he was a stickler for having things set down in black and white. He took pride in the fact that none of his decisions had ever been reversed. Not many judges could say that.

I grabbed a burger and a malt at the drive-in before I went to Randall's. I might not have a chance later on and it looked like a long evening. There were a number of kids from high school there, laughing and talking loud enough to be heard over the jukebox playing in the corner. It was playing the new music, what they called rock and roll, and the volume was turned up. I wondered why they spent their money for music they liked and then didn't listen to it.

What I was thinking must have been written across my face because a woman at the next table passed me a note. I recognized her from church and the note read, "Need ear plugs, Sheriff?" I smiled at her and nodded. I knew she was a widow, as was her companion, and both of them were at least ten years older than I was. I also knew that they were both interested in me as a man and I thought about moving over to their table. That would give the rumor mongers something to talk about.

Just then the jukebox finished its last number and fell silent. Conversation in the dining room died down for a couple of minutes before two of the kids wandered over to feed the machine. They took their time deliberating the choices and I decided to finish my malt in the cruiser.

"That's too loud for this guy," I told the widows, wiggling a finger in my ear. "You ladies have a good evening."

When I got outside and into the cruiser I could still hear the band playing. Even with the windows up I could still understand the words they were singing. I wondered why it needed to be so loud. I'd run into this in the service, too, and the only thing I could figure is that a lot of people are afraid of silence. They have to fill it with noise to feel safe. Not that they would admit it.

Things were quiet when I got to Randall's, for which I was grateful. The only sounds came from the soft clicks of the bones being handled by several old men playing forty-two. They were at a couple of tables off to one side and most of them had a tall paper sack sitting on the floor by their chair. Every once in a while each of them would pick up his sack and unscrew the cap of a bottle inside. Then they would take a sip or two.

Nor was this illegal, at least, not in my understanding of the law. Public consumption of intoxicating spirits was illegal but I had no way of knowing what was in any given sack. So long as they minded their manners, I didn't care what they were sipping. It might be white lightning or it could be ice tea or soda pop. It wasn't my business unless things got rowdy, and for these old men, their rowdy days were done.

My business with Tony didn't take long. He had typed up his statement and dated it, and he signed it in my presence. I witnessed his signature, and we did it again for the list of damages. "Damn," I said, looking at the sheet of damages. "Morris and Ollie really busted up the place. I didn't realize it was so bad."

Tony nodded. "Yeah, I had to go to clear Ft. Worth to replace four tables and six chairs. I was lucky they didn't break the mirror behind the soda counter, too."

I nodded and looked over Tony's statement. "This looks good but why don't you just tell me how it happened."

"Well, they were both drunk when they got here. I didn't see them come in or I'd have bounced them right out. When I saw them at the soda counter I could tell they were woozy. So I told them to hit the road. Morris took offense and swung at me but I ducked. He ended up hitting Ollie in the jaw and that made Ollie mad. So he knocked Morris down and Morris come up swinging a chair. Ollie jumped back and it hit one of the tables. It was lucky nobody was sitting there because it busted the table right in two. Then Ollie grabbed a chair and busted it over Morris' head and he damn near killed him. Morris was so drunk it didn't slow him down a bit and he grabbed another chair and swung it."

Tony paused and shook his head. "I've never seen anything like it, Sheriff. Oliver had another chair by then and was swinging it, too. When they hit they both broke up, but it threw Morris off balance. He landed on another table and busted it flat. Then they started a shoving match that smashed two more tables, and a couple more chairs got broke when two men fell over them trying to get out of the way. Then Morris fell down, bleeding from the head and Ollie took off. About then the night watchman showed up and he carried Morris to the hospital. When he got him there, the doctor said Morris had a concussion, a busted wrist, and a couple of busted ribs. He said he didn't know how Morris lived through it, either."

I asked a few more questions but Tony didn't have much to add. I thanked him for getting the information and asked if he wanted to press charges against Morris and Oliver. "I don't know," he told me. "I hate to make trouble for them. I've been drunk and done some stupid things, too. I think if they pay the damages it will be enough."

"I notice you didn't list gas to take you to Ft. Worth and back," I said. "Or the time it took you to make the trip. We can add it in if you want. It's legitimate."

"I don't know," he said. "I don't think folks around here would like that. I've got to make a living."

I nodded. I knew what he was saying. The good folk of Live Oak would understand a bill to replace the furniture. That was fair and square. Adding freight and labor might be seen as greedy. Tony was telling me the extra money wasn't worth the risk of public disapproval. He wasn't from Rutherford County. As an outsider he had to live with these people to make a living. I was sure that was why he didn't want to press charges, either. Oliver and Morris might be drunken bums, but the were our drunken bums. It was up to us to take care of the problem, not some outsider.

I thanked Tony for his efforts and took the documents he had signed out to the cruiser. I locked them in the evidence safe in the trunk and then drove around a couple of roads I hadn't patrolled for a while. I was back in town by nine and went back to Randall's. The parking lot was full by then so I parked in Charlie's used car lot across the street. Charlie was just locking up when I got out of the cruiser and he laughed when I asked him not to sell it out from under me.

Buzz was with Charlie and asked if I wanted him to work the

domino tournament. "No, but thanks for asking," I told him. "I think Claude and I can handle it." Claude was the retired Texas Ranger the city paid to be their night watchman. "How come you guys are working so late?"

Charlie shook his head. "Quarterly inventory," he told me. "It's time to pay taxes and order more parts."

I offered my condolences and both men laughed. Then Buzz walked across the street with me. "I need to get home," he said. "I'm just going to stick my head in and watch a while. Some of these guys are really good."

"Then get your badge and gun belt out of the car," I told him. "I can't put you on the clock but it will help you get a good spot."

※

It was well past ten the next morning before the jailer and I got Oliver Bates halfway presentable and then down to the courtroom. He was still feeling the effects of the load he'd taken on and woke up screaming about the black widow spiders all over his cell walls. He was the only one who could see them and it was scaring the hell out of two other inmates, and the jailer, as well. The city night watchman had thrown them in the clink for disturbing the peace the night before, jailing them mostly so they wouldn't hurt themselves or someone else driving home. Being dragged out of a drunken stupor by Oliver's screams must have been quite a shock.

I released one of the inmates and told him to get down to the hospital and bring a doctor. He was back in fifteen minutes with the new man in town, Dr. Winston Pettigrew. He took one look at Oliver and took a small bottle of clear liquid out of his baby bag. That's what they used to call the little black bags doctors used for house calls. He waved the bottle under Oliver's nose and then told Oliver to drink as much of it as he could. It looked like it might hold a quarter cup.

When he drank this, Oliver stiffened up like he'd touched a live wire but it calmed him down right away. I caught the odd smell of what was in the bottle. "That smells like white lightning, Doctor," I said. "Vinegar, too."

"That's about what it is," the doctor answered. "It's

paraldehyde mixed with pure ethanol, drinking alcohol. It's to keep the poor man from going into convulsions."

"Well, it sure settled him down," I said. "How long does it last? He's supposed to be in court at ten."

The doctor looked at his wristwatch. "It should carry him through that. You might want to warn the judge, though. Mr. Bates may not be very responsive. I'll leave another bottle you can give him, if need be, but vodka or any kind of distilled liquor will work almost as well at this point."

"You better give me the bottle. It wouldn't look good if we had to give him a drink from a liquor bottle in court."

The doctor nodded and smiled. "There is that. Keep a close eye on him if you have to jail him. He's a pretty sick man. You want me to admit him to the hospital, Sheriff? We can dry him out there."

I shook my head. "No, not unless the judge orders it. I'm not sure it would do much good, either. He'll be drunk again thirty minutes after we release him."

"I take it you've dealt with him before?"

"Oh, yeah. He's been in jail five times already this year. It's always for drunk and disorderly."

There must have been something in my voice because the doctor said, "Look, Sheriff, he's a sick man. Hate the disease, not the man."

I looked the doctor square in the eye. "It's hard to separate them out, Dr. Pettigrew. Oliver beats his wife when he gets drunk and I don't think I've ever seen him sober. Not since we were kids and maybe not then."

"Even as a child?" It was clear the good doctor was having a hard time believing me.

"Even then, doctor. His dad was a drunk, too. He started out as a moonshiner, just like Oliver's granddaddy. Liquor was always handy."

"I was told this was a dry county."

"It is," I assured him. "The Baptists and the bootleggers like to keep it that way." The doctor just shook his head and left.

Thing went a lot smoother after that. Once we got Oliver

up to the courtroom, I told the clerk I needed to see the judge before he was arraigned. This was unusual but he agreed to tell the judge since it was a medical problem. Unfortunately, the judge was running late that morning and we had to wait almost an hour.

The judge was surprised to see me but he listened carefully while I told him what happened at the jail. "The man seems to be trying to drink himself to death," he said. "There's no question in my mind that he's an alcoholic." He shook his head. "The American Medical Association claims it's a disease, some kind of compulsion to drink the alcoholic can't control. Trouble is, the law doesn't make that distinction and there doesn't seem to be an effective treatment, either. Any thoughts, Sheriff?"

I told him what Dr. Pettigrew said about drying him out so he didn't go back into DTs and the judge nodded. I also warned him that Oliver might smell from the paraldehyde the doctor gave him, and the judge chuckled. "You know, the worst part of my job isn't seeing humanity at its worst. It's smelling it."

The hearing itself didn't take long at all. Thank God Oliver didn't go into DTs or a convulsion, either. He did smell like a distillery but that was partly medication. The Honorable David Allen White did take judicial notice of his earlier episode of DTs for the record, and once Oliver plead guilty, he ordered him to receive medical treatment before serving ninety days in jail. He also ordered Oliver to pay for the hospital stay and to make restitution for the damages he had done before he hit the tree. Then the judge went on to order Oliver to be chained to his bed for the duration of his hospital stay and to have no visitors except clergy, lawmen, and officers of the court.

I don't know if Oliver understood any of this or not. It seemed like he was having trouble keeping his eyes open but he was docile enough when I transported him to the hospital. Just to be safe, I shackled his feet and cuffed his hands behind him. When we got to his room, I secured him to the bed with a ten-foot chain. I also made sure that the door could only be opened by a key, inside and out, and I had them empty the room completely except for the bed.

By the time we got done with Oliver, it was almost one. The

Bates' phone was on a party line so I didn't try to call. That would be like publishing what I had to say on the front page of the newspaper. I just took off for the Bates' place at a good clip hoping Miss Milly wouldn't be too offended.

I need not have worried. Milly greeted me warmly at the door and just shook her head when I told her what had gone on. "I thought something must have happened," she said. "It's good that Oliver has medical attention. Since he can't have visitors until he's in jail, I won't need to visit him." She brushed back a wisp of hair and I realized she was wearing a dress I'd never seen. Even though it was June and quite warm, she was wearing long sleeves buttoned at the wrist.

"That's a pretty dress," I told her. "It looks Sunday-go-to-meeting."

She smiled. "That's exactly what it is, John. It's not every day that the high sheriff comes to dine."

"Would I be out of line observing that it's the lady who makes the dress look good?" I asked.

"You might," she answered, looking around. "But there doesn't seem to be anyone here but us. I'm certainly not offended."

We stood there a moment, looking at each other and neither of us knowing what to do next. "You must be hungry," she murmured at last. "Our lunch is in the ice box and it won't take a minute to serve."

The food may not have taken long to serve, but Milly had gone all out preparing it. First we ate a garden salad with spinach and dandelion leaves combined with vine ripe cherry tomatoes. This was followed with fresh cornbread, black-eyed peas, early squash, and fresh baked chicken. All served with dark iced tea and rhubarb cobbler for dessert.

"Gracious!" I said when we were done. "You're going to have to roll me out to my car."

"It's your reward for having to put up with Oliver drunk," she told me, smiling sweetly to take any rancor out of the words. "Bring your tea and let's sit out in the shade."

We sat there for a while in pleasant silence before she spoke. "So, John Stone, tell me more about yourself. Have you ever been married?"

I shrugged. "No. There were two or three near misses."

"Two or three? Can't you remember?" There was a playful edge to her words, almost challenging.

"Well, one of them wasn't exactly available," I answered.

"So she was married?" Her tone was still playful, but I knew this was important to her.

"Yes," I told her simply. "I was still in the Coast Guard and she was a Navy wife. Her husband was always off to sea and I didn't know she was married until we were...involved."

"Until you were lovers," Milly said simply. She must have sensed my discomfort for she reached out and touched my arm, giving it a gentle squeeze. "Don't be upset, John. I'm not here to judge you. Just don't lie to me. I take it this wasn't a pleasant experience?"

"It was wonderful at first. Then I found out and I felt betrayed. That seems funny but I did. I mean, I was the one who was...."

"Taking her to bed," Milly said softly. "Yet, you felt like you were the one being betrayed." She looked at me gravely. "Don't misjudge me, John Stone. I'm a real woman, not a prude. I have real desires and real needs and I know all the blue words. I just save them for special occasions." She smiled sweetly to make the point. "I understand why you felt betrayed, but I also understand why she took you into her bed, despite being married."

I knew very clearly what Milly was saying. All I had to do was reach out and we would spend the afternoon in one another's arms. "I really feel uncomfortable with this, Milly," I told her.

"I know you do, John. You're very sweet and very honorable. I hope my candor hasn't ruined our friendship."

"No, it hasn't. I'm just surprised."

"Then let's talk about other things. What about the other two?"

"They were both very sweet and very intelligent young women," I told her. "What they wanted in life turned out to be different from what I wanted."

"That's interesting. How so?"

"It was like they wanted everything in their life to be nailed down and on a schedule. They even knew what color they wanted to paint their house, what kind they wanted it to be, and what they wanted for furniture. They weren't comfortable with just letting things happen as they naturally did. It didn't leave much room for surprises."

Milly nodded. "No, it wouldn't, good or bad. That's very sad."

I nodded. "Yes. They were so afraid of all the bad things that might happen. It shut the door on a lot of good things that can happen, too."

"Like us," Milly murmured. I didn't know quite how to take that. Seeing the question in my eyes, she went on. "Think about your job. Think about how things are for me. Neither of us knows what's going to happen next. So we live life as it happens and enjoy it as we can."

Suddenly Milly looked embarrassed. "I'm afraid I have a confession to make, John Stone. I hope it doesn't offend you but I'm glad Oliver got drunk and ran over the judge's bushes. That made this wonderful afternoon possible. I'm only sorry we can't make it perfect." She held up her hands. "No, I take that back. This afternoon is perfect just the way it is. It has to be. I don't want to ruin it."

We were quiet for a while. Then we talked for a good while longer. One thing I learned was that Milly was seven years younger than I am. I had always thought of her as older and told her so. She was only thirty-one.

"It's the gray hair," she said, smiling and touching her temple. "It runs in my family. We turn gray early, especially the women. I guess I could color it. They have all kinds of things now, but who would I color it for?" What she left unsaid was that Oliver would never notice.

"I think it's good the way it is, Milly. I think raising a family at sixteen had a lot to do with it, too. You've earned every one of those gray hairs. Coloring them would be like gilding the lily."

"My goodness, John Paul Stone," she said sweetly. "You're not only a gentleman, but a poet, too." I was surprised she knew my middle name. I usually went by JP Stone or John P.

"That's the first time I've been accused of that," I laughed.

"Well, it's certainly no sin. Do you like poetry?"

"You mean other than country songs? I'm afraid I haven't been terribly exposed. What's your favorite poem?"

It was an innocent question but she flushed and I felt like a fool, yet not knowing why. "I'm afraid I need to ask you to wait for that answer," she told me. "I can tell you I'm quite fond of Elizabeth Barrett Browning. Emily Dickinson, too, especially the poem that starts with 'Hope.'"

"I'll have to look them up," I told her. "About all I'm really familiar with are a couple of poems my dad used to read me for a bedtime story. They were about the gold rush in Alaska."

Milly laughed. "Robert Service! I suppose your favorite was 'The Cremation of Sam McGee,'" she laughed.

"Yes! How did you know?"

"I used to read it to my brothers. It was their favorite, too."

I looked at Milly and was surprised. Her face looked much younger than when I first came. Once again I was tempted to take her in my arms and it was all I could do to fight it down. "Milly," I said softly. "I think I better go now."

She looked in my eyes, surprised. Then she nodded. "Yes, perhaps you better. I'm sorry, John. I didn't set out to lead you astray. It's been a wonderful afternoon." Then she surprised me again, leaning forward quickly and kissing me on the cheek. "Don't be a stranger," she said.

It was all I could do to keep from turning the car back as I drove toward town. Then I came to the road leading to Neville Pierce's place and as I turned I saw Clint Farley's truck headed my way from town. When I did I was glad I'd left when I did. Clint is the kindest man you ever want to meet, but he can't keep his mouth shut. There is no way he could have failed to see the county car parked at the Bates', and if he had, it would be all over the county by the time I got back to town. He lives just a couple of miles down the road from the Bates, and his wife was as bad about running off at the mouth as he was.

This meant I would have to be careful when I came calling on Milly. Nor did I realize that I intended to see her again until that moment I thought "when" and not "if." There was no question in my mind how I felt for her. Nor was there any doubt that she had feelings for me, too. I had no idea why, but

I was damned glad she did. Nor did I care that she was legally a married woman. To my way of thinking, her marriage to Oliver Bates was a sham.

A week later I asked the librarian if she had any poems by Elizabeth Browning or Emily Dickinson. This surprised her and she dug out an anthology for me. I know she wanted to know why I was interested but she didn't say anything. "Somebody told me they were worth reading," I said. "There was something I saw on a gravestone. Something about Hope."

"Oh, that's Emily Dickinson," she said. "Elizabeth Browning's most famous poem was about love. Didn't you read them in school? I thought you went to college."

I shrugged. "The names are familiar, so we must have covered them in English. There's been a lot of water under the bridge since then."

"Tell me about it," she said. "You want to check this out? It has poems by Robert Frost and Walt Whitman, too."

"Let me look at it first," I said. "It might not be my cup of tea." The librarian laughed and told me to let her know.

Ten minutes later I left the library without the anthology. Seeing Elizabeth Browning's most famous poem told me what I needed to know. I was sure it must be Milly's favorite, the one she didn't want to mention. Yet, knowing this didn't help. The whole situation was a recipe for disaster and I felt a cloud of melancholy settling over me, one that was hard to shake it off. I thought about getting drunk, but I knew that wouldn't help, either. I didn't want to lower myself to Oliver Bates' level, either. So I headed for the house and spent the rest of the afternoon splitting firewood until I could barely stand. The next day my whole body ached and my hands were sore as a boil, but I felt better. The dark cloud was gone and I had plenty of firewood to last me through the winter.

THREE

A Rainy Day

The next time I saw Milly Bates was ten days after she fed me lunch. I called to let her know Oliver was out of the hospital and was allowed to have visitors. It was raining that day and I offered to pick her up if she needed a ride.

"Thank you, Sheriff. That would be very kind. I'll carry him some fresh clothes."

"I'm sure his cell mates will be obliged," I said and I heard a man's chuckle. The neighbors were obviously listening in and I decided to rub their noses in it. "I'm surprised none of your neighbors has offered to bring you," I said.

"Oh, they have but I doubt anyone is going into town in this weather," she answered. "The roads must be pretty bad. They wouldn't want to get stuck. I hope you don't, Sheriff."

"I'll drive the county jeep," I told her. After the war, the Army had donated a couple of surplus trucks. One of these was the military version of a Dodge Power Wagon with cleated tires and four-wheel drive. The ride was rough as a cob but it could go just about anywhere, and it had a winch in case we mired to the hubs. "We may get a little muddy but we'll get there."

As it turned out, the roads weren't that bad at all. The ride was still rough but I took it slow and easy coming to town. That was mostly to stretch the time we had together and at one point we hit a pothole that bounced Milly clear over next to me. Without thinking, I stopped and put an arm around her. She took her time pulling back. "My goodness, John," she whispered, her eyes less than six inches from mine. "I don't suppose we could do that again, could we?" Her hand was on my leg and she squeezed it gently.

I raised my hand to touch her face but it brushed her breast and her eyes grew wide. "I beg your pardon," I said, pulling back. "I didn't mean to do that."

"Oh," she said, laughing at my discomfort. "I thought you were having your way with me. Shoot!"

Just then I saw a gleam of headlights through the rain. "There's someone coming," I told her and she scurried back to the other side of the seat. I started moving again and eased ahead.

The headlights turned out to be someone coming home from town and they turned off before we reached them. After we passed them, she reached out her hand and I took it. "This is so romantic," Milly said. "Driving in the rain and holding hands like two young folk."

"We are two young folk," I reminded her. "Most of the county is a good bit older than us. We're also playing with fire, Milly."

"I know," she replied. "Only, I don't care. You don't understand how much I missed you these last eleven days. I thought about you all the time." Seeing my surprise, she said, "I told you I was a sinner, John. It was all I could do to keep my hands off you when I got in the truck. I hope that doesn't shock you, but it's true."

"It doesn't shock me, Milly, but we need to talk about some things. I don't want to do anything to hurt you."

"My goodness, John," she said playfully. "You sound so serious." Seeing the look on my face, she said, "All right, then. I'll behave. At least, I will for now. Just being around you gets me all...." She sighed and we rode the rest of the way into town in silence.

The rain let up after we got to town. Milly had some sewing to deliver after she was done visiting with Oliver and I had a few things to attend around the office. A couple of complaints had come in that morning about cattle on the road and I called around to find out whose they were. I didn't have much luck getting in touch with anyone, so I headed to the feed store. Sure enough, I was able to talk to one of the farmers I called, but he assured me he had moved all his cattle to the back pasture the week before. He also told me where he noticed a fence sagging along the road, and it belonged to one of the people I'd not been able to reach.

Milly was waiting for me when I got back to the office, and

I told Cheryl I was going drop Milly at her place and check on the stray cattle. "I may be away from the radio for a while," I told her. "So don't worry if you can't get me. I'll call in when I get back to the jeep if the radio's working." One of the reasons the old Power Wagon was not used much was because its radio was always going out. It worked all right whenever the radio man looked at it, but the minute it was out of the shop it started acting up. My deputy, Buzz, claimed it was possessed.

Milly was quiet on the way home. When we got to her place, she turned to me and said, "We need to get the sad stuff behind us, John. I think it's time I told you how I came to be married to Oliver. Can you stop back after you're finished with the cattle?"

"Sure, Milly. I don't think it will take that long. You think maybe I should park in the barn?"

She nodded. "That might be a good idea. I hate sneaking around but I don't want to cause talk. You're up for election next year, John. I'd hate it if you lost because of me."

"It would be worth it," I assured her and she began to cry. Yet when I tried to comfort her, she shook her head and ran into the house.

❧

Taking care of the cattle took a lot longer than I thought. It was getting late in the afternoon by the time I could shake loose. The radio in the jeep was being cantankerous, so I borrowed the farmer's phone to call my office. Cheryl was just about to leave for the day and told me that nothing urgent had come up that afternoon.

"I need to check on a couple of other thing while I'm out this way and I may be late getting home."

"What do you need to check?" She asked.

"I'll tell you tomorrow, Cheryl. This is a party line."

I knew that would get folk buzzing, so I asked the farmer, "You had any trouble with road hunters lately, Walt?"

He laughed. "Not likely, John. Folks know I shoot back."

"You need to be careful with that," I warned him. "I'd hate to have to arrest you for killing some damn fool."

"Now, I didn't say I was aiming at them, Sheriff. It works right fine to put a round or two ten or twelve feet over their heads. Makes them shit their pants and what they don't know don't hurt me."

I drove away in a different direction from the Bates' place and circled around to get there. I know a couple of people saw me go by and that was good. Word would go out that I was scouting for road hunters and that might keep them honest for a few days. By the time I got to her house, Milly had supper waiting. Dark clouds had rolled in, making it hard to see, and a soft rain was falling. When I got into the house I could hear it beating gently on her tin roof.

I took off my cap and my rain jacket and hung them by the door. I turned around to greet her and Milly came into my arms and held me close. I could feel her breasts and legs pressing against me and I felt myself begin to respond. I started to say something, but Milly pulled back and kissed me lightly on the lips.

"Milly...." I tried to say but she laid a finger on my lips.

"You need to eat first and then I need to tell you some things. Let's enjoy supper first. I hope you don't mind an omelet. I was out of meat and I didn't want to kill a chicken. There's cobbler for dessert."

The omelet was wonderful and the peach cobbler was even better than the rhubarb. After she served me, Milly lit a couple of candles on the table and turned off the overhead light. Yet, we didn't talk much and Milly only nibbled at her food. It was clear to me that she was nervous, and at one point I reached out and took her hand.

"Don't worry, Milly," I told her. "There is nothing you can tell me that would make me think less of you."

"I hope not, John Paul," she said, so softly I could barely hear.

"You don't even have to tell me," I added. "Now or later. It's really not any of my business."

"I want you to know," she said. "You need to know what you're getting into. I'm damaged goods, John."

"Milly!" I said, more sternly than I intended. She flinched and pulled back, but I didn't let go of her hand. "You're about to make me very angry," I told her. "I don't want to ever hear you talk about yourself that way. I won't have it. You are not damaged goods. You are a wonderful woman."

"You don't know, John," she replied, tears in her eyes."

"Then tell me," I said gently. "Don't try to pretty it up. Just tell me the simple truth."

She nodded and took a deep breath. Then she began to talk and the way she looked worried me. Her eyes turned inward and there was no emotion in her face. She looked the way people sometimes look after a car crash or a bad fall, keeping a tight rein on her feelings. It was almost as if she wasn't there. Maybe she wasn't.

"I met Oliver through my daddy" she told me. "He was my daddy's drinking buddy and I really liked him at first. He was funny and he treated me like a queen. He even taught me how to drive. I knew he drank, but he always seemed to have it under control. I know now that he didn't. He just seemed to." Her eyes were incredibly sad.

"Oliver came over one day when my daddy was gone. He was drinking heavily and he got me to take a drink. I never had before and the first sip was awful. It burned my mouth and made me cry, but Oliver convinced me to take another drink. He said to take a bigger drink this time and it would take the pain away. So I did and he was right. It didn't burn so bad that time. He said each drink would take more pain away and he was right."

Milly shook her head, as if she couldn't believe what she was saying. "After a while I got to feeling happy and taking a sip didn't burn at all. Before I knew it I was so drunk I could hardly stand and I thought it was funny. I started laughing and at some point I discovered all my clothes were gone and I was lying on my bed. Oliver was, too, and all his clothes were gone. He looked so funny naked that I started laughing so hard I could hardly get my breath.

"That was when my daddy came home and he scared me to death. He was drunk, too, and I thought he was going to kill Oliver. When I tried to defend him, my daddy hit me so hard it knocked me clear across the room. He'd hit me in the stomach and I started throwing up. This made him even madder."

Milly was so pale by then I thought she was going to pass out. I tried to get her to stop, but she refused. "I have to do this now, John. I don't know if I'll have the courage later on. Please let me get it out."

I nodded and she continued. "We really hadn't done anything yet but we were naked on the bed and my daddy made us get married. I assure you I have repented at leisure. Oliver is a different man when he's not drinking. It's like Dr. Jekyll and Mr. Hyde and Oliver has not touched me since then. To tell the truth, I think he prefers men. That may be why he drinks the way he does."

She paused, then added, "I know Oliver blames me for his drinking, but I can't see how. He was a drunk long before I met him. He also blames me for him being the way he is, but I know that's the liquor talking. So I suppose you're right, John Stone. I'm not damaged goods. I'm still a virgin."

"Good Lord, Milly," I exclaimed. "You're not really married, not according to the law. Why did you stay with him? You could have had it annulled."

"I've stayed with him because I made some promises, John." I was relieved to see that her color was coming back. "I didn't have anywhere else to go, either."

"You made those promises at gunpoint, Milly. They don't count, not legally. The marriage was never consummated."

"I know, but I don't want to shame Oliver. Up to now I've not had a reason to leave, but I can't right now. He's a sick man."

"He's already done a pretty good job of shaming himself, Milly. He doesn't have a reputation worth protecting."

"Yes, but he needs me and I promised for better or for worse. Do you want to know the ugly truth, John?" I nodded and she said, "My youngest brother was out of school and in the Army by then, by the time we got married. Things were getting worse and worse with Daddy, and I was sick of it. The truth is that I wanted out of Daddy's house, John. Oliver gave me the opportunity and I'm grateful to him for that. That's the ugly truth. I was too weak to just leave home, and I used Oliver to get away." She began to cry. "Do you hate me?"

I got up and knelt down beside her, holding her close. When

I did, she began to weep, great aching sobs wracking her thin frame so hard I was afraid she might die. Yet, I didn't dare let go, either, and after fifteen long minutes, the sobs began to diminish. I am not a spiritual man but I offered a heartfelt prayer for the gift of that grace.

A few minutes later Milly looked up, her wonderful gray eyes full of doubt. "You didn't answer me, John Paul," she said. "Do you hate me?"

"How could I hate you, Milly? You're the most wonderful woman I ever met. Thank you for trusting me and telling me the truth."

Milly smiled weakly. "Thank you for being so patient with me. I need to ask you to do something for me, a small favor."

"Of course," I told her. "If I can, I will."

"I wanted us to be together tonight, to make love and listen to the rain. Now I'm so exhausted I can barely stay awake. Would you mind going home now?"

"Are you sure you'll be all right by yourself?" I asked. "We don't have to do anything."

She reached up and touched my cheek tenderly and I kissed her hand. "Of course, I will be, sweet John. I promise you there will be time for us later, too. Just not tonight."

"Let me walk you to your room," I said, getting up and lifting her in my arms. I was surprised how light she was. Then I carried her into the bedroom and gently laid her on the bed.

"I like to feel your arms around me," she said. "Now kiss me goodnight. Call me tomorrow."

"On a party line?" I asked, chuckling.

"Yes," she told me, smiling. "Let's scorch their ears."

FOUR

House Arrest

I didn't get to see Milly again until two days later when the Queen Bees Book Club held a square dance fund raiser in the high school gym. It was an annual event they put on to benefit our local library and they started the evening with hot chili and cornbread, along with potato salad, cole slaw, and iced tea. The potato salad and cole slaw were from secret family recipes brought over from the Old World a century before, and these had both won first place at the Texas State Fair years before. After the write-up in the Fort Worth Star Telegram, people came from all over the next year to sample the food and to listen to the well known country fiddler who always showed up to play. His sons came with him, too, and took turns, one accompanying their father on a banjo while the other called the dance.

Since half the county was Baptist, the event was billed as a picnic and "circle game." This allowed all but the most hard shelled Baptists to kick up their heels, and there was a fierce rivalry between them and the Methodists for first prize. To keep everything fair and square, judges were brought in from Cowtown.

It was my job to make sure that drinking was kept at a minimum. Nor did the county commissioners complain about my taking on a couple of extra deputies for the evening. These were young men from surrounding counties and I put Buzz in charge of them while I circulated among the crowd. To make our presence known, we all wore khakis, western hats and boots, and light blue uniform shirts. We also wore our badges and gun belts, and each of us had a night stick and two pair of handcuffs.

Of all our local events, the Queen Bee dance was Milly's favorite. When she hit the dance floor, she was a different woman. Since it was a custom to come to the dance with a partner, Milly always brought Landon Cable. He was what we called "simple" or "slow" back then, what they call "disabled" or "challenged" these days. Yet, he was the best dancer in the county. His family had been in the area since before there was a Rutherford County and they had become quite wealthy, first with cattle and then with oil.

I have to hand it to the Cables for how they treated Landon. Some families shut children like him away, as if being slow is something shameful. Yet the Cables did not. What they did, instead, was to find out what their son was good at and, then, to help him become the best at that. Since Landon was good with animals, they hired the best horse handler around to teach him horse whispering. When he showed an interest in dancing and gymnastics, they hired professionals to drive over from Ft. Worth a couple of days a week to train him. They also brought in a resident tutor to teach Landon the basic skills for reading and math, and the tutor discovered he was a prodigy when it came to math. To round things out, he was taught to sing and he and Milly would do an occasional duet at the church. He was a tenor and their voices seemed to weave together into one.

The result of this rearing was a good looking young man with a sweet disposition. No one would suspect was challenged until they were around him a while. Even then, it was easy to forget his disabilities. Landon was smart enough to keep his mouth shut most of the time, which some mistook for depth or wisdom. He also delighted in number puzzles, and was not adverse to showing off his skills. Yet his greatest passion was dancing and his favorite partner was Milly.

When the fiddle started that night I saw Milly smile and her foot began to tap. It didn't take Landon long to find her and they moved to the center of the gym floor with three other couples to form a square. Since the gym floor was varnished hardwood, no one was allowed to wear street shoes on it and everyone danced in socks.

After the first tune was done, the fiddler walked over to the microphone. He gave the Episcopal padre a hard time about having a hole in the toe of one of his socks, accusing him of being a tightwad. His friend hollered back that all he had was holy socks. There was a collective groan at this and the fiddler answered the pastor with a fast reel. To the delight of the crowd, the padre began to dance, keeping time with the music. The crowd was surprised when Landon walked over and watched the padre for a few moments. Then he began to dance with him in perfect step. The crowd applauded and began to clap in time.

The fiddler picked up the pace, and both dancers stayed with him until he began to fiddle even faster. The padre shook his head then and dropped out but Landon stayed with it until the fiddler finally gave up. When he stopped, there was tremendous applause for Landon and he smiled and waved. Then he rejoined Milly and the other couples forming up the square. It didn't seem to me like he was even breathing hard.

I glanced at Milly just then and I had never seen her happier. She was as radiant as any bride I've ever seen, and I felt a pang of jealousy. Then I felt silly. How can you be jealous of Landon? I asked myself. He's just a nice kid. She likes him and she needs every friend she can get. Yet, scolding myself didn't work. It rarely does but I was able to set the feeling aside.

The next square dance began after that and I went outside to relieve Buzz. I figured I had just seen the main event of the evening and I needed some air and some space, too. Crowds are a lawman's worst nightmare. They can turn from being a happy bunch into a mob at a moment's notice, and I had seen these very folk do that at a Friday night football game. I'd also seen it more than once and when it happens, there is no telling what's going to happen. A night stick and a pistol aren't much defense against collective insanity.

The full dance set lasted about three-quarters of an hour. The fiddler and his sons took a break and those who smoked came outside for a cigarette. The gym was one of the few public buildings where smoking was not allowed, mostly because of the fire danger. Varnish is almost as volatile as gasoline and a dropped match could set the floor ablaze in nothing flat. With the limited exits we had, ninety percent of the crowd could be burned to a crisp before they could get out. Even if the fire was put out quickly with extinguishers, a lot of folk would be trampled to death in the inevitable stampede. I'd seen any number of magazine and newspaper reports about places where this had actually happened. The Cocoanut Grove fire comes to mind.

I was thinking about this when Milly brought Landon over to meet me. "That was some dance," I told him. "I've never seen anything like it."

Landon grinned happily. "It was fun. I wish he didn't stop so soon."

"Well, I bet you'll get lots of requests after tonight. Have you ever danced like that before?"

"No," said Landon happily. The concession stand caught his attention and he added, "I want a coke, Miss Milly. You want one, too?"

"No, but I'll go with you," she said. She smiled at me.

"You have a good evening, Miss Milly," I told her, trying not to grin like a fool. "It was good visiting with you."

Landon was tugging her arm, but Milly smiled at me. "You, too, sheriff. I hope you catch those poachers."

"You doing my job now, John?" a familiar voice asked from the other side. It was the state game warden assigned to Rutherford County. He was a good bit younger than me and still a little green. I wondered why they had sent him out here all by himself.

"Not for a minute," I answered, offering the man a hand. He shook mine warmly. "Who I'm after are spot-lighters. Farmers have been complaining. Nobody has lost any stock yet, but they're worried."

"They have every right to be," he agreed. "I caught a bunch of kids in a pickup last night. Aside from being underage and having beer, they had four deer rifles with them and all kinds of ammo. I asked them what they were trying to do, start a war?"

The warden lit up a Lucky Strike. He offered the pack to me but I shook my head. "That's a habit I never cultivated," I told him. "My dad smoked a pipe and if I was going to smoke, I think that's what I'd try. But I'm afraid that's too much fooling around for me."

The warden laughed. "That's for damn sure. You light it and you have to tamp it down just right and smoke it at the right speed or it goes out. Then you have to tamp it and light it again and you got to clean the damned filter all the time or get a mouthful of tar. Takes forever to get a good briar broken in and then you have to scrape out the bowl with a special tool."

I must have been looking at him oddly because he added, "My dad was a pipe smoker, too."

I chuckled and nodded. "By time I did all that, I'd loose interest. You didn't mention that if you smoke it too fast, you can burn up your pipe, not to mention your tongue."

He nodded. "I think I'll stick to these." He stared intently into the crowd. "Now there's a pretty lady I'd like to meet."

I looked where he was staring and laughed. "She's the daughter of the biggest poacher in the county," I told him. "So I'm told. I never caught him."

"I think I'll give her a try, anyway," he said, hitching up his gun belt. "She looks kind of wild to me."

"I'm told that, as well," I said. "But it could just be talk. Good hunting, Pete. Be careful. You know what the hunters say."

He was clearly distracted. "What's that, John?"

"Sometimes you get the bear and sometimes the bear gets you."

"Now wouldn't that be nice," he told me.

❧

I was getting ready for church the next morning when I got a call from the district judge. He told me Oliver's appendix had ruptured the night before and the doctor had taken it out. "That means Oliver will be convalescent for at least six weeks, Sheriff. What I need to know from you is whether or not you can handle him at the jail. Or do I need to send him home when he's released from the hospital? They're not willing to keep him for more than a few days."

"I don't think we're set up for taking care of him," I answered. "Have you thought about the prison hospital?"

"I did, but the man is not a felon. There are some legal issues that would be hard, if not impossible, to negotiate and time is of the essence." I think one of the reasons the judge was first elected was the way he talks. His delivery combines the style of a preacher and the vocabulary of a professor of law, and in the courtroom his deep voice resounds like rolling thunder. Or, maybe, the voice of God.

"Let me do some thinking," I told him. "Maybe I can come up with something that will work."

"I hope you can, Sheriff, because otherwise I'll have to release him to the custody of his wife. He would still have to serve out his sentence when he is recovered, of course."

"Has his wife been notified?"

"Yes, I believe a neighbor brought her into town last night and again this morning."

"Let me talk to her and see what she thinks. Maybe I can work something out with the hospital or the nursing home."

"Ah, that's a good thought, the nursing home. I suppose you could hire someone to be a temporary deputy. Doesn't Mrs. Bates have any means of transportation?"

"Ollie's truck, maybe. I'll check it and see about getting it fixed. He took out a fender and one of the front axles was bent. Maybe someone from church could lend her a car. I'll talk to the pastor, too. I'd rather keep Ollie off the road as long as we can."

"I certainly concur with that! When he's behind the wheel, the man's a menace to society."

"Couldn't you revoke his license?"

The judge nodded. "I can and I may do that. However, I doubt it would keep him from driving."

As it turned out, the simplest solution was to repair Oliver's truck. It was not as badly damaged as it first appeared and the wrecking yard had a fender and an axle. The owner agreed to put them on for fifty dollars. When I told him it was for Miss Milly, not Oliver, he dropped the price to twenty-five. He also told me her credit was good. "She come and set with my mother while she was dying," he told me. "I offered to pay her but she wouldn't take a dime. And if I was to offer to fix the truck for nothing, you know she wouldn't take it. But if she never pays me, I'll be happy as a hog in mud."

I thanked him and asked how long it would take to get the truck fixed. "We're kind of behind, Sheriff. So it could take a while. In the meantime, I've got an old heap she can borrow. It may be a little rough looking but it's clean and it runs good. It won't give her no trouble."

The nursing home was a different story. "I'd do it in a minute for Miss Milly," the owner told me. He sounded pretty smug to me. "She does a world of good for our patients. She leads the singing at our chapel services and spends the afternoon visiting the sick who can't get there."

The man shook his bald head. "Oliver is something else. I don't want that useless, egg-sucking hound anywhere near this place. I don't care if he is sick. Put him in jail where he belongs, and if he dies, good riddance!" I wondered if he'd sound as smug if I flattened his nose.

"Then do it for Miss Milly," I said. "Otherwise, she'll have to take care of him at home until he goes to jail. She may not be able to be here."

"No, it's out of the question. We'll just have to do without her."

This didn't surprise me. I'd never had direct dealings with Thom Jacobs before, but I knew him by his works, as the Good Book says. He was a deacon at the biggest church in town. Yet, from what I'd seen, he was always the one willing to cast the first stone. I'm not much of one for religion, but his faith didn't seem to make it out the door on Monday morning. Nor did I think it showed up again until the next Sunday.

Maybe I'm being hypocritical here, judging Thom the same way he was judging Oliver. However, I don't make any claims on piety or goodness. As I said, I attend the Methodist church for political reasons. At least, I did at first. Then I found a better reason. Milly sang in the choir and I went more to hear her than the preacher.

The thing is, the preacher at the Methodist Church tells me that God loves us all equally. I understand why he believes that and I hope he's right. Only, if He does, I cannot imagine what He sees to love in Thom Jenkins. I've never met a crook with a meaner streak, and the way Thom acts in public made me question how he treats the old folks in private. I wondered if I needed to investigate. It occurred to me that might be better than flattening his nose.

It also crossed my mind that Thom might be singing a

different tune if the judge had put his request in the form of a court order. Thom didn't know how lucky he was that the judge didn't. Or how glad I'd have been dragging him out of the nursing home in handcuffs for violating a court order. Oliver Bates may be a drunken bum who beats his wife and plows up the judge's rose, but I'd much rather deal with him than with Thom Jenkins. Oliver was only a surly drunk. Thom struck me as totally rotten.

❧

Oliver Bates ended up spending a week in the hospital before he was discharged. Nothing else worked out so Oliver was released to the custody of his wife. I was surprised when the judge made a special trip to the hospital the day Oliver was released to make it clear to the man exactly how the cow would eat the cabbage. The judge asked me to go with him as a witness, and when we got there, he was glad to find Miss Milly visiting Oliver, too. So was I and when I shook hands with her, Milly held onto mine just a moment longer than she needed. It was all I could do to keep from grinning like a lovesick monkey.

The judge handed Oliver a formal court order and spelled out the details. Oliver was under house arrest and was ordered not to go any farther from the house than the privy or the well house. He was not to drink alcohol in any form or to use the telephone, and I, or one of my deputies, was authorized to check up on him at random times. When Miss Milly needed to be gone, I or one of my deputies would take her place. Should Oliver violate any conditions of his house arrest or walk away, the judge would issue a bench warrant for his arrest. For walking away, the charge would be the same as breaking out of jail, which the judge explained was a felony. At that point, Oliver would be remanded to the state to serve out his sentence.

The judge also pointed out that the order required Oliver to be chained to the bed at night or whenever Miss Milly had to leave the house to take care of chores. "What if the house catches fire?" Oliver asked.

"Then you better make sure it doesn't," the judge answered. "Since that's a concern, you will not be allowed to smoke or to have matches."

Oliver tried to argue, but the judge cut him off. "One more word, Mr. Bates, and you'll be placed in the county jail. Your home is much more comfortable, I'm sure."

Oliver shut up but I knew he didn't accept what the judge was saying. I told the judge as much when we drove back to the courthouse. "I know, John," he said. When he used my given name, I knew he was speaking off the record. "Between me and thee and the fence post, I expect he'll try to escape or weasel his way out of her custody. So I need you to keep a close eye on the situation. There is to be no tolerance of any infraction."

After I dropped the judge off, I went back to the hospital to see Milly. When I walked into the room, Oliver was raising hell with her about something, but he stopped when I came in the room. I told her I needed to have a word with her and we walked down the hall to a conference room.

Nobody was there and when I shut the door, Milly came into my arms. "I'm so glad to see you," she said, giving me a kiss that damn near curled my toenails. I kissed her back with interest, and somehow my hands ended up on her backside, pulling her close. When I did, she moaned and pressed hard against me, and there was no hiding how glad I was to see her.

When somebody tried to come into the room, it was lucky I was standing with my back to the door. I turned around and opened it a crack. It was one of the clerks and I told her we'd be out in a minute. She told me there was a phone call for me from my office and I could take it on the extension in the room.

When I picked up the phone, it was Cheryl. There had been a car wreck west of town and someone had been hurt. I told her I was on the way. "We can talk later," I told Milly, explaining what was going on. "I can give you a ride home when I get back."

"Oh, Martha is supposed to come by for me," she said. Martha was one of their closest neighbors. Even though Milly was talking normally, I could tell she was disappointed. "Something always seems to interfere, John. I don't know what to make of it."

"I think we just need to be patient for a bit," I told her. "Trying to push the river won't help. I'll talk to you later this evening if I can. If I can't, we can talk tomorrow. Now I need a private word or two with Oliver."

Oliver was surprised to see me come into the room alone and he started to say something. I cut him off quickly. "Shut up, Oliver!" I said as sternly as I could. I also took my leather sap out of my pocket and shoved it under his nose. My face was less than a foot from his and I could smell the rancid odor of coming off a drunk. "You know what this is and you better believe I know how to use it!"

Oliver's eyes got as big as saucers. "You're in a world of shit, Ollie!" I assured him. "One word! One word that you're giving Miss Milly any trouble and I'm going to take you out behind the woodshed. Do you understand me, Ollie?" He nodded so hard I thought he'd get whiplash.

"And do you know what's going to happen then?" I asked is a soft, menacing voice. Oliver was sweating so hard it was drenching him. "Then I'm going to put you in a cell with Deke Barnes!" Deke was one of the meanest people I ever met. He was in jail awaiting trial for beating his last cellmate to death.

It was then Oliver's sphincter let loose and he started crying. I looked at him sadly. I founded it impossible to feel anything but pity for the man. I put my sap back in my hip pocket and walked out into the hall. "You better get the nurse, Miss Milly," I told her. "Ollie's messed his bed."

"I'll change it," she said and tried to get around me to the door.

I blocked her way. "No, Mrs. Bates," I told her gently. "You need to let the nurses do that. It's their job."

Milly started to argue, but I didn't move. She looked in my eyes and then smiled. "Thank you, Sheriff," she told me. "You're right. I'll get the nurse." I watched her walk down the hall and stayed where I was until the nurse came.

❦

As it turned out, I really needed to be at the car wreck, and not just to be seen doing my job. The Highway Patrol happened to be close by and got there first. So I directed traffic while the trooper investigated. When he was done, I asked him to switch with me while I had a look around, too.

No one is ever happy about being in a car crash, but this one was particularly sad. The two passengers in one of the cars were teenagers. They were killed when the other driver swerved into their lane and plowed into them at high speed.

The other driver smelled like a brewery and the highway patrolman agreed with my reading of the tire marks. I ended up taking the drunk driver into custody and carrying him to the hospital for a blood alcohol test and a physical exam. The test showed he was well over the limit for drunk driving, and the physical revealed that he was healthy enough to be incarcerated. All that was wrong with him was a broken jaw and a couple of teeth knocked out when his face hit the steering wheel. They fixed him up as best they could and I took him to jail.

It was well after six by the time I got the drunk driver booked and into a cell. I was glad Milly had not waited for me and I called to ask if she had a ride to town the next morning. I said we needed to discuss her husband's house arrest. She told me she had not planned to come to town and I asked if it would be convenient for me to stop by in the early afternoon. She told me it would and I added that I needed to look over the house to see what arrangements we needed to make.

I felt like a fool saying this but I wanted the information to get out so there wouldn't be talk about my frequent visits later. I decided to tell her that I had found a car for her to use until the truck was fixed and that we needed to talk about that, too. Milly knew what I was doing. She understood the need to get the information out quickly so the neighbors wouldn't worry about seeing a strange car at the Bates.

I grabbed a quick burger at the drive-in and a group of young folk came over to my table asked me about the accident. I explained what had happened, and stressed that their classmates had not been at fault. They were very upset and asked me what would happen to the drunk driver. I told them I had booked him for involuntary man-slaughter and that I was pretty sure he would eventually come to trial for it.

"The decision rests with the prosecutor and a jury, but this is a clear cut case," I told them.

"He should get the death penalty!" one of the girls told me.

She was tall and thin and well dressed. She also had bright red hair and a fiery disposition to go with it. "He killed two people."

"I understand how you feel," I told her. "I've lost good friends to drunk drivers, too. However, the law reserves the death penalty to intentional murder, and this guy didn't set out to kill anybody."

"He decided to drink!" the young lady declared. "This is a dry county and he decided to drink here anyway! That's intentional."

"I can't argue with that," I replied. The young lady was the elder daughter of one of the community pillars who made sure our county stayed dry and that the bootleggers stayed in business. I wondered if she knew how many people drove the thirty-two miles coming back from the nearest liquor store drunk. I was pretty sure the man I incarcerated was doing just that when he plowed into the two kids and killed them.

"I'm certainly not defending what he chose to do, either, Mandy. All I'm telling you is that I don't think the courts will see it that way."

"That's because it didn't happen to them!" Miss Firebrand of the Year told me. "They would if it was their son and daughter who got killed."

"I'm sure they would," I agreed. "What you can do is talk to the prosecutor. He can bring other charges if he thinks that's justified. The point is that right now the man's in jail. Tomorrow or the next day I'll take him before the judge and the prosecutor will bring charges. Until then, he's a guest of the county, and the food ain't that great."

Most of the kids thought that was funny, but the firebrand was not satisfied at all. I hoped she would follow through and go to the prosecutor. He was coming up for election, too, and he needed to share the heat on this one. Let her chew on his ear. It would be good for his soul.

When I left the drive-in I was feeling restless. So I decided to prowl the county roads for a couple of hours. I headed south of town to look for rustlers and road hunters in an area I hadn't patrolled in a while and I stopped to talk to a farmer whose lights were still on. He hadn't seen any sign of road hunters. Nor had he lost any stock.

"It's been a while since I heard about anybody night hunting," he said. "But it's getting about that time of year."

"Well, put the word out that I'm prowling for them," I told him. "That may slow them down a bit. I'll get Buzz to follow up in a few days."

I covered the southern part of the county pretty well and was heading north again when I realized I was circling back toward the Bates' place. By then I was almost there, so I swung by to see if there was a light on. It was after eleven then and I figured Milly was already asleep, but when I looked up their drive, one of the front windows was lit. So I pulled in the driveway and drove around to the back of the house. When I did, the light on the back porch came on and Milly stuck her head out.

"I was hoping you'd come by," she said as she hugged me. She was wearing a patched old robe that revealed about as much as it hid. As I ran my hands over her back, I confirmed what I suspected. She wasn't wearing much under it. When I pulled back and began to pull at the ends of the cloth belt that held the robe together, she smiled. "Oh, good. You're going to have your way with me now." Then she added, "Be gentle with me, John. It's my first time."

※

I was sleeping soundly when Milly touched my shoulder. "It's a little past five, John Paul. You might want to go before it gets light."

"I might want to do a little more loving before I go, too," I replied, taking her in my arms. "How are you feeling?"

"I'm a little sore but it feels wonderful," she told me. "Three times was a lot more than I'm used to."

"Well, I'll just fool around a bit, then," I said. I opened her robe and started kissing her. The night before I had discovered something she really liked and I turned to that. It didn't take long and she loved it. I was miles away before the sun came up.

FIVE

Break-Out

The next few weeks were a real trial for me. Because of the court order, I got to see Milly several times a week. That was good but we couldn't do much about it. Having Oliver around really cramped our style and it felt strange pretending we weren't lovers. It's a good thing nobody else was around besides Oliver or I'm sure they would have seen right through us. Oliver was too bound up in his own misery and self-pity to see much else and I made sure I spent some time with him whenever I went out to their place. I also made sure to search the place for hootch, and I made sure Oliver was aware of it. I also warned him what would happen if he broke custody or gave Milly any trouble.

This made it hard for Milly and me to talk much, but at the end of my visits I'd shackle Oliver to the bed so Milly could walk me out to the car. We couldn't touch or embrace, but we could talk, and this was better than nothing. "This feels like waiting for Christmas before my mother died," Milly told me one day as I was leaving. Then she gave me a coy smile. "I wonder what Santa's going to bring me."

"Well, it sure won't be a lump of coal," I assured her.

"You mean I haven't been bad?" she teased.

"I mean you've been absolutely wonderful," I told her. "Very, very good. You remind me of that nursery rhyme."

"Oh?" she asked. "What nursery rhyme is that? Little Miss Muffet?"

"No, it's another one you know," I told her. Then I recited.

> There was a little girl
> Who had a little curl
> Right in the middle
> off her forehead.
> When she was good

She was very, very good,
And when she was bad
    she was torrid.

"That's not what it says," she said, pleased but pretending to be indignant. "I'll show you torrid, John Paul Stone!"

"I certainly hope so," I answered with a grin.

❧

One day early in the third week of Oliver's house arrest I asked Buzz spell me so I could take the day off. I headed down to the river to my fish camp in the neighboring county and Milly drove out and joined me for a good part of the afternoon. She told Buzz she was going to visit a sick friend, but she told me she hated lying about it.

"It's not a lie," I told her. "I'm a friend and I'm sick. Love sick."

"You're love sick?" she asked with a shy smile. "Does that mean you're in love with somebody, John Paul?"

I smiled. "It sure does, but I haven't told her yet."

"I don't suppose it's anyone I know, do I?" She was looking down at her hands.

"Oh, I bet you do. It's a lovely lady everybody calls Miss Milly. I even made up a song about it." I lifted her chin and kissed her tenderly.

"You did? How does it go?"

"I just have the first couple of lines finished, but I think you'll recognize the tune." I began to singing to an old Hank Williams tune. "Hey, Miss Milly, I'm feeling silly. How about doing something silly with me?"

I was surprised when Milly started to cry. "Did I do something wrong? I didn't mean to upset you."

"No, you silly man," she told me, grabbing me around the neck. "That's the first time any man ever told me he loved me."

"Well, I do," I said. "I've admired you since the first time I ever saw you."

"Admiring someone is not loving them, John," she pointed out.

"You're absolutely right," I said. "I've loved you since the second time I saw you. I couldn't say anything about it, of course, but I was really jealous of Oliver."

"You were? I had no idea."

"Well, I couldn't let you know it, could I? I mean, you were a married woman."

"And you got hurt by a married woman," she said, touching my face gently. "Are you uncomfortable with what we're doing, John Paul?"

"No, not a bit. I don't consider you married and I was the first man you gave yourself to. I feel honored. I'd marry you tomorrow if I could."

"Well, if that's a proposal, I accept." Then she laughed. "This is all so wonderful but it's also very strange." A moment later she was sad. "The fact is, I can't marry you, John. I can't leave Oliver."

I took her face in my hands. "Hey, sweet lady, I know that. I'm not asking you to leave him. What we have is wonderful and I don't want to do anything to ruin it. Let's enjoy what we have as much as we can. I'm not going anywhere, and you aren't either. My proposal is good for the next fifty years or so." What I didn't say was that if he kept drinking, we would both outlive Oliver.

"So is my acceptance," she told me gravely. "I don't want to be married to anyone else but you, John."

"Maybe we need to do something to celebrate that," I told her.

She gave me a wonderful smile. "Maybe we do, at that."

❧

The next week Dr. Pettigrew drove out to the Bates place and certified that Oliver was healthy enough to be incarcerated in the county jail. All our cells were full that day due to a birthday celebration that turned into a public brawl down at the American Legion the week before. So I told the judge we would need to either release someone early or wait until their sentences were up to have a cell for Oliver.

Somehow Oliver got wind of this and tried to escape the next day. His truck was fixed by then and he forced Milly to give him the keys. To make sure she didn't call for help, he tore out the phone line and Milly had to walk to the nearest neighbor's place to call us. I was on the other side of the county and by the time I got word of it, Oliver was long gone.

All I could do at that point was put out an all-points bulletin that he was wanted for assault and jail break. I had no idea where Oliver might be, and once the APB was out, I drove down to the hospital to talk to Milly. She was beaten up pretty badly and her neighbor had insisted on bringing her in to town to see the doctor.

When I saw the way she was bruised, I went cold as ice inside. Later, Milly told me it was frightening to see me that way. She said she was afraid I was going to hunt Oliver down and shoot him. "Please don't shoot him, Sheriff," she begged me.

"There's no way that's going to happen, Mrs. Bates," I told her. "Not unless he threatens me or someone else with a weapon. He may get roughed up a bit if he tries to resist arrest but there is no way I'm going to allow him to be shot."

The neighbor was hanging on every word and I told her I needed to talk with Mrs. Bates privately. When she left I leaned close to Milly's ear. "There's no way I'm going to risk being separated from you by killing him. I promise." Then I leaned back and said in a louder voice, "Is there anything else you need to tell me, Mrs Bates? I'll keep it to myself if I can."

Milly knew as well as I did that the neighbor was listening at the door and she smiled. "No, Sheriff," she said, touching a finger to her lips and then to mine. "There's nothing else."

"He didn't hurt you in any other way than you told the doctor?"

"No," she said. "He just beat me. He has before but this time it was much worse." She told me later that the look on my face when she said that scared her even more. "Please don't hurt him, Sheriff," she said. "When he's drunk he doesn't know what he's doing."

❧

I might have been angry about Oliver beating Milly and escaping, but the judge was livid when I told him what I'd seen. I've never seen a man with a face that purple and I was afraid for a while he was going to have a stroke. "That brass-plated shit-heel!" he declared. "Treating her like that, and after all she's done for him!" It was one of the few I ever heard him resort to profanity.

Then he pulled himself together and I could see the effort it cost him. "Well, Sheriff, we did warn him what would happen," he said. He had a cold, wicked look in his eyes. Taking a form out of his desk, he filled it in and signed it, and handed it to me. "Here is a warrant for his arrest for unlawful flight. He is also in contempt of court and we will file any other charges you may come across catching him."

"His wife could swear out a complaint for battery," I told him. I wondered why he hadn't mentioned that.

The judge shook his head. "No, I don't want to see Miss Milly on the witness stand if it can be avoided. She's suffered enough." Then he gave me a stern look. "I am aware of your feelings for her, John. Be very careful when you catch Oliver Bates. Take Buzz with you. I'll talk to Charlie about it."

As it turned out, catching Oliver was like falling off a log. I got a call from Neville before I left town looking for Oliver. "I'm calling to do you a favor, Sheriff," he told me. "I may want a favor in return some day."

"I'm not buying a pig in a poke, Neville," I told him. "I'm in a rush at the moment."

"Yes, but hear me out. I didn't expect you to be that stupid, but you're an honorable man," he told me. There was no irony in his voice. "I trust your judgment about the favor. Oliver Bates is here at my place and he's drunk as a skunk. I've got his truck keys and he's not armed, but you need to get here quick. He's been trying to buy a gun from me. I put him off with a bottle of whiskey."

I picked Buzz up at Charlie's dealership and we got there in under fifteen minutes. We were both armed but we kept our weapons holstered when I knocked on the door. Neville answered right away. "He just ran out the back door," he told us.

Buzz was a faster runner than I am so I told him to go after Oliver. I ran back to the cruiser and called in, telling Cheryl we were in pursuit of Oliver Bates and where we were. Then I roared around to the back of the house in the cruiser and had to laugh. Oliver was so drunk he had fallen over a fence into a mud puddle and got himself all tangled up in barbed wire trying to get loose. Buzz was there grinning like a fool and holding his pistol by his side. "Right considerate of him, Sheriff. He cuffed himself with bob wire."

"How'd you know I was here?" Oliver demanded as we were cutting him out of the fence. He glared at Neville who was watching us from his back porch.

"Who you kidding, Ollie?" I answered with a grin. "You're a falling down drunk. Where else would you go but to the closest place for liquor?" I looked at my watch. "You've been free three hours now. I hope it was worth it."

I called ahead on the radio and asked Cheryl to let the judge know we were on the way in with Oliver. He was shackled with his hands behind him in the back seat and Buzz was following us into town driving Oliver's truck. Three minutes later Cheryl called back and told me the judge wanted to see Oliver right away when we got there. So Buzz and I dragged him up the broad stairs to the courtroom, mud and all. The judge was taken aback by the sight, but he had to work hiding a smile when Buzz told him what happened.

"Good work, officers," he told us. "Unless my nose deceives me, I believe it must have been a hog wallow."

By the time we got to court, the prosecutor was waiting along with the judge. I wish I had a recording of what the judge had to say to Oliver that afternoon. I have never heard such a tongue lashing as he gave the man. His Honor must have talked for ten minutes and he never resorted to profanity or repeated himself. When he was done, the judge turned to me. "I want him here at ten tomorrow morning," he said. "We have enough to send him to Huntsville for at least a year and I am going to request maximum security." Oliver paled when the judge said and the prosecutor was surprised. Then the judge asked Buzz to take the prisoner back to jail.

"Don't worry, Emory," the judge told the prosecutor when Oliver was gone. "We're not going to go to the expense of a trial. Tomorrow I'm going to find Oliver in contempt of court and sentence him to six months to a year, less a day. That sentence will commence once he has served out his original sentence of ninety days." The judge looked at me. "That means we're going to have to feed Oliver for at least nine months. Will your budget stand that, Sheriff?"

I nodded. "I'll talk to the commissioners, judge. They'll whine and moan, but they'll go along. Ollie's made a lot of enemies."

The prosecutor smiled and said, "If you need me to, Sheriff, I'll explain what it could cost the county to try Ollie." The judge nodded.

After the prosecutor had left, the judge said to me, "Keep Oliver safe, John, and Miss Milly, too. Let me know if she needs a peace bond against the man."

"I doubt that she will ask that, judge," I told him.

"I do, too, but we have to keep her safe. From what the doctor told me, Oliver came very close to killing her this time when he hit her. An inch to the right and she'd be gone." Seeing my face he nodded. "I told you this now so you could get a grip on how you feel about him. Do you want me to see if one of our neighboring counties will jail him for us? I was thinking of Buford County."

I chuckled. "That would serve him right, wouldn't it." The sheriff of our neighboring county was notorious for his treatment of prisoners. When an area newspaper reporter had confronted him with his reputation, he replied, "Hell, kid, punishment's what jail's for, ain't it?" By comparison, our jail was the Hilton.

"Or, we could save that threat to keep Oliver in line."

"Why don't we do that?" I suggested. "I have no problems with it but Miss Milly might."

"There is that," the judge replied. He sighed. "Just keep him safe, Sheriff. We don't need the Rangers coming in to investigate us. I like to think we're better than that." Then he looked at me over the top of his glasses and I realized he knew exactly how things were. "So be discreet, John."

As things turned out, we had to transfer Oliver to the Burton County jail, anyway. Two weeks after we brought him in there was a big fight at the Roadhouse. This was a private club about fifteen miles south of Live Oak on a lake the club owned. The powers that be in Rutherford County allowed it to stay in business despite its reputation as a rowdy bucket of blood. It brought a lot of business into the county. There was live entertainment that drew rough folk from as far away as Cowtown and it was public knowledge that you could get anything you wanted there. The waitresses were from out of town and they were known to meet customers in the single room "fishing" cabins down by the lake. These were generally rented out by the hour and held nothing but a bed and a bathroom. That didn't keep them from staying busy all evening and most of the night.

There was also a back room where five or six poker games took place on certain nights of the week. These were very carefully set up so that players bought boxes of custom-made chips for a couple of hundred dollars. At the end of the night a player could cash in his chips, and where the house made out lay in the fact that each box of chips only held a hundred and eighty dollars worth of chips. With six players to a game, that meant a minimum of a hundred and twenty dollars for the evening, and six full tables would bring in seven hundred and twenty dollars. At least half the players bought more than one box, and rumor had it that the management brought in two or three professional gamblers who played on a split with the house.

The gambling and prostitution were highly illegal, of course, as was serving liquor by the drink. The Road House got around this by calling itself a private club. Private clubs could serve liquor by the drink from a common stock owned, in theory, by the members. Daily memberships at the Roadhouse were sold for ten dollars a pop at the door, or you could pay annual dues of fifty dollars.

Where the county made out was in sky high property taxes and private club licenses. I am sure there was a lot of under-the-table cash that went directly to the county commissioners, too. I had been discreetly sounded out to see if I would take a bribe. I refused the bribe but the commissioners did accept the gift of a new police cruiser every couple of years for the sheriff's department.

I accepted the situation and kept quiet because there wasn't much I could do about it. The first year I was in office as sheriff,

I did try to raid the place. Word got out that we were on the way and when we arrived at the Roadhouse, there were only a few people playing dominoes in the back room. There was no sign of cards or poker chips. Later I found out that we had not been gone from the club house fifteen minutes before the games were in full swing again.

After that I confined my efforts to catching rustlers, road hunters, and thieves, and being highly visible on the back roads. Nor am I sure where the judge fit in this scheme of things. It was one of many things we never talked about. The closest we came was when I reported the attempt to bribe me. He pointed out that all I had was my word against theirs and nodded when I told him I wanted someone else to know. Other than that, he didn't say much but I think he felt the same way as I did. I think he stayed clean. At least, that's what I'd like to believe.

Where all this came to bear on Ollie was that there was a stabbing at the Roadhouse one evening and I was called in. The bouncers had the offender, one Horace Stringer, tied to a chair in an empty office, and there were half a dozen witnesses in another room waiting for me to interview. These were all paid employees of the club. When I asked why there weren't members on the list, I was told none of them had seen a thing.

We all knew this was a lie but there was nothing I could do about it. Stringer had a history of violent behavior in our files, mostly assault and battery, so it was an open and shut case. I had written statements from a half dozen witnesses, and all of them would be available to testify. Emory was there when the defendant was arraigned, and there was no mistaking how disappointed he was when Stringer pled guilty. Emory had thought he was looking at a slam-dunk trial where he could show off his prosecutor's skills. Being denied the opportunity to strut his stuff really made Emory mad and he tried to get the judge to throw the book at the defendant.

What we didn't know when we brought him in was that Horace Stringer held a grudge against Oliver Bates. Two minutes after Buzz put him in the cell next to Ollie, Stringer had grabbed him through the bars and was strangling him to death in a choke hold. We were lucky the other prisoners started yelling and Buzz pulled Horace off Ollie. Other than being scared out of his wits and gaining a few bruises, Ollie was fine.

The upshot was that late the next afternoon, Buzz and I were driving Oliver to Burton County. Ollie raised hell about this but all the other counties around us had dealt with him one time or another before and refused to take him.

"Your buzzards are coming home to roost, Ollie," was how Buzz put it. "No one to blame but you. You picked the wrong man to cheat. You oughtn't have tried it with Horace. You can't blame the other counties for not wanting you, neither. You done wore out your welcome."

That was about as good a way of putting it as any. When I told the judge the next day, he nodded. "Oliver has worn out his welcome around here, too," he told me. "Unfortunately, John, he's our problem, not theirs." Then he smiled. "Perhaps the sheriff of Burton County will be able to help Oliver see the error of his ways. It's probably too much to ask for, but I certainly hope so."

SIX

Respite

Having Oliver Bates incarcerated in Burton County was a real blessing for Milly and me. I spent a lot of time at her place, going out on patrol at night two or three nights a week and ending up spending several hours with her. To make it work I had to do a lot of extra work going after a gang of rustlers, but it paid off. I never caught anybody red handed but I did interrupt an attempt to steal thirty head of cattle one night. The gang took off in two pickups and had too big a lead for me to catch up. They got away before I could organize a series of roadblocks. However, I impounded the unregistered trailers the rustlers abandoned and these brought in a good price at auction. The proceeds, of course, went to the county.

After that, word got around and cattle loss in Rutherford County dropped off to nothing. The farmer whose cattle I saved sang my praises to the county commissioners, as well as to his neighbors, and the weekly paper ran a story on me. The only complaint I heard was that sometimes I wasn't in the office until late in the day. I told the commissioners this was true. I was busy making up for the sleep I lost on night patrol and going after rustlers. They agreed that's what I needed to be doing.

About two months after I took Oliver to Buford County, our jail census dropped off. Once Horace Stringer had done his time and was released, I went to talk to the judge. What I wanted to know is how he felt about bringing Oliver back to Live Oak to finish out his sentence.

"Well, things have certainly been a lot quieter since he's been gone," the judge pointed out. "It's amazing how much court time he consumed. Between me and thee and the chair you're sitting on, I would rather keep it that way. What do you hear from the sheriff in Buford County?"

"Not much," I told him. "I called him a couple of times and

he said Oliver's being a model prisoner. He told me that Oliver was a bit difficult at first, but they had a come-to-Jesus meeting. He said Oliver's been cooperative ever since."

"A come-to-Jesus meeting?" the judge asked. "What's your take on that, Sheriff?"

"All I know is what I've heard, Judge. Huck Rawlins has a reputation for not putting up with much from prisoners. He told me he believes in giving them lots of opportunity for exercise and fresh air exercise. I gathered they do a lot of work on county roads. I do know he's been investigated by the Texas Rangers, but they didn't bring charges. On the other hand, the Rangers are not known for being light handed."

"Do you think this come-to-Jesus meeting might have involved corporal punishment?"

"I wouldn't be surprised at all, sir. I can't imagine Oliver being all that reasonable, otherwise."

The judge nodded. "I think you need to make a trip to Buford County, Sheriff. I need you to personally evaluate the situation there and report any irregularities to me. I don't know if Mrs. Bates has been over to see her husband, but take her with you. Perhaps that will mask your real purpose. That's assuming you don't mind taking her, of course." He smiled when he said that.

"I don't mind, sir. I believe she mentioned going over there a couple of times but she told me that visiting hours are quite limited. She said Ollie would hardly talk to her when she visited him in jail here."

"Well, take her anyway and warn Sheriff Rawlins that she will be coming with you. Tell him that it's our pleasure that he grant this visit and that you will be there with her during it. I'm sure there must be some legal or domestic matters she needs to discuss with her husband."

So the next morning I drove over to Jerome, the county seat, to talk to the sheriff. Milly agreed to go with me to visit Oliver and we took our time getting there. During the drive, I could tell she felt nervous, and I told her she didn't have to see Oliver if she didn't want to do it.

"No, John, I need to see him," she told me. "I am his wife and it's my duty. For better or for worse."

"Well, you know how I feel about that," I told her. "You may be his wife under the law, but I am your man. Or have you changed your mind about that?" I smiled to take rancor out of my words, but I was serious.

"You don't have to ask, John Paul. You know that in my heart you are my beloved husband." She smiled. "In the rest of me, too, silly man. Or do you need reminding?"

"That's the best offer I've had all day," I chuckled and we didn't do much talking for a while. I knew where there was a big shade tree in a secluded spot not far off the road and we stopped there to linger a while. We were taking a risk, but on the other hand, Milly didn't seem to mind. Not at all.

"So that's what people do in the back seats of cars," she said with a smile as we were driving away. "I don't suppose that's your first time in a back seat, is it, John?"

"Let's just say that's my first time in the back seat of a police car," I told her and she laughed. Then I looked at her seriously. "I don't kiss and tell, Milly. Not even to you."

"Well, I wasn't asking about kissing," she told me, but she smiled. "Thank you," she added. "I didn't think you did but hearing it is reassuring."

I had to pick up the pace to get us to Jerome by noon and we made it with fifteen minutes to spare. Huck Rawlins was still in the office and waved off my apology. He was quite cordial to Milly, too, which surprised me.

"I am very happy to finally meet you, Mrs. Bates," he said. "Your reputation proceeds you." Seeing her surprise he added, "You helped several of our families here in the county after the last flood, and some of them were my kinfolk. That's one of the reasons I agreed to take Oliver and it's the main reason I'm allowing a special visit today."

"Thank you, Sheriff," Milly said. "I really appreciate it. I have some fresh clothes for Oliver." She held up a sack and the sheriff took it.

"I'll get him these in the morning," Rawlins replied. "That's when they shower." He didn't say as much, but I knew the sack would be searched for contraband. He glanced at the wall clock. "Why don't you all get a bite to eat over at Wanda's? It's about time to feed the prisoners and I'll let Oliver know you're here. You can see him about one."

We walked across the street to Wanda's Bakery & Cafe and took a seat at a table in the back. I picked that one because it was off to one side by itself and it gave us a little privacy if we wanted to talk. The chairs were hard and worn smooth with years of use, and they didn't invite lingering. I wondered if that's why the owner bought them.

The food was much better than I expected. It wasn't fancy, roast beef with a side of okra and black-eyed peas, served with biscuits and iced tea. The tea didn't do much to mask the mineral taste Jerome's water is known for, but it helped. So did the lemon slices served with the tea but we both drank very little. Travelers from Live Oak believe the water has a purgative effect and I didn't want to put it to the test. It was a long drive home and places to answer nature's call were few and far between.

Milly didn't have much appetite and only ate half of her food. When the waitress asked if something was wrong with it, Milly shook her head. "I hate to waste good food," she said, "but I'm just not very hungry." Once we were alone again, she told me, "I'm really nervous about this visit today, Sheriff. I don't know why, but I am."

"Could have something to do with the company you've been keeping, Miss Milly," I replied softly. "You might feel a bit...." I shrugged, at loss for the word I wanted.

"Guilty?" she murmured. "Maybe that's it."

"I was thinking more like awkward." I told her. "You don't have to do this visit if you don't want to. Huck Rawlins will understand if you change your mind."

"No, I need to do this. Guilty is the right word, too. I feel like the woman caught in adultery. I'm still feeling the glow from the stop we made."

"I'm sorry," I said. "I didn't stop to think."

"Oh, I'm not," she told me. "I'm glad we stopped. I think that's what I feel a little guilty about. I love it so much."

I felt a sinking feeling in the pit of my stomach. "Are you saying we need to stop, Milly?"

"Oh, heavens, no!" she declared. "I don't know if I could

take that. It's what makes my days worth living, John Paul." She smiled sweetly.

I nodded, relieved. "Well, just so you know, that's the way I feel, too. You fill up an empty place inside me I never knew was there."

Milly smiled, then blushed furiously. "What did I say?" I asked. "I didn't mean to embarrass you."

"Oh, it wasn't what you said, sweet man. It was what my silly imagination did with it. I'm awful!"

"I can't imagine what...." I started to say, but then the coin dropped and I grinned. When I did, Milly covered her face with her hands. "Well, I'm glad you find our time together fulfilling," I added and she wouldn't look at me.

"You're not helping!" she said from behind her hands. I didn't reply and after a moment she peeked out between her fingers.

"Are you all right, honey?" the waitress asked. I'd not seen her approach and wondered what all she had heard.

"She's all right," I told her. "She just swallowed the wrong way. She'll be all right in a minute."

The waitress looked at Milly, who nodded. "I hate it when that happens," the waitress said. "You all done with these plates?"

※

Our visit with Oliver Bates was strange. The jailer had us wait in a large room much like the one we had in Live Oak. A few minutes later he brought Oliver in and I was astonished by the change that had taken place. He had lost at least thirty pounds and his coveralls hung loosely from his shoulders. His long, unkempt hair had been severely clipped into a military burr, and he was shaved.

This was a real change because it was always a challenge to get Ollie to clean up for court. We had to wash him down with a fire hose and he fought us tooth and nail getting undressed. The only reason we didn't cut his clothes off him was because Milly would have to buy him new ones out of her egg money. We knew this was a good part of what she had to live on. Getting Ollie to shave was out of the question. We just ran a hair clipper over his face to cut the brush back.

The change I saw didn't stop with Ollie being clean and neat looking. There were deep lines in his face on either side of his nose. The skin below his ears was deeply tanned, as were the back of his hands and the deep V where his shirt collar lay open. So was his face below his hat line, and to all appearances, he looked healthier than he had in years.

Yet, what really struck me was Ollie's eyes. As healthy as he might appear, the man looked haunted. It was like he had seen things his mind could not fathom. Who his eyes reminded me of were pictures of Korean War soldiers just back from the front. Their eyes were flat, almost lifeless, and Ollie's were the same. I was certain it was not a lack of alcohol or the rigors of withdrawal that caused this and I wondered what Huck and his deputies had done to him. When I glanced over at Milly, I could see that she was as shocked by this as I was.

As profound as the change we saw might be, it was nothing compared to the change in Oliver when Huck Rawlins entered the room a minute after we did. When Huck came, Oliver's eyes were filled with stark, craven fear. He only spoke when he had to, and then only to answer direct questions. The answers he gave were short and of few words, and he kept his eyes averted the whole time.

It was no surprise that we exhausted every topic of conversation within ten minutes. When Milly looked at me, I knew she was disturbed. "I think that's all we need, Sheriff," I told Rawlins. "I really appreciate your doing this for Miss Milly."

"Well, as I said, she earned it," the sheriff told us. He pushed a button and a moment later the jailer came to take Oliver back to his cell. When he was gone, I said to Milly, "I need a moment with the sheriff, Mrs. Bates. Do you mind waiting in the vestibule?" She shook her head and left the room.

"I'm impressed, Huck," I told Rawlins. I needed to know what the sheriff had done to Oliver, but I certainly didn't want to antagonize him. Oliver was still in his custody and I didn't want him to suffer the consequences of my raising hell with Huck Rawlins. "How in the world did you do that? I've never seen anything quite like it."

Rawlins shrugged. "Nothing to it. Consistent discipline. We never let him get away with anything. Whenever he messes up, he knows that discipline will be swift and painful." He smiled and his mouth became a tight, grim slash across his face. "What I call it is a come-to-Jesus meetin'. It's good for the soul."

"Well, it's certainly effective. What do you do?"

Rawlins smiled again and I knew that if Ollie had been in the room, he'd be scared to death. "That's a trade secret, John. Suffice it to say, pain is a very good teacher, and so is fear, but you'll never find a mark on any of our prisoners. Where we leave marks is on their soul."

Then Rawlins chuckled. "I'm sure you noticed the weight the prisoner lost since he's been here. That's from the water. We give them plenty to eat but it goes right through them until they get used to the water. Bates seems to be more affected by this than most others. We had to put him on bread and water for a couple of weeks to tighten his bowels up. He seems to be doing a lot better lately."

Jesus, I thought. Nor was I being irreverent. As bad as he was, Oliver Bates didn't deserve whatever Huck was doing. From what Huck was telling me, they must have worked Oliver over with something besides a rubber hose. Contrary to common belief, rubber hoses do leave marks but these can be made in painful places where they normally don't show.

I was so troubled I almost missed the next thing Huck said. "You know I was in the Marine Corps, John. I served in Korea and was captured when we got over-run by Chinese troops. I spent seven months in a prisoner of war camp and I learned a lot from them. They knew how to break a man down. I never broke but a lot of my buddies did. Some of them were pretty tough, too."

"That must have been awful," I replied. I hoped Rawlins would tell me more, but he didn't.

He shrugged. "Yeah, it wasn't no picnic, but it didn't kill me. And you know what they say. What doesn't kill me makes me stronger."

I wondered if Huck knew he was quoting Friedrich Nietzsche. My guess was that he didn't.

Milly was quiet on the way home. We were about halfway

there before she spoke softly. Her beautiful eyes were troubled. "What did they do to Oliver, John?"

"I don't know, Milly. Whatever it was sure scared him."

"Did you see how he looked at the sheriff? He looked like a whipped dog. One that's been kicked too much. And he's lost so much weight. Do you think they're starving him?"

"No," I told her. "Part of it is not being able to get any liquor and part of it is the minerals in the water. The sheriff told me Ollie had a hard time getting used to it but he's been eating better lately."

Milly nodded but she said nothing. "What do you want me to do, Milly?" I asked.

"Could you move him back to Live Oak?"

"Of course. He's our prisoner. We only moved him to Buford County to keep him safe. Let me talk with the judge."

"Thank you, John," she said. "I appreciate it."

Milly didn't add anything else and we drove for several miles before she spoke again. Yet it wasn't a comfortable silence. I knew she was still troubled and after a while I asked. "What's bothering you, Milly?"

"Pull over for a minute, please," she asked. When I did she looked at me gravely. "I need to ask you something, John. I don't want you to be offended, but I need to ask."

"Sure, Milly. What do you want to know?"

"I overheard you talking with the sheriff. You sounded like you admired what he's done with Oliver. Were you aware how he would treat him before you took him there?"

"No, I didn't. I knew Huck Rawlins has a reputation for being tough but I had no idea he'd do whatever he did to Oliver. I was just pretending, Milly. I wanted to kick Huck's butt from here to Denver but I needed to know what he'd done to Ollie."

"You think he tortured Oliver?"

I nodded. "Yes. I think he must have to make Ollie as scared as he was. It may not have been physical torture, but Huck did something. For what it's worth, I'd already decided to move Oliver back before you asked."

Milly's gray eyes searched mine, then filled with tears. "I'm so sorry, John. You sounded so convincing. I couldn't believe it was your voice saying those awful things the way you did. I should have known better. Please forgive me for doubting you."

I took Milly in my arms. "It's all right, sweetheart," I assured her. "You haven't had much luck with men before. I'm sorry I scared you but I didn't want to make Huck mad. I was sure he'd take it out on Ollie if I did."

Milly shivered. "You're right," she said. "He would. That man could make a snake seem hot-blooded."

"I'll talk to the judge just as soon as we get back. I'll drive back to Jerome the first thing in the morning."

❦

The judge was very concerned when I talked to him late that afternoon. He questioned me closely about what I'd observed and agreed that we needed to get Oliver out of there as soon as possible. "I believe you are quite correct in your assessment, Sheriff. I would have never have sent Mr. Bates there if I had known. Do you have any idea what they did to him?"

I nodded. "The Chinese and North Koreans were pretty hard on prisoners of war, Judge. The people I've talked to about it say that the psychological part was worse than the physical torture. They used our troops to experiment with brain-washing. They used drugs, too, and some of our guys never got over it. I think that's what Huck did to Oliver. I told you what he said about learning a lot from the Chinese. Forcing him on a bread and water diet was part of it. I think that was punishment. I don't think the water is that bad. Unless Huck put something else in it. That wouldn't surprise me a bit."

The judge nodded. "I think we had better respond immediately." He pulled a legal form out of a file cabinet and filled it in quickly. "Here is a writ of habeas corpus, if you need it. I would urge you to serve it tonight and to get Oliver out of there. Tell Sheriff Rawlins I have ordered you to have Mr. Bates in court here the first thing tomorrow morning."

The judge paused and I waited. "I hate to ask this of you, John, but we do need to get Oliver out of there right away."

"I think you're right, judge. I'll phone Huck right now and ask him to have Ollie ready to go."

"Let me know if you have difficulty," the judge said. "If

need be, I can telephone my counterpart in Buford County. Assuming he's sober." He looked at me sternly. "You didn't hear me say that, Sheriff."

I smiled. "I didn't hear what, sir?"

"Precisely."

⁊

When I talked to Huck Rawlins ten minutes later, he was surprised. "I can have him ready, John," he told me. "No problem. Why didn't you pick him up when you were here?"

"I would have if I'd known, Huck, but his honor doesn't always keep me in the loop. Something came up and the judge wanted to get on it right now, if not before. He called me in and told me to have Bates in court first thing tomorrow morning."

"Something came up?" Rawlins asked. "What was it?"

"Hell, I don't know, Huck. You know how judges can be. When I asked he told me it was complicated and he'd explain later."

Rawlins chuckled. "Well, I guess I'm lucky. Our judge doesn't pull stunts like that. I'll have him ready. It's better if you're here by eight."

No, I thought. You probably have your judge in your pocket. "Hell, I'll be back here by eight!" I growled. "I'll be running both ways with lights and siren. Judge wants him there, so I'll, by God, have him there!"

"No need to take the Lord's name in vain," Rawlins admonished me.

"Sorry," I said. "I don't normally do that. No offense meant."

"None taken," he replied.

⁊

The trip to Jerome went well and I ran with red lights only. Nor did I have to use the siren except with some cows on the highway. When I cut loose with the screamer, they scattered like a flock of birds and some of them even jumped back into the pasture. I was still in Buford county by then so I didn't have to worry about them. They were Rawlins' problem and taking care of it would give his deputies something to do besides torture prisoners.

Thinking of that reminded me of Oliver's weight loss. The more I thought about it, the more convinced I was that his gut problem had little to do with the public water supply. All Huck had to do would be to force Ollie to drink lots of magnesium hydroxide, or, failing that, to give him soapy water enemas. The dehydration from either would make him weak and dizzy, easy to control. I knew from experience that being given an enema could be painful, particularly if you're forced to retain the fluid. I also knew that if it was repeated too often, it could have serious medical effects. Given the choice, I suspected that Ollie would choose to drink the magnesia. I also suspected the doctor might find evidence of rectal damage.

When I got back to town and I called the doctor and asked him to come to the jail. His face grew grim when I explained what I suspected and he asked me to bring Ollie to the hospital. "I can do a better job of examining him there," he told me.

Once he had examined Ollie, the doctor confirmed my suspicions. "I found evidence of scaring in the rectum and lower colon," he told me. "The scars look recent but it would be hard to say when they were made. Not knowing what you told me, I would have guessed Mr. Bates had engaged in rough homosexual behavior or had been raped. The thing is, I found wood splinters in his anus, too, and signs he had been burned."

"You mean with a cigarette?" I asked.

"No, it's more like a match was inserted, leaving the head on the outside. Then it was ignited, either with another match or something like a cigarette. It then burned down, and as it did, the pain would be excruciating. There are large bundles of nerves in that area."

I just shook my head and the doctor asked, "Who did this to him, Sheriff? The scars aren't that old."

"I'm not sure," I replied. "For the last couple of months he's been in jail in Buford County. The thing is, I don't see how we can prove anything. They could always claim that it happened in our custody."

The doctor shook his head. "Actually, they couldn't. Those scars have been made since I last saw Mr. Bates. I'm sure of that. I checked him out from stem to stern. I would have seen the rectal scars. They'd be hard to miss."

"Could they have been self inflicted?" I couldn't imagine anyone I knew doing that, but people do crazy thing to themselves.

The doctor nodded. "Yes, and I see what you're driving at. Even if I testified that the scars were made during their custody, they could claim self-abuse. I've never seen a case of that but I've certainly read of them. Some people cut themselves and others hurt themselves with fire." He sighed. "So I suppose there's nothing to be done about it."

⁂

The judge came to the same conclusion the next day. His face was solemn when I began and it grew more and more grave as I reported. When I finished, he sighed and shook his head. "I had no idea we were consigning Oliver Bates to that kind of hell when we sent him to Buford County," he told me. "Did you, John?"

"No, sir. I would have never agreed to sending him there if I had. I would have tried to send Horace to some other county, instead. He doesn't have as bad a reputation as Ollie does."

"There is that," the judge agreed. "It might have been kinder to send Oliver to Huntsville, but there was no way we could have known. What do you suggest we do now? I don't suppose he's had the devil scared of him, so to speak. If he had, we could simply release him."

"I don't think you should release him," I said. "I don't think anything has changed with Ollie. The minute you let him out he's going to get drunk."

"What did the doctor tell you?"

"The doctor says Ollie needs to go somewhere where they can treat his disease. He knows of a place in Minnesota called Old Lodge that's supposed to be pretty good. They keep them there for a month and when they're done they go to another place for six months."

The judge shook his head. "I don't know, John. I'm no physician but I think Oliver Bates may be a hopeless case."

I nodded. "That's what I told the doctor. He told me the people up there specialize in hopeless cases."

"The question is who is going to pay for all these months of medical treatment? I'm sure it doesn't come cheap and Oliver can't pay. I don't think he's ever held a steady job other than bootlegging."

"What about the state mental hospital?" I asked. "The one in Austin?"

"That's a possibility," the judge said. "I'll take that under advisement. Talk to the doctor, John. See what he says. If he's willing to sign the commitment papers, that might be a solution. I certainly wouldn't describe Oliver as sane."

⁂

When I talked to Dr. Pettigrew that afternoon, he wasn't encouraging. "I know alcoholism is considered a disease, but there is some question whether or not it's a mental illness," he told me.

"That doesn't make sense, doctor. Ollie doesn't seem to be able to live without alcohol. Then, when he's drunk, he's crazy."

"Yes, he is crazy when he gets drunk. The question is whether he can control this. I think he can."

"Well, if it's a disease, how can he control being sick?"

"It's like having diabetes. Diabetics can control their disease by the way they eat and with insulin. I have no doubt Oliver bates is an alcoholic. I think he prefers being drunk. He doesn't have to be responsible then."

"Doctor, you saw him in the jail when he was seeing spiders. He may have been drunk then, but he didn't choose that."

Dr. Pettigrew shook his head. "I take your point but I don't think the state hospital will accept Mr. Bates as a patient. At least, not until he experiences alcoholic encephalopathy. That's wet brain in lay terms. Wet brain is a recognized psychosis and they might take him then. I don't think he's there yet. I'd rather try disulfiram."

"What's that?" I asked.

"You may have heard it called Antabuse. It's a powerful drug given to people who want to stop drinking. When they drink alcohol after taking disulfiram, they become quite ill. It can cause nausea and vomiting, extremely painful headaches, and a loss of coordination and mental functions. The way it was described to me is like having the worst hangover imaginable."

"The problem is that Ollie doesn't want to stop drinking," I pointed out. "We can force him to take Antabuse while he's in custody but I don't think he'll continue to take the stuff once he's released. He doesn't see the need."

We kicked it around a while longer without coming up with a good solution. It looked like the best we could do was to keep Ollie sober while he was in jail and make him serve out every day of his sentence. When I talked to the judge again, he agreed to impose the maximum jail time rather than a fine. A fine would only hurt Milly and neither of us wanted that.

SEVEN

Twister

Oliver serving out his sentence took us through the last weeks of spring and most of the summer. It was good having him gone. Milly and I spent more and more time together, and sometimes it was hard to remember how we were supposed to act when we were in public. We were very careful and nobody caught us doing anything improper, but soft whispers began to move along the county grapevine. What I noticed was the way people looked at me when they didn't think I was looking, but nobody said anything. A few times, when they realized I'd caught them at it, they just smiled.

Summer didn't last forever. Oliver Bates was released the day after Labor Day and I drove him out to their place. When I did I made sure he knew I would be keeping a close eye on him. I stopped the cruiser half way there and took out my black leather sap. "Do you remember this, Ollie?" I asked.

Oliver's eyes grew wide with fear. He nodded his head. "Good. Now do you remember what I told you the last time you saw it?"

Again, he nodded, but that wasn't good enough. "I want to hear you say it, Ollie. What did I tell you?"

"You told me not to give Milly no trouble," he said.

"That's right. And what did I say would happen if you did?"

"You'd put me back in the cell with Horace."

"Yeah, that was part of it. What did I say I'd do first?"

"You'd take me out behind the woodshed."

"I'm impressed, Ollie. You remembered. Now I'm going to tell you one more thing. Are you listening?" I pushed the sap up under his nose and Oliver nodded furiously. "Now smell this." He did.

"Good," I told him. "Now remember this. If you ever hurt Milly again, by hitting her or shoving her or in any other way,

I'm going to use this to break both your kneecaps. And when you smell this again, it's going to have your blood on it." To make my point, I gave his knee a soft rap and he yelped.

"Are you clear on this point, Ollie?" Again, he nodded frantically.

"Let me hear it," I told him.

"You're clear on that point." His voice quavered when he said this. I knew that the first time he took a drink, he'd forget it.

"Are you going to drink, Ollie?"

"No, sir, I'm not. I promise."

"You understand how angry I'm going to get if you break that promise?" He nodded and I said, "Knee busting angry. Do you understand? I want to hear it from you."

"Yes, sir, I understand," he told me.

"How angry will I get?"

"Knee busting angry."

"Very good, Ollie," I said, starting the cruiser's engine. "I'm glad we had this talk."

Less than a week later, Milly told me that Oliver was drinking again. Yet, when he did, he didn't abuse her. It seemed like that part of my message had gotten through his thick skull, but I didn't put a lot of faith in it. Instead, I rode close herd on Ollie and for a while it looked like he was keeping his drinking in control. He still got drunk but for over a month he didn't get into a fight and he didn't hit Milly. I know because if he had, I would have seen the bruises. No matter where he tried to hide them, I would have seen them.

I don't know if Ollie knew Milly and I were seeing a lot of each other, and I really didn't care. Under the customs of that time he could have probably got away shooting both of us if he caught us together, but I made sure he didn't. I also made sure he knew I was watching him like a hawk and he avoided me whenever he could.

⁂

That fall we had an awful twister blow through. It came late in the season and was the worst one I ever rode out. As it turned out, it was one of the worst storms the state ever had. It tore up three towns and left forty-six people dead. Most of them never knew it was coming. It roared in behind the worst thunderstorm anyone could recall, leaving hailstones the size of walnuts in its wake and God only knows how much rain. Some folks claimed six inches came down in half an hour. Others said they got nine. I don't know. The wind blew my rain gauge right off the post and I was surprised it didn't take the house, too. The barn and sheds were all left untouched, as well.

We were all lucky out where I lived. Most of our damage was to fences and a few livestock. The twister wiped out most of Curtis and jumped Live Oak. Then it came down on Bole's Well and plowed its way cross country before ripping through Ashtown. All that was left standing there was the rikety outhouse behind the new Baptist church. The storm took out the church house and tore out the wrought iron fence around the graveyard, but it didn't even turn over the ash bucket in the privy. That's what was strange. The outhouse wasn't anything but a flimsy board shed held together with baling wire and hope. They had indoor plumbing in the new building and only used the fresh air toilet for urgent need.

I knew the damage was going to be bad when I came out of the root cellar that morning, even though it was so early I couldn't see much. The wind sounded like a freight train coming right at us as it roared by the night before, and I knew what it was when I first heard it. I lit a coal-oil lantern and grabbed my boots. I was lucky I grabbed my gun belt, too, before I took off for shelter like a scared cat.

I was also lucky I lay down with my pants and shirt still on when I went to bed early that morning. There was late call the night before. Oliver Bates had gotten drunk and ran his truck square into a tree again. That was just about dark and no one spotted him for several hours. He was lucky it was September and still warm. A couple of months later we had a hard snap freeze and he could have frozen to death.

It took some time to get the crash sorted out and to get Oliver treated for a few cuts and settled in jail. When I left the courthouse, I drove out to the Bates place to let Milly know Oliver wouldn't be home that night. I stayed longer than I intended and by the time I got home it was just after four. I was too beat to do much but kick off my boots and undo my gun belt when I got home. It seemed like I no more than closed my eyes than the wind came up and woke me.

I was glad I lit the lantern when I grabbed my gun-belt, too. As I flung back the root cellar door and ran down the steps, I damn near stepped on the great granddaddy of all copperheads. I might not be telling this if I had. He was nearly as big around as a woman's wrist and ever bit of four feet long. The way he was laying stretched out across the floor was right where I would have stepped, and if he had bit me, I might not have survived. Copperheads may not be as poisonous as rattle snakes, but a big one can kill you.

I don't recall drawing my pistol, but when it went off it damn near ruptured my ear drums. It was good the cellar floor was dirt, too. The walls were solid masonry and I didn't need a .45 bullet bouncing around a space that small. I apparently made the shot by instinct, too. I didn't have time to aim and my first shot took the snake's head clean off. The rest of him coiled up around where his head used to be, of course, but I knew there wasn't any danger. I could see his head lying off to one side.

That woke me up completely, of course. I couldn't have slept even if I wanted, and there wasn't much to do but sit there listening to the wind and the rain. I couldn't help thinking about the wreck that night, either. I hated to admit it, but it wouldn't have hurt my feelings if Oliver Bates had broken his neck while he was at it. I saw too much of him those days and I can't say I ever saw him at his best. Or maybe I did. I don't know. Maybe being drunk and disorderly was the best he could manage. I know got tired of arresting him, but that wasn't all bad. When he did, I got to see Miss Milly more often.

The storm missed my house, but it took down my power line and knocked out phone service in some parts of the county. I don't know why, but I still had service and the first thing I did was to call Milly. There wasn't any answer and I was worried sick. From what I could hear when the twister passed my place, it sounded like it might have hit theirs. I'm not a religious man but I found myself praying that she was all right. Their place did have a storm cellar and I hoped she had time to make it.

I knew I needed to get to town right away, but I headed for Milly's place first. It was lucky the cruiser had just missed being hit by a falling branch nine inches across. I guess I could have driven my pickup, but it didn't have emergency lights. So I took off in the cruiser with the big red light on top flashing. I didn't get half a mile before there was a tree down across the road and I had to take a different route. This took me by a lot of places the storm had hit but I didn't stop until I got to the Bates'. When I got there I could see the house was still standing and I thanked Whoever is in charge for that mercy.

Power was out at the Bates', too, and I drove around to the back of the house and shut of my red light. Using my spotlight, I could see the barn was gone, along with the windmill, too. Several trees were down and it looked like the hog pen was crushed under one of these. All that was spared was the chicken shed, the outhouse next to it, and the woodshed. I had a sealed beam flashlight in the cruiser and I got out and walked over to where I knew the cellar was. I saw a big tree had fallen across the top of it and a big branch lay across the door. "Milly!" I shouted, banging on the tin cover. "Are you in there?"

"Yes, Sheriff, I am." She was talking very loud but I could barely hear her. The wind wasn't as bad, but it was still blowing and making noise with the trees. "We're all right. We just can't move this door." I wondered who "we" might be but I didn't ask.

I looked around with the light and saw an axe leaned up against the woodshed. I grabbed it and turned the spotlight of the cruiser on the tree limb across the door. Then I propped my flashlight on the ground to give more light and started chopping like fury. "I'll have you out of there in a minute," I yelled. Later, looking at the branch I cut in two, I was surprised. It was a full fourteen inches across and I cut through it in no time, like it was a sapling.

When I was done, I dragged the branch back out of the way. Then I tried to open the hatch but I couldn't budge it. "I guess you might need to unlock the door," I yelled and I heard Milly laugh. I was relieved to hear it. She wouldn't laugh like that if she was hurt. A moment later I heard the latch snick back and I pulled open the door.

"Thank you, Sheriff," Milly said. She was carrying her cat and I wondered why she was being so formal. That was for when we were in public. I tossed aside the axe and was about to give her a big hug when I saw the dark faces that followed her out. They were two young people, a boy and a girl, and it looked like they were about eight or nine. Turned out they were a couple of years older, but they were smaller than most kids their age.

It took me a minute to recognize them. They were the children of a wetback Mexican who worked for Milly's neighbor. He and his wife lived in a shack set off by itself and when the storm hit, their dad had told them to run for the Bates' place. The kids made it just in time, but not their parents. The boy and I took the light and went to look, but their shack was gone and there was no sign of the mother or dad.

There wasn't much else we could do right then, so I took the boy back to Milly's. She had a fire going in the cook stove by the time we got there and was cooking breakfast by the light of a coal oil lamp. I told her I needed to head for Live Oak, but she persuaded me to have a bite to eat first. "It's going to be a long day, Sheriff," she told me. "You need a good breakfast to carry you through it." Then she smiled. "You had a short night, too."

"Do you mind keeping the kids here for a while?" I asked. "The parents may come looking for them." When I said this, the boy looked at me and I realized he knew his parents were probably both dead. I looked at his sister and realized he had already told her what we'd found. It looked to me like she was trying very hard not to cry. So was her brother.

"Of course not," Milly replied and I knew she was aware how things were. "They're welcome here as long as they need to stay." She walked over to the girl and stroked her head gently. "It's going to be all right," she assured her and gave her a hug. After a moment, her brother came over and Milly hugged him too. "We're going to do just fine," she said.

※

Things were chaotic by the time I got to town. As I went, I made sure to stop at every house still standing to check on the folks living there. I asked the men to check on their neighbors and to come into town when they were done. "There are going to be lots of folk that need help," I told them. "Some of them may be trapped in the wreckage, so bring your tools. I'm putting together search teams."

When I did get to town, the judge was glad to see me. "Thank God you're here," he told me. "This is a disaster. We need someone to take charge." I told him what I had in mind, organizing search teams and sending them into every part of the county, and he agreed. By then there were a number of men on the courthouse square and I sent them out in pairs to rouse the town folk. "We're going to need lots of help," I said. "Ask the women to start cooking for our volunteers. Tell the able bodied men we need them to help us search for survivors. Ask them to gather together here at the courthouse to get assignments. The women need to take the food to the school gym. We need to do this quickly."

I looked around the crowd and called a half dozen men to join me in my office. I had a large county map on the wall and I drew off sectors and appointed one of the men as the team leader. I told them to get three other men to make up their team and told them not to send anyone out alone. "It's a dangerous situation," I said. "Use the buddy system."

The next thing I did was call the school superintendent and ask him to unlock the gym. I also asked him to call other towns in the county and to request their gyms for emergency shelters. While he was doing that I organized men with trucks to stand by to take food and fresh drinking water to the survivors we knew about. When the superintendent was done calling, I asked him to supervise food delivery.

That's the way the whole day went. About two that afternoon one of the ladies who was helping with food for the volunteers brought me a plate. I didn't feel much like eating, but I did and was surprised how hungry I turned out to be. I guess I was running on nervous energy because the food made me sleepy. I dropped off for a couple of minutes while I was taking a turn monitoring the radio and phone in the office. Then an incoming call woke me up and I hit it again so hard I was surprised when it started getting dark outside. I thought it was another storm coming through at first, but the wall clock told me it was after eight-thirty.

I asked Buzz to cover the radio for me and told him I'd be in the cruiser if he needed me. Nobody was using the phone at the moment, so I called Milly. I told her I needed to check storm damage but that I'd be there as soon as I could. She told me things were all right there and to take my time. She added that the kids were asleep and asked if there was any news of their parents. I told her there was nothing so far and asked if she minded them staying there with her until we found them.

"Of course not, Sheriff," she replied, reminding me it was a party line. "I was able to talk to my neighbors and they are all safe. The only ones I couldn't reach were the Farleys. You might want to check them. They were directly in front of the storm."

"Clint and Mary are all right, Miss Milly, but I'll check their place. They were in Ft. Worth when the storm hit. They're helping out with the search and rescue teams."

"That's where I should be, Sheriff," she replied. "Helping out."

"You are helping out," I reminded her. "You're taking care of those kids."

I could tell she didn't like this but she saw my point. "Well, there may be other children in the same situation. Don't hesitate to bring them here, too."

It turned out that the Farleys were not as lucky as the Bates. Their house was severely damaged by a falling oak tree, but the barn and sheds were still standing. Nor had the twister taken any of their livestock. "That's all right, by me, Sheriff," Clint told me later. "The barn is the main thing. The house can be rebuilt. It's the barn that builds the house, not the other way around. Mary and I have our health and we have each other. We've been blessed to still have what we do."

The next stop was at the Bates' and Milly opened the door before I could knock and greeted me with a warm hug. "I was so worried about you," she whispered. "I'm so glad to see you safe."

"I'm fine," I told her. "I just need a good night's sleep."

"I wish it could be with me," she answered and kissed me. It reminded me exactly what I'd be missing by sleeping alone. On the other hand, I was dead tired. I wouldn't get much sleep with

Milly there with me. When I told her this, she laughed softly. "There is that," she said. "Why don't you stretch out on the bed. I promise not to pester you."

The offer was tempting but I shook my head. "I need to be at my place if someone calls." She kissed me again. As I drove away I told myself I was crazy to leave, but I didn't turn around.

I was up early the next morning and made myself a big breakfast before I left. Milly had sent some cornbread home with me along with a half dozen eggs, and I scrambled three of them. I drank a half a pot of coffee to go with them and filled a thermos with the rest. By the time I got into the cruiser, I was wide eyed and bushy tailed, raring to go.

The clouds had cleared the night before and it was a beautiful morning. If it hadn't been for the storm, it would have been perfect. Yet the bright light showed the scars the storm left in its passing and I was amazed at the damage it had done. Even where there weren't any buildings, it had leveled acres of scrub oak and ripped huge branches from the largest trees. The pastures and peanut fields were littered with broken limbs and storm trash, and I knew it would be a good while before things looked normal again.

The Red Cross pulled in just before noon and I was glad to see them. The governor had declared Rutherford County a disaster area and after two days there were more volunteers than we knew what to do with from as far away as Iowa. I set them to searching for missing people and helping clean up storm debris.

Once the Red Cross arrived, there wasn't much for me to do. They had a disaster coordinator and I told him what we had done so far. Then I left to take a look around in the cruiser. I left the office for Cheryl to manage and asked Buzz to be available to respond to calls for help in the county jeep. I told him to take someone with him if he had to make a call.

One of the families I was worried about was the Krauses. They were two elderly sisters, Lucy and Lacy, and a brother, Morton. They lived on the family farm in an isolated area in the far southwestern corner of the county. They didn't own a car and none of them could drive, but they did have an old John

Deere tractor their dad had left them. Morton, the brother, used that to get around, occasionally driving thirty-six miles into Live Oak when they needed something they couldn't make or mend. Yet, they had good neighbors and when one of those folk was heading for town, they would generally stop by and offer the Krauses a ride.

I'm not sure just how the Krause sibs had come to be the way they were. I know the family they grew up in spoke an odd German dialect, and for some reason they were never sent to public school. None of them seemed to be able to speak, though they seemed to understand what all was being said to them, and they could read and write. They were able to communicate with each other somehow and could make their wishes known to others.

What I remember about the Krause sibs was that the three of them were always smiling. I think this may be how they came to be labeled as simple. But my sense of it was that there was a sharp mind going on behind each one of those placid smiles. I think they were shy and used being thought of as simple as a way to deal with a strange and fearsome world.

When I got to the Krause place that afternoon, I was given a warm welcome. Lucy, the oldest, brought me a glass of cool tea and Lacy, the youngest, pointed me to an old rocking chair that must have been their father's. As old as it might be, the woven twine bottom was perfectly strung, and the joints did not creek when I sat in the chair.

"This is really a good chair," I said. "Did your father make it?"

Lacy, who I had asked this, smiled happily and shook her head. She pointed to Morton. "You made this?" I asked and he smiled and nodded. "You really did a good job weaving the bottom," I added. Morton shook his head and pointed to Lucy, who smiled and nodded.

That's the way the conversation went. I did all the talking and they did the smiling and pointing. When I asked how much rain they had from the storm, Morton pointed toward a rain gauge and held his thumb and forefinger about three inches apart. To my question about the wind, Lacy nodded and pointed toward the storm cellar and then to a stack of large branches piled by the woodshed. My question about storm damage was answered by them all shaking their heads, and when I asked if there was anything they needed, all of them smiled brightly and shook their heads again.

When I got up to leave, Morton tugged at my sleeve and beckoned for me to follow him. He led me around the house and we passed a huge garden that was done for the year except for a large patch of pumpkins and late squash. High chicken wire guarded the whole area from marauding rabbits, and it occurred to me that the Krauses grew most of their own food. Then we passed a well kept chicken yard full of hens and I followed Morton through a wooded area and out into a broad pasture.

Morton stopped at the edge of the clearing and pointed to something lying in the grass. I looked at him and he was no longer smiling. "Something bad?" I asked and he nodded. He seemed reluctant to go farther so I stepped around him and approached the object. All I could make out clearly was a fancy cowboy boot, but then I saw that it had a leg sticking out. It looked like it had been wrenched from the rest of the body and raggedly sheared off above the knee, but there was very little blood and no evidence of trousers. When I drew close I could smell the odor of decomposition.

"Where did this come from, Morton?" I asked.

Morton shook his head and pointed upward, circling his hand around in a rapid motion before pointing it down. "The wind dropped it here?" I asked. He shook his head and repeated the swirling motion. "You mean the twister dropped it here?" I asked.

This time Morton nodded emphatically and pointed to another area of the field. Looking where he was pointing I saw the body of a large black dog and walked over to look. Like the severed leg, it was beginning to rot, but I saw a bright red collar. Moving upwind of the dead dog I reached down and took off the collar. When I did I discovered a rabies tag. This was someone's pet and the number on the tag would tell me who the owner was. I checked this out several days later when I had time and found out that the dog had disappeared from a farm sixty-something miles from the Krause place.

I asked Morton for a gunny sack and a shovel. He walked back toward the house and I looked around the area for more storm debris. There was none and when Morton came back I put the boot and leg into the sack. This did nothing to abate the smell, but it did make it easier to handle.

I told Morton I needed to take the leg to the morgue but the dog could stay. I asked where he would like me to bury it and he shook his head. He pointed toward himself and then to the dog, and I understood. Morton was telling me he would take care of it.

I thanked him and then asked, "Have you all found anything else from the twister?" Morton shook his head and I told him I needed to get back to town. Yet, when I was about to put the gunny sack into the trunk of the cruiser, Morton tugged my sleeve and shook his head. He rushed off to a shed and came back with a large paper feed sack. Holding the sack open, he gestured to me to empty the gunny sack in it and when I did, he quickly closed the paper sack and tied it with a string. He shook his head and held his nose and I had to laugh. Morton was telling me it would stink less in the paper sack.

As I drove off, the three Krause sibs waved goodbye. They were smiling, of course, and as I drove back to Live Oak I had an odd thought. The Krause children might be considered simple, but they weren't stupid. As a matter of fact, they were a lot sharper than a lot of those who called them dim witted.

※

I was out on patrol again the next afternoon when I got a call over the radio that Clint Farley needed to talk to me right away. Since I was only a couple of miles from town, I went back to the office and called him. When I asked him what he needed, he said he had found a couple of bodies while he was rounding up his livestock. He said he wasn't sure who it was and I told him I'd be there right away.

"What do you want me to do while I wait, Sheriff?" he asked.

"Are you sure they are both dead?" I asked.

"Yeah, I tried to get a pulse but they were both cold."

"Then stay them and leave them the way they are until I get there. Fifteen minutes."

When I got to the Farley place, Clint was looking grim. "I didn't want to say it over the party line, but it looks like that wetback and his wife."

I didn't have to ask which wetback and it turned out Clint was right. The two bodies were starting to decompose, but I recognized them. They had been around for years. I called the office on Clint's phone and asked Cheryl to send somebody with a truck and a couple of blankets to pick them up. Our local mortuary was overloaded and we needed to get these people out of the sun. I dreaded having to tell the children what had happened. The saddest thing was that all four of them would have been all right if they had run the other way.

When I got to the Bates', Milly knew something was wrong by the look on my face. The kids could speak good English. So they understood what I was telling them and they clung to Milly, sobbing. I waited for a while and then told the boy I needed to talk to him, but his sister came along, too, as did Milly. We all sat at the kitchen table and I took out a pen and tablet.

"I need to know some things," I told them. "I need your full names. That includes your middle names."

They told me and I wrote down Luís Xavier, and Maria Alicia, Rodriguez y Degas. "They call me Louis at school," the boy told me. "They call her Mary Alice. They have our last name as Degas, not Rodriguez."

"What are your parents full names?" I asked.

"Papa is named Domingo Rodriguez. I don't know his middle name," the boy answered.

"It's Carlos," his sister said. When her brother frowned at her, she said, "That's what Mama told me. My mother was Anita Hortensia Degas before she married. They got our last names mixed up when we were born. We're twins," she added.

I got as much information as I could, birthday, places where they lived, and kinfolk. I was surprised to learn that the children were born in Alice, Texas, which was why that was Mary Alice's middle name, and that they had no memory of any other relative besides their grandmother. "She died before we came up here,"

Mary Alice told me. "She was very sick. I don't remember her too well. We had to talk to her in Spanish."

Nor were the children sure where their parents were from in Mexico. "I don't know," Mary Alice said and Louis shook his head when I looked at him. His sister added, "My mother told me their families didn't want them. They didn't like to talk about it."

"Papa told me that, too," Louis added. Seeing his sister's surprise, he said, "He was a little drunk one day and he told me lots of things. He told me I was born first." He looked a little defiant when he said this.

This was clearly news to his sister and I could almost see the wheels turn in her mind. She struck me as the dominant twin, and their whole relationship had just been turned upside down. Not only was Louis the oldest son of the family, he was the first born, as well, which meant she was number two. I could see she didn't like his knowing this, either. I don't think her mother had told her she was first, either. I think Mary Alice had simply assumed this because her brother usually let her take the lead.

Milly smiled at this and stopped preparing our dinner to hug each of the kids. "It doesn't matter who was born first," she told them. "What matters is that you have each other. Now, if the sheriff is done with his questions, I need you to help me set the table."

I almost smiled when she said this. Milly is never bossy but that was her way of telling me enough was enough.

Dinner that day was a wonderful relief from the disaster. Before we ate, the four of us held hands and Milly asked me if I would say grace. I was surprised but I stumbled through being grateful for the food and for being alive and together. When I looked up, Milly had tears in her eyes. She told me later that was the first time grace had been said in her home since she got married. I told her it wouldn't be the last and the floodgates let loose. That night after the kids were asleep she showed me just how much it meant to her.

※

Having the kids in the house changed our lives. School was back in session three days after the twister, which meant that

Milly and I had to take our time together in the morning after I drove the kids to school. I spent a lot of time on the phone over the next week trying to run down family, but the kids seemed to be right. Degas and Rodriguez were both very common names and I ran into a dead end trying to track their parents' origin. I did, however, manage to confirm they were born in the little town near Corpus Christi and I requested a copy of their birth certificates from the state.

I went to see the judge that Friday afternoon. After I explained what I had found out, the judge thought a minute. "Milly Bates is the logical person to take care of them," he said. "That's to whom their family chose to send them and she certainly qualifies in terms of character. The problem is Oliver, John. I can't in good conscience assign temporary custody to a family where the husband is a known alcoholic and is violent, as well."

"Could you assign custody to me?" I asked.

"It would be simpler if you were married, John. They need a mother."

I shrugged. "We're talking about temporary custody. They could live at my place and I could hire Milly to keep house and take care of them."

"You do realize the talk this will foster," the judge pointed out. "There are already rumors going around about the two of you. It could be a political disaster, Sheriff. I would be remiss not pointing that out."

"Judge, I think the welfare of those two kids is more important than my political career. I think most people will understand that. If they don't, then I'll do something else."

The judge looked at me a long time. Then he nodded. "All right, John. I'll draw up the necessary papers and issue the order of temporary custody. You do need to understand that it will be contingent on whether or not any extended family show up to claim the children. The term will be for six months and we will review the situation then."

When I told Miss Milly about it that evening, she cried. "Oh, John. This means we have a family together. Even if it's only for a little while."

Then she pulled back and looked at me seriously. "I hope you understand I'm not going to accept any money for this. I'm not doing it for the pay."

I nodded. "I understand that, but that's the only way it will work. The judge is cutting us a lot of slack but we need to keep up appearances. We have to be able to swear under oath that I've hired you to look after the kids. You're going to have some expenses, too."

She looked at me for a long moment. "I need to be very clear what we're about, John. I'm doing this for the sake of the children. I'm not taking charity from you or anyone else."

I sighed. "Milly, this is not charity. I'm asking you to take care of my kids. I'm going to have to hire someone else if you won't do it. Since we can't get married, this is the only other way we can do it. You can put the money in a savings account and give it back to me later. I don't care."

Milly gave me an amused look. "All right, Sheriff. Mrs. Bates will take care of your children and do the housework. However, I can't give you any work related references. I have never worked outside the home."

"How did you live? Someone had to pay the phone bill and property tax." I was certain Ollie had never coughed up the money for those. Nor had he been gainfully employed aside from bootlegging and petty theft.

"I was very frugal," she answered. "I made a little money selling eggs and doing sewing and ironing. I could have made more as a store clerk or as a secretary. I was offered several jobs but Ollie wouldn't let me take them."

"Why in the world not?"

"He thinks it's shameful for a woman to have to earn the family living. Not that he ever did!" A flash of bitterness crossed her face, but a moment later she was contrite. "I shouldn't have said that, John. I'm being disloyal and Oliver is not here to defend himself."

"You're being truthful, Milly," I assured her. "The real truth is that Oliver would hit you if you said that to his face. At least, he would if I wasn't around."

Milly looked at me in alarm. "You must never hurt Oliver, John. Not even if you see him strike me. It's the drink doing it."

"Then I'll whale the tar out of the drink!" I declared. "I am the sheriff and if I see an assault going on, I will stop it, whatever it takes. Tell me this. Have you ever seen him completely sober? "Even when you were growing up?"

She shook her head sadly. "I can't honestly say that I have, but he is my husband and divorce is a sin, John. I can't get around that."

"What do you think the judge would say about the situation if he knew all the facts?" Milly shrugged and I plunged on. "He would tell you that to be a real marriage, the vows must be consummated. Do I have to explain what that means?"

I smiled when I said this and Milly tried to remain serious. I could see her fighting a smile, and then she snorted. "I think you already did, John. Maybe you should explain it again." When she said this she gave me a look that I'd come to know well.

I laughed and she added, "All right, then, I'll be your housekeeper and your children's nanny. At the moment, however, what I feel like being is your lover. What do you think about that, John Paul Stone?"

I took her in my arms. "I think that's a great idea, Miss Milly."

EIGHT

Complications

The kids accepted the move to my house quite well, though I know they missed their folks terribly. They didn't say much, but, as kids do, they seemed to accept the situation and adapt to their new life. After a while they began talking to Milly about their parents, and sometimes it happened at the supper table. I made it a point to always be there for supper and they grew comfortable talking about these things with me, too. I think this was because I made it a point to listen without criticizing.

I also made it a point to spend special time with each of them. Mary Alice was partial to the soda fountain and I took Louis along with me in the patrol car sometimes, which he really liked. Later on, I taught them both to drive, and then how to shoot and handle firearms. I was surprised how much I enjoyed all this.

I think one of the things they liked most was having their own rooms, particularly Mary Alice. She said Louis tended to be a slob. I guess he was, compared to her. She always wanted everything just so. I was taught how to keep things in order when I was in the Coast Guard, and it took with me. So I showed Louis how things were supposed to be, and why. He understood and it wasn't long before he was giving Mary Alice a hard time about how sloppy her room got.

Then there was Ollie, always there in the background, affecting even the simplest decisions we made. One was a car for Milly. When Ollie crashed his truck the day before the twister, it was a total loss. I set up a deal with the owner of the junk yard for Milly to buy the old car he told me about before. He gave her a good price and I gave her the money to pay for it. Yet she didn't want to take it at first, and I had to put my foot down.

"Look, Milly," I told her. "This is for the kids, just like the household account I set up for you to draw on at the bank."

We'd had a long talk about that one. "You need some way to get from your place to mine every day, and to pick up the kids when I can't. I'd be happy to have you drive my pickup but that would cause talk."

"No, John," she smiled. "That might cause more talk. People are already talking enough because I'm your housekeeper. I'm feeling like a kept woman with your paying me for that."

"Milly, we've had this conversation, several times. I'm paying you to take care of the kids because I'm their legal guardian. That was the agreement I made with the judge. I'm not paying you to share my bed." Then I grinned at her. "I guess, if it would make you feel better, we could stop sharing a bed."

"You don't mean that for a minute, John Paul Stone!" she declared with a laugh. "Unless you think there would be more room on the floor!"

"It would look better if you had your own car," I pointed out.

"What would look better?" She fluttered her eyes and spoke with a deep South accent. "Making love on the floor? Or in the back seat of the car?"

I laughed. "Well, then we could truthfully deny going to bed together."

"And ruin all their fun?" She shook her head. "Who is this woman?" Her deep gray eyes were filled with wonder. "Whenever I'm around you, she just pushes my normal self out. I like her but she scares me."

"It's not a bad thing, being who you are," I reminded her.

"No, it's marvelous. I can't see it as anything but a gift from God. You set me free, John Paul."

There was a flaw in that last statement. If I was a gift from God, then He was the one who set her free. I was just the tool God used, but I didn't point this out. Instead, I started to ask her to finish the job by leaving Oliver. Yet, I kept the thought to myself and a moment later I was glad I did. "I know you want me to set myself all the way free, John. I just can't right now. I don't know why. It doesn't seem right. I think of myself as your wife, too, and that doesn't make any sense, either, does it?"

Again, I kept my peace and once again she echoed what I was thinking. The longer we knew each other, the more often this happened. "I also know what the judge told you. I think if we were married, he would probably grant full custody right now. That makes it even more tempting but I just can't." She looked at me gravely and the desolation I saw in her eyes almost broke my heart. "I hope it doesn't mean I lose you."

"No, it doesn't, Milly," I told her. I spoke softly, and I hoped my words carried the utter conviction I felt. I wanted her to know I was there for as long as she would allow it. "I do understand. It's just the way you are and that's who I love."

"Warts and all?" she asked. I was glad to see the desolation give way to a look of amusement.

"Especially the warts," I assured her. "There's one I really like to kiss."

She rewarded me with a smile that warmed me from the inside out. "Yes, I noticed. You better watch out, talking like that, John Paul. Here comes that woman I was telling you about."

❧

Normally, Oliver's original sentence would have carried him up to the first of December. Yet, nothing about Oliver Bates was normal. I'm not sure just how he did it, but he managed to get a bottle of rum smuggled into the county jail. Nor did he share it with the other prisoners and he got roaring drunk. I mean that literally. He started off happy enough, singing drinking songs that grew progressively more profane. Then, when the jailer told him to be quiet, Ollie started shouting and swearing at the deputy. This made a couple of other prisoners angry with Oliver for not sharing the bottle, and they started shouting and cussing right back. Ollie offered to whip their butts, but the jailer told me he was careful to stay out of their reach.

Finally, the guard had enough and called me. The two of us could have handled it but I called Buzz. I'm glad it did. When I got there, Ollie got quiet at first. He watched me like a dog waiting for me to turn my back so he could bite. When I asked him where he got the bottle, he clammed up. Then, when I pointed out how much trouble he was in, he swore at us and threw the bottle at me. It broke on the bars and a big piece of it struck me on the cheek, cutting me deep enough to bring blood. Fortunately, I ducked my head when he hurled the bottle and I didn't get any glass in my eyes.

"That's it, Ollie," I told him. "You just assaulted a peace officer. I hope you like it in Huntsville."

Oliver swore at me again and I added, "Or would you rather go back to Buford County?" As angry as I was, I wouldn't have done this and the judge wouldn't have gone along with it. But Ollie didn't know that. He was full of Caribbean courage cussed me out again. Among other things, he told me exactly what I could do with Buford County and Sheriff Huck Rawlins, too.

"Sweep up the glass and bring the fire hose," I told the jailer. When I glanced at the other cells, I saw that the prisoners who had been fighting with Ollie were now putting as much distance between themselves and him. "You men stay quiet," I ordered, glaring at them. They hadn't said a word since I got there.

"Yes, sir!" They answered in unison.

When the jailer had cleared the glass from our area, I told Oliver to stand out of the way while Buzz washed down the floor of his cell. He started to argue but Buzz let him have it with a burst of water. Nor did he hit him full force, which was a good thing. Buzz is not mean. If he was, he wouldn't be my deputy. On the other hand, he doesn't put up with a lot of crap and he told me he was aiming at Ollie's chest. I took his word for it. Unfortunately, Ollie opened his mouth open to cuss us again and got hit full in the face. He got more than he could swallow and he choked. He fell on his bunk and started coughing, and Buzz began washing the glass to the back wall of his cell.

"We're going to have to move you to another cell so we can clean up your mess," I told Ollie. "We can do it easy or hard. It's up to you."

Oliver was still coughing but he chose to do it the hard way. So I stood aside while Buzz and the jailer took him down and cuffed him. He tried to fight back and swung a punch at Buzz. He was lucky Ollie was too drunk to be effective and the punch only grazed him. After that he and the jailer managed Oliver easily.

I was sorely tempted to put Ollie into the cell with the other two and let them straighten him out. I'm glad I didn't. That would have been a mistake. Instead, we moved him to another cell and gave him a towel and a dry blanket. We also scrounged up some surplus dungarees and a t-shirt shirt so he could change. These were damned near worn out and they hung loose on his frame. This surprised me. I always thought of Oliver as being a big man. Yet the liquor had robbed him of his appetite for anything else and turned his muscle to fat.

Oliver calmed down after that. By the time Buzz and I left, he was passed out on his bunk, still wearing his wet clothes. I did have Buzz drape the wool Army blanket over him and I asked the other prisoners to yell for the jailer if Oliver started choking or having a seizure. Nor was there any doubt in my mind at the time that I was doing this for Milly, not for the drunken bum who was her lawful husband. Or I could say, her awful husband. That pretty well summed up the kind Ollie was.

❦

I went to see the judge the next morning. I told him what had happened the night before, stressing the fact I had not laid a hand on Ollie. When I was done, the judge sat there a while, cogitating. Then he sighed. "We could certainly sustain a charge of assaulting two peace officers against Mr. Bates. It is enough to send him away for a year or two, but I would rather not see it come to trial. I know what the defense could make of Mrs. Bates being your housekeeper, and I don't want to put her through testifying at a trial."

"She can't be called to testify against him, can she?" I asked. The rule is that husbands and wives cannot be compelled to testify against one another except in certain cases.

"No, but she might be called to testify for the defense, not as a character witness but as a ploy. Her refusal might be considered grounds for a successful appeal, if it comes to that."

I knew he wasn't done, so I kept quiet and waited. "Another consideration is how Oliver might pay for his defense. He doesn't have the proverbial pot to piss in, but I happen to know he does own his farm, free and clear. A good lawyer might take a lien against that, which would eventually leave Mrs. Bates without a home. You do understand that this whole conversation is completely sub rosa, don't you, John?"

"Of course," I answered. Then I added, "I don't suppose

Oliver might see his way to pleading guilty, would he? That would do, wouldn't it?"

"Yes, it normally would, but that could come back to haunt us, given Mrs. Bates' situation. We have to consider that."

"I don't understand, sir. The assault was not on me, but on my deputy and on the jailer. There's also the charge of smuggling contraband into the jail."

"Yes, Sheriff, but you are a witness to the assault and if the prosecution doesn't call you to the stand, the defense can." I saw him come to a decision. "Let me talk to Emory. Perhaps there is some way we can convince Mr. Bates to accept a plea to a lesser charge."

I experienced a moment of utter clarity just then. The way the judge said this told me that what he was really worried about wasn't me being a witness or even Milly. We could work around that. The judge was concerned about Emory's ability to prosecute the case and win. Even though Ollie had let the fences and the buildings run down, there was a lot of oil drilling business going on in the county. That made the property an attractive prize for some hungry shyster from Cowtown or Dallas. Nor would Ollie be that hard to manipulate.

That made me wonder where Ollie had come up with the money to buy the property in the first place. I asked Milly about it and she told me Ollie had inherited it from an distant cousin. I was curious, so I did a little research and discovered she was right. The cousin was on his mother's side and died intestate, unmarried and without issue. Ollie was his only kin.

Something didn't seem quite right about this to me, so I did a little more research. Sure enough, there were all kinds of liens filed over the years against Ollie's property. Ollie had been wise enough to declare his farm as homestead property and under Texas law it could not be taken away except to pay taxes or to pay off the original mortgage. The taxes had been kept current over the years, probably by Milly, so there was no way Ollie's creditors could take his farm to pay off his debts. Nor could they come after Milly.

❧

I didn't think about this much at the time. Then one night

when I was out on patrol my mind made a connection. One thing I've learned over my years ion law enforcement is that people are consistent. A man who is honest in small ways will be honest in big ones. So when I see a man doing things a certain way in one area of his life, I know he will do the same in others. The connection my mind made was that Oliver Bates was a man who let anything he didn't have to do right now slide. So rather than take care or his truck, he'd put off changing the spark plugs or replacing the tires as long as he could. The fact that taking care of things ahead of time saves money and aggravation simply didn't occur to him.

This made me wonder about something. So one evening after supper I asked Milly if she remembered where she was married. "Yes, I do. It was at a little church in Fulger County, Oklahoma. We went there because my daddy knew the preacher and Oklahoma didn't have a waiting period." Then she smiled. "The preacher was really old and he kept forgetting our names. He kept calling Oliver 'Alfred' and he called me 'Lilly.'"

"Do you remember his name?" I asked.

"Yes, he was Brother Ruben James. Why do you ask?"

"Oh, you know me. I've got a lawman's mind and I like to know the full picture. It's no big deal."

Milly nodded but I knew she wasn't satisfied with my answer. She started to ask me to explain but just then the phone rang. It was the manager of the Roadhouse. One of the county commissioners had died of a heart attack and they needed me there. "He was having supper with a friend of his," the manager told me. "He just keeled over."

After a while, peace officers develop a nose for trouble and I knew there was a lot the manager wasn't telling me. I knew it wasn't a simple heart attack, but I didn't ask questions. Like everyone else, I was on a party line. So the manager hadn't told me the commissioner's name and I hadn't asked.

When I hung up the phone, I explained to Milly what was happening. "I don't know how long I'll be," I told her. "Do you mind staying with the kids until I get home?"

"Of course, not," she told me. "Do you know who it is who died?"

I shook my head. "No, but I know who I'd pick for the honor." Louis thought that was funny and laughed. Mary Alice smiled, but she was watching how Milly responded.

I picked up the phone and listened. No one was on the line and I dialed the number for the Pettigrews. When the good doctor came on the line, I told him who was calling. "Someone's apparently had a heart attack, doctor," I told him. "I may need a medical opinion. You mind going with me?"

"Give me ten minutes," he said. "You can pick me up here at home."

"Please give your wife my apologies if you're in the middle of supper."

"I owe you one, Sheriff," Dr. Pettigrew told me as we drove away from his home. "You saved me from a fate worse than death. We had dinner guests and the woman drives me crazy. She laughs at the least provocation and it sounds like a horse whinny. Her husband cheats at cards, too, and it's all I can do to restrain myself from confronting him."

I was surprised at his being so candid and wondered why he was telling me this. "They're my wife's distant kin," he added. "They only descend on us twice a year and only stay two days. Marge doesn't like them any better than I do. They take advantage of her good nature."

"Well, you know what Mark Twain said about fish and relatives," I pointed out.

The doctor laughed. "Yes! They both smell after three days. So what's the situation, Sheriff?"

"One of our commissioners had a heart attack at the Roadhouse. I don't know which one of them it was or even if that's how he died. That's why I called you. Has anyone filled you in about the place?"

He told me no one had and I outlined the setup for him. "So what you suspect is that the commissioner was visiting one of the waitresses at one of the lake cabins."

"That's right. The manager called me because he wants it kept quiet. His version is that the commissioner was having supper when it happened. I don't mind saving the commissioner's family some embarrassment, but I want your medical report as accurate as you can make it. My report will tell it like it is, too." Seeing the look on the doctor's face, I added. "I'm not suggesting for a moment that you'd pull any punches, doctor. I'm just telling you that you won't catch any flack for it from me. I think I can speak for the judge, too."

"Fair enough," he said. "I appreciate your candor. I know how convoluted things can be in a small community."

Convoluted doesn't begin to describe what we found at the Roadhouse. The commissioner who died was one of the more honest ones, and he left a wife and three small children behind. His death also left an opening in the board of deacons at the largest church in town, and one less member of the Klan. They weren't that strong in Rutherford County, but they were there and I kept close tabs on the members. I knew more about them than they probably thought. I grew up here and did well playing high school football and baseball, so people seem to trust me. They tell me all kinds things they might not tell their husbands or wives, and they know I don't pass along where I find things out, either.

Getting back to the late commissioner, I say he was more honest than most, but I don't mean completely honest. Most folks are what I'd call fairly honest. They might tell a diplomatic lie now and then, and they may fudge a bit on their taxes or how fast they were going when I clocked them. Yet, they don't claim it's the utter truth. They call lying to keep from hurting someone's feelings a white lie, and lying to the government is giving themselves the benefit of the doubt. They may even tell an outright whopper, like the fishing story where everybody hearing it knows the truth is being rigorously stretched. The thing is that they know they're lying but it's generally accepted to fib this way.

On the other end of the line are people who couldn't tell the truth to keep from hanging. The way you know these people are lying is that sound is coming out of their mouth and their lips are moving. Lying is a way of life and a lot of these people really don't stop to think what they're doing. The lie is out there flopping around like a chicken with its head cut off before they realize they said anything. So they pile on more lies to cover the first one, and instead of one chicken, they're dealing with a whole flock with its collective heads cut off.

These compulsive liars are different from what I call sport liars. A sport liar is one who is out to see what he can get away with. Even though honesty may be the best policy, and a lot less work than lying, these people are always after an angle they can shoot, a corner they can cut, or a loophole they can hide in. The payoff is putting one over on someone and these liars go to great lengths to set up their deceptions. These are the con artists and they seem to breed like flies. For them there's a sucker born every minute.

Maynard Gentry, the late commissioner, of Rutherford County lay somewhere between a compulsive liar and being honest as the day is long. He was fairly honest, which means he was a politician who stays bought. Better offers might come his way, but once Maynard was in your pocket, he stayed there. That didn't mean he wouldn't shake you down for a few more dollars now and then, but he was careful to keep his graft within reason.

At least, Maynard had up 'til then. When I learned who it was that died, it crossed my mind that he may have gotten a little too greedy. When the doctor looked him over in the guest cabin where his body lay, he told me that Maynard appeared to be in very good health. "I'll need to look him over at the hospital and run some blood tests, but he appears to be a man in his mid forties who doesn't smoke and gets plenty of exercise. His hands are calloused and scarred, so I suspect he makes his living from a manual trade that lets him keep them fairly clean."

"He works down at the feed mill," I told him.

"Well, that accounts for the dust on his clothes. Some of it, anyway. I do not see any obvious wounds, but I will take a closer look. If there are any, I'll find them." The doctor looked at me. "I did a short residency with a Boston pathologist, you know," he confided. "The thing I like about the dead, Sheriff, is that they don't lie. They can't if you know what you're doing."

"So when in doubt, shoot the bastards?" I asked and he chuckled. "Any idea when he died?"

"I'd say between two to three hours ago," he told me. "I'd say at least an hour before you called me. It took us twenty-three minutes to get here."

Just then there was a knock on the door. When I opened it, the manager let me know the hearse from the funeral home was there to pick up the body. "It's not going to the mortuary. The doctor is going to do an autopsy."

I could tell the manager didn't like this but he was a smooth operator. "You think that's necessary, Sheriff? The man had a heart attack."

"We always do one when there's a death under suspicious circumstances," I replied.

"Suspicious circumstances? What do you mean?"

"You tell me. A man in good health dies during a rendezvous in a guest cabin with a woman who is not his wife? He's not known to drink or smoke and is a public official. It was also at least an hour before anyone notified me."

"I was thinking more of embarrassment to his family," the manager said. "I would think this would be better kept quiet."

"Well, if he was doing something that might embarrass them, he should have thought of that first," I replied. "We will respect his privacy as much as we can, Mr. Smith, and yours, but we have to rule out foul play."

"I'm done here, Sheriff," the doctor told me, slipping off the surgical gloves he put on before examining the body. Seeing my surprise he explained that was how he was trained by the pathologist. I told him that was how I had been trained, too, but it wasn't common practice in rural Texas.

"You can ask the funeral home people we won't be long," I told the manager. "I will need to talk to the woman he was with when he died."

"The woman he was with?" the manager asked and I knew it was a lie. His tell was a tightening around the eyes. "I only told you he died in one of our guest cabins."

"Or the man," the doctor replied before I could respond. "There is quite a bit of evidence of sexual activity, both on the body and on the sheets. The late commissioner apparently came as he went." I wondered who he was quoting and made a mental note to ask.

The manager weighed his options and came down on the side of profit. He nodded and left, and when we were alone again, I spoke to the doctor. "I would like you present during this interview, doctor. I need to be sure that the woman they bring in is the one who was here."

"That's easy enough," the doctor smiled. "There are a few things she couldn't help noticing. Unless they questioned the original hostess." I smiled when he used the term. "Or should I say, Mata Hari?" he added.

The first woman the manager brought us was a middle aged matron and the doctor tripped her up very quickly. "Did you notice anything unusual on the gentleman's nude body?"

"Nude, we never got nude!" she said indignantly.

"Then who stripped the body?" the doctor asked, nodding to the still form on the bed. It was completely covered with a sheet.

I could see the matron thinking up a lie and I told her to stand in the corner furthermost from the door and to be quiet. "Not one word," I warned her, putting as much steel in my voice as I could. The doctor told me later that I was quite convincing.

I opened the door and the manager was there, obviously trying to overhear what was being said inside. "You have a choice," I told him. "You can either get the woman who was with him in here or we can shut the place down for the evening while we interview all your staff." It was a busy night and I knew he wouldn't want to lose the income. His bosses would not be happy at all.

"What about the one you have?" he asked.

I shook my head. "She's going to stay here until we talk to the right woman. One more ringer and I'm shutting you down."

The next woman we brought in looked like she couldn't be more than fifteen, if that, and when I asked her name, she told me it was Sally Jones. I nodded to the doctor who asked if she had noticed anything unusual on the commissioner's body. She accurately described a distinctive birth mark high enough on the right thigh to be covered by underwear. It had been the first thing I had noticed when I looked at the body. I was surprised when the doctor asked a second question. "Thank you," he said.

"Now, can you tell me if the man you were with was circumcised or not."

"No, he wasn't," she said. This was correct and I told the other woman she could go. She wasted no time getting out the door.

"Now I need to see your driver's license," I told her.

"It's in my locker," she told me.

"Then I'll go with you to get it."

"You can't! That's in the women's dressing room."

"We'll warn them that a man is coming in," I assured her. "Do you mind guarding the body, doctor?" I asked. "We won't be long." He told me he didn't.

Once we got to the young woman's locker, I told her to stand aside once she had opened the combination lock. Then I looked through the young woman's purse, removing a nasty looking little automatic and putting it in my pocket. Looking through her billfold, I took out two documents. One was a driver's license made out to Sarah Jones and the other was a food handler's permit issued to Nancy Hiller. "All right, Nancy," I said. "Let's go back to the cabin." When I said this, the young woman blanched so fast I thought she might faint, and the way two of the other women looked at each other told me the name was news to them. Somehow Nancy managed to stay on her feet and I was sure I had just learned who she was.

I saw the funeral home people waiting as we were walking back to the cabin and told them it was all right to remove the body. I also told them to deliver the body to the hospital for autopsy. This surprised them but they assured us they would, and when we got to the cabin I told the doctor I was ready to go.

The doctor looked at the young woman with me and I told him her name. "Aren't you going to interview her before we leave?" he asked.

"No, I'm going to interview her at the office while you do the autopsy," I answered. "Or are you going to wait until tomorrow?" He assured me he was not and before we left I phoned Cheryl. I told her I needed to interview a female suspect and asked her to wait for us at the office. This was long before having a chaperone became standard police practice, but I was taking no chances.

There were some shady owners associated with the Roadhouse. I wouldn't put it past them to try to make me look bad.

It was after ten before I got to the office but Cheryl was there waiting for me and I thanked her for coming out. "It was either that or put Nancy in jail for the night," I said. My words had the effect on the hostess that I intended. She looked scared to death and Cheryl knew better than to try to comfort her. "I need you to witness the interview," I added and Nancy looked even more scared.

"Nancy, the only thing you are in trouble for at the moment is having a driver's license that doesn't belong to you. You do need to tell me the truth from here on, and I assure you I can tell if you are lying. Lying to me will get you into real trouble. Are you clear on that?"

She nodded and I asked, "All right, who is Sally Jones?"

"I don't know, sir. They gave the license to me when I went to work there."

"Who gave it to you?"

"Mr. Smith, the manager," she answered and the rest of the interview was pretty straight forward. By the time we were done, I had enough to shut the Roadhouse down. Not that the commissioners would allow it. They'd find some way to either shoot me or get me fired if I did.

I took my time as I interviewed Nancy Hiller and the picture which came together was sad, mostly because it was true of so many young girls her age. As I listened, I was struck by the fact this could have been true of Milly because Nancy came from a similar background. Her father was a mechanic at a large truck dealership in Ft. Worth and her mother was a waitress in a greasy spoon cafe not far from where the family lived. Nancy was the next to youngest of six children and her parents had to work long hours to feed and clothe their children. This meant that there was little adult supervision of the kids and they mostly raised themselves.

Nancy had not done well in school and dropped out at age sixteen to work at the same cafe as her mother, who had become deeply religious and started to question her closely about her personal life. A year later Nancy had enough of this and moved out of the family home. She began living with two older girls in an apartment above a music store on the other side of town. Nor did she let her mother know where she was living, even though Nancy still worked at the same cafe.

One of the girls Nancy roomed with was over twenty-one and there was always liquor around, mostly beer and cheap wine. There were also men and one of them had gotten Nancy drunk and taken advantage. Yet, he had also left her ten dollars for a present, and this became a habit. He would come over from time to time and he always left her ten dollars. Then one day morning when the other girls were out, he brought a buddy along. Nancy agreed to service the friend, too, and her take that day was twenty dollars, far more than she could earn in tips as a waitress.

When another apartment over the music store came open two months later, Nancy moved in by herself. By then there were four or five men visiting her every week. Fortunately, one of her roommates had explained the need for birth control and Nancy never became pregnant. Unfortunately, one of the local crime bosses soon got wind of her operation and a detective on his payroll shut Nancy down. The option he gave her was to go to jail or to go to work for the crime boss, which is how she ended up as a hostess at the Roadhouse. Needless to say, her income had taken a nose dive even though she was servicing more clients.

As I said, the saddest thing about his story was how common it was. One of the things that made the interview interesting for me was watching Cheryl out of the corner of my eye. Cheryl was seated to the right of Nancy at the conference table and I was at the end to Nancy's left. So when Nancy was talking to me, Cheryl was out of sight. Nor was this an accident. I wanted the hostess to focus on me and forget about Cheryl.

As Nancy told her story, I saw a wide range of emotions cross Cheryl's face. At first all I could see was harsh disapproval, but as Nancy's story came out, that changed to indignation over Nancy's seduction to outrage with the crooked detective. Yet, by the end of the interview, there were tears running down Cheryl's face. This confirmed something I suspected about Cheryl but had never seen so clearly. Below that facade of stern religious matron there was a deep well of compassion.

When the interview was done, I asked Nancy where she wanted to go. She was surprised she had a choice. "I guess back to the Roadhouse," she said.

"Are you sure?" I asked. "You don't have to go back there if you don't want to. As a matter of fact, I'd rather you didn't."

"Why?" she asked.

"I'm concerned about your safety," I told her. "What you could testify to in court could cause a world of trouble for the owners and the management. I'm certain that Mr. Smith is aware of this. I don't want you to disappear."

Nancy paled when I said this. "You've seen it, haven't you? You know of people who just disappeared one day, don't you?"

Nancy nodded. "Where else can I go?" she said. "I don't have much money. I haven't been paid this week."

"My deputy and I will take you out to pick up your paycheck and your clothes in the morning," I told her. "I brought your purse with us. We'll figure it out." I handed it to her.

"You mean I'm not under arrest?" she asked.

"No, but we won't share that information with Mr. Smith just yet."

"What about my pistol?"

I smiled. "I think I better hang onto that for a while, Nancy. Along with the fake driver's license. I can't see how either one will bring you anything but grief. You're still a minor, so ask me for the pistol when you're twenty-one. The main thing right now is to find you a safe place to stay."

NINE

Outlaw In-law

The next morning when Buzz and I stopped by the Parker Hotel to pick up Nancy Hiller, the clerk told me she had checked out. This made me suspicious. "When was this?" I asked.

The clerk looked at a registration card. "Jimmy checked her out about five-thirty this morning. Says here she left a five o'clock wake-up."

"Did she check herself out or did someone else do it?" I asked. I had a bad feeling about this. I didn't think Smith would move this quickly but he could have.

"Just a minute, Sheriff. Let me ask Jimmy. I think he's still here."

The clerk picked up a house phone and dialed. We could hear it ring in the dining room and I looked through the door. Jimmy was sitting there finishing up his breakfast. "Never mind," I told the clerk and he hung up, puzzled. I signaled Buzz to follow me and we walked over to Jimmy's table.

Jimmy the Night-man is an elderly gentleman. He has been the hotel's night auditor for more years than anyone can remember. He's also been called by his sobriquet so long that few remember his last name, which is Ferguson. He looked up from the newspaper he was reading and smiled when he saw us. "Sit down, Sheriff, Buzz. Have a cup of coffee on me."

"Coffee will have to wait today, Jimmy," I said taking a seat. "Thank you all the same. Spunk just told me you checked Nancy Hiller out at five-thirty this morning."

"That's right. She left a five o'clock wake up call and caught the 5:48 train headed west." He smiled. "She was traveling light and seemed to be in a hurry, don't you know? I asked if she forgot her luggage but she hadn't. Room was paid up, too. Should I have called you?"

I shook my head. "No, Jimmy, we weren't holding her. Did

she check herself out, or was there someone with her?" I asked.

"All by her lonesome," he said, shaking his head sadly. "So young, too. I didn't think she was twenty yet."

"She isn't. You didn't see anybody hanging around looking for her, did you? Or anybody asking for Sally Jones?"

"Not a soul," he told me. "It was just she and me and the good Lord, too. Is she in trouble, Sheriff?"

"Not as far as I'm concerned, Jimmy. She's been hanging around with a rough crowd, so who knows?"

"Did she have anything to do with that murder last night at Roadhouse?"

Few things approach the speed of light but local gossip is one of them. I decided to put it to use. The truth might not be as entertaining, but it needed to be told. "It wasn't a murder, Jimmy. Put out the word on that. One of our county commissioners went out there for dinner and had a heart attack."

"I heard it was Maynard Gentry," Jimmy told me. "Seems young to me to be having a heart attack."

I shrugged. "That's how the doctor called it and he was very thorough. I remember Maynard's dad having heart problems, too."

Jimmy chuckled. "Maybe so, but maybe Maynard got lucky with an inside straight. The only time I did, I like to wet my pants." He shook his head sadly. "I never saw a royal flush, either," he told us. "Not even playing for peanuts." He grinned. "I did have a few straight flushes, but those were in the dealing, not the cards, don't you know?" He sighed. "Then the good Lord gave me arthritis to clean up my act. Can't hardly cut the cards any more."

⋇

I asked Jimmy to keep quiet about Nancy Hiller, and he said he would. Buzz went home to change his clothes and then headed for work. There were some things I wanted to check out, so I spent the rest of the morning on the phone. This was mostly chasing my tail. Police work is often like that but I did learn a few interesting things. Among other things, I learned that I was probably going to have to make a trip to Oklahoma if I hoped to dig out the information I was after.

I was just about to walk out the door for lunch when the phone rang and Cheryl picked it up. I was surprised to see her. I'd told her to take the morning off since we worked late, and I didn't expect to see her until one. Then I looked at the clock and saw I'd worked straight through the noon hour.

Cheryl told me that a man named Smith wanted to talk to me. She added that he was the manager of the Roadhouse and I closed my office door before I took the call. This doesn't give much privacy. Cheryl has ears as sharp as a wildcat, but it did let her know the call was very important and I knew she would be listening by the door, if not on the extension.

"Sheriff Stone," I told the caller.

"This is Gaylord Smith at the Roadhouse. I'm calling about one of our employees, a young woman named Sally Jones."

"I don't believe I know a Sally Jones," I replied. "There are at least four women named Sally in the county, but none of them are named Jones."

"Sheriff, you took her in custody last night. She was the young woman who was there when Mr. Gentry passed away."

"Oh, your hostess. Her name is Nancy Hiller. At least that's what her food handler's license said. Why are you calling her Sally Jones?"

"We tell all our employees not to give our customers their real names. It can cause trouble. Sally Jones was the name she chose when she went to work here."

"This isn't making much sense to me, Mr. Smith. We found a fake driver's license in her purse that made her twenty-one. The name on that was Sarah Jones and I imagine Sally is short for Sarah. However, Nancy told me she was given the driver's license when she started work there."

"Well, of course, she did. These girls will lie at the drop of a hat. No one else gave her the fake license, Sheriff. She showed it when she came to work for us. I couldn't have given her a job if she hadn't."

I was certain that Smith knew that I was aware he was lying. He was a smooth operator and I doubted it was worth trying to catch him in a direct lie. So I played along. "All right, then, Mr. Smith. Let's call her Sally Jones. I'm not sure Nancy Hiller is who she is, either. What can I do for you?" I tried to give the impression there were other things I needed to do.

"She never came back here last night. I need to send someone in to make bail if you're holding her."

"We're not holding her," I told him. "We interviewed her last night and then let her go. Aside from the fake license, she hadn't done anything wrong. Unless the drug tests show different, Maynard Gentry died of natural causes. Rumor has it his heart couldn't take it when he filled an inside straight."

Smith ignored my jest. "So where is she, Sheriff?" The man was persistent.

"I don't know. I thought she was going back to the Roadhouse. She told me she needed to get paid. Other than that, I'm not sure. She did mention something about heading north, maybe to Minnesota or Wisconsin. We had no cause to hold her."

"Minnesota? What the hell's in Minnesota?"

"Your guess is as good as mine, Mr. Smith. Tons of snow and lots of dumb Swedes?"

At that point Gaylord Smith thanked me and hung up.

❦

The death of Maynard Gentry sank into the oral history of Live Oak within a week. It was replaced as a topic of conversation by a juicy scandal. One of the community pillars was arrested for soliciting an undercover police officer in a bar in Cowtown. It would have been bad enough had the officer been female officer, but the banker chose to solicit a young man who appeared to still be in his teens. The accused hired a good lawyer and beat the charge, of course, but that only added fuel to the small town fire. Even so, the titillation that offered soon wore out and the community settled back into the humdrum of daily life.

Nancy Hiller was another matter, though she never became a hot topic for gossip. A couple of weeks after Maynard died Milly had a visitor and Nancy's name came up. It was on a Sunday afternoon and the kids and I were over at Milly's place for dinner after church. We had just finished washing up when a car came up the drive and a young man walked up to the door.

When Milly saw the young man getting out of the car, her smile disappeared and she looked worried. When she invited him in, the kids and I came into the living room to see who it was and Milly introduced him as Sammy Brown. He looked familiar, though I couldn't place him at first, and I didn't recognize the name. Yet I sized him up as a crook and I'm sure he knew I was a peace officer. It was significant that neither of us offered to shake hands. We seemed to recognize one another as natural enemies.

The visit didn't last an hour, though it seemed a lot longer. Milly offered the stranger a glass of iced tea, and as the two of them visited, I looked him over. The suit he was wearing was a good one, better than an off-the-rack Sunday suit, and it fit him well. His shoes and socks were expensive, too, as was his white silk shirt and stripped tie, and from the neck down he looked like a successful lawyer.

From the neck up, however, he looked like a punk. At least, he did to me. His dark hair was slicked back in a duck-tail and his face looked like he rarely saw the sun. His cheeks were marked with old acne pits and there was a faint scar that ran down his forehead and across his left eyebrow. He was also cultivating a thin black mustache on his upper lip but he didn't have strong enough features to make it work. His normal expression looked to me like a petulant sneer, and combined with the mustache, it made him seem silly. What he reminded me of was a spoilt little boy playing pirate and trying to come across as mean.

To put it in a nutshell, Sammy Brown struck me as a phony, and I had him pegged as a liar, too. Even so, he projected an undefined air of menace and I thought he would probably dangerous if he could intimate his victim or sneak up from behind. Or maybe this was only the scar, or the result of my imagination. Whatever it was, I had no use for Sammy Brown at all. I wondered what hold he had on Milly.

I noticed the kids were very quiet in the stranger's presence, too. After a while they drifted back to the kitchen table and began playing cards quietly. I would have liked to join them but I sensed that Milly wanted me to stay. It was clear that she knew the young man well, and that he knew both her and her husband, too.

"So how is Oliver, Sheriff?" the young man asked. He looked

at me. "I understand he's a guest of the county these days."

"Ollie's doing all right," I answered. "He doesn't like it, but at least he's sober and off the road for a while. He's gaining a little weight, too."

"I understand he found a way around staying sober in jail," Sammy said, smiling. "That's Oliver for you."

"All that did was earn him a longer sentence," I pointed out. "The judge was not amused. Ollie assaulted two of my officers, too, and the prosecutor is still thinking about charging him with that."

The young man nodded. "That's probably the only way you'll ever keep Oliver even halfway sober, keeping him in jail. Is he allowed visitors?"

"Of course," I said, telling him the visiting hours. "Don't be offended if you show up and are searched," I added. "After that last stunt Ollie pulled, we're a lot more careful."

"I'm sure you are," he said. "I appreciate what you've done for my sister." While I was certain he meant that, there was an unmistakable irony in his words. I realized he knew exactly how things were between the two of us. I also knew he would not hesitate to use that information against me or Milly. I suddenly realized that this was the source of the subtle air of menace Sammy projected. He knew things and he let people know he knew. What was implied was that he was not someone you wanted to fool with. Yet I doubted Sammy had the sand in his craw to carry through. At the first sign of strong resistance, he would take off at a dead run.

Just then the dime dropped and I placed where I had seen him. "You work for Gaylord Smith," I said. "You're a bartender out at the Roadhouse. I didn't make the connection with Miss Milly at first. Brown's a common name. You must be Miss Milly's youngest brother."

I could tell he didn't like being called the youngest but he let it go. "Yes, I am. I'm also one of the assistant managers at the Roadhouse. I tend bar sometimes to keep the regular bartenders honest."

The conversation when on for a while after that and Milly seemed to relax. When Sammy left, he offered me his hand and

I shook it. He also gave Milly a hug and said he'd try to come by again soon. She assured him he would be welcome.

After her brother left, we sat down for a while in a couple of rockers on the front porch. The kids came out and joined us for a while, but we must have been too quiet for their liking. So they went back into the house and I could hear them playing cards on the kitchen table, laughing and occasionally arguing.

"They seem to like living with us, don't they?" Milly observed and I told her I agreed. She was quiet for another minute or two, and when she started speaking, it was like she was talking to herself. "I wonder why Sammy came to visit just now? He works right here in Rutherford County, and he must have worked here for a while if he's an assistant manager. But I had no idea he was anywhere close by."

Then she looked at me. "So why now and not before. Oliver and I have lived here for years."

"I think it may have something to do with his working for Gaylord Smith," I said.

"So why he didn't come to see us before? He and Oliver were the best of friends. Oliver was Sammy's hero growing up."

Milly looked at me, her eyes pleading, and I wanted to take her in my arms. I sensed there was something more she wanted to say and I wanted to hear what it was. So I simply put my hand to her cheek and said, "It's all right. Go ahead and tell me. It's about him, not you."

Milly nodded. "Thank you, John Paul. You're right. It is about him, not me. I'm only his sister, not his mother." She gathered her thoughts for a moment and went on. "Sammy always seemed close by when trouble came knocking. He was not a bad boy, not really bad. After Mama died he did some very stupid things and later he took after our dad with his drinking. He thought the world of Oliver, too, and looked up to him like an uncle when he was growing up."

"Then he and Ollie may have been in touch for some time, Milly," I pointed out. "From what you've told me, Ollie seems pretty close-mouthed about what he does, even with you. Or am I reading things wrong?"

"No, you're right. He doesn't tell me anything except when he needs money. Then he makes up some outrageous lie, as if I couldn't see right through it. I have to keep my egg money with me all the time or he'll steal it. He's good at figuring out hiding places."

When Milly said this, there was an edge of bitterness in her voice, very unlike her. It was as near as I'd ever seen her to being angry. Then she shrugged and the resentment left her eyes. "Or maybe I'm not very good at hiding things."

When she said this, Milly tried to smile but it didn't work. Instead, she shook her head sadly and sat quietly for a long while, rocking her chair gently in rhythm with mine. It was almost like we were making love, and maybe we were, at that, creating love between us. Then she turned to me and asked, "What did you mean that Sammy's showing up might have something to do with his working for Gaylord Smith?"

"I think they're still looking for Nancy Hiller. I think Gaylord Smith sent Sammy here to see you." I started to say more, but stopped. What I thought was based on how I look at things. I wasn't working from solid information.

"What are you not telling me, John?"

"Well, figure it out for yourself. You and Sammy aren't close now, are you?"

"No, not any more. Not since he left home. We were very close after Mama died, but even before he left home he started pulling away. That's been what, twelve or fourteen years? I haven't seen him a dozen times since the day he left. Not even when Daddy died. He didn't even show up for the funeral."

"So you didn't know he was working at the Roadhouse, right? Oliver didn't ever mention him, either, did he?"

"No, John, Oliver didn't. Why are you asking all these questions? Why don't you just tell me what you think."

"I don't want to speak ill of your brother, Milly. What I have to say may hurt you and I don't want that."

"Silence can be even more hurtful, John. Please tell me straight out."

"Well, I may be wrong, but I think his boss, Gaylord Smith, sent him here to find out if you knew anything about Nancy

Hiller. That's the girl who witnessed Maynard Gentry's death."
I gave her an abbreviated version of the story Nancy had given
me. "She is trying to break free of Smith and the people who
own the Roadhouse. I think they're trying very hard to find her."

"Why do they think I might know something?"

"They probably think I might have told you where she is. I'd
be willing to bet that Sammy will be back out here sometime
when I'm not around. Probably within the next week. They
must be really worried about what she told me. That means
Nancy is in danger."

"Did she tell you anything? Is she a witness?"

"She didn't tell me anything I didn't already know. She
confirmed some of my suspicions but she didn't really bring
me any new evidence except for the driver's license. That's her
word against hers and they know it would be a waste of time
to prosecute. I think maybe they're afraid she told me about
something else she saw. I think they must be really nervous and
I wish I knew what it was. Nancy must know some real dirt to
get them stirred up like this."

"Or maybe not," Milly said softly. "The wicked flee when no
man pursueth."

I recognized Milly's quotation from Proverbs. It was one of
a handful of Bible verses I know by heart. One of my Coast
Guard chiefs used to say it all the time and one day I looked it
up and surprised him by quoting the rest of the passage. "Yes,
but the righteous aren't always as bold as a lamb," I pointed out.

Milly laughed, delighted at my word play. "It's a lion, silly
man. The righteous are as bold as a lion, like you are, John."

I leaned over and nuzzled her neck. "Especially between the
sheets."

"Or in the back seat of a police cruiser?" she murmured. "You
must be reading my mind." She glanced over her shoulder. The
house was very quiet. "We need to wait. The kids are still up."

"The kids are probably eavesdropping," I told her and she
blushed.

Later that evening, long after dark, we were lying entwined
in Milly's comfortable bed. "I have a small confession to make,

John Paul," she whispered. "I meant to tell you before."

I was almost asleep. "What's that?" I asked, barely able to speak.

"I noticed you the first day you came to church," she said. "Then I started noticing you all over town and sometimes I'd make sure I was where I thought you might pass by. I even thought about.... Well, you know! I'm terrible, aren't I?"

"Yes, m'am, you are," I muttered. "You're terrible wonderful and you're terrible good for me, too. And right now I'm terrible...." I don't recall finishing whatever I was trying to say.

❧

The next morning we took our time saying goodbye once the kids were off to school. I had scheduled a couple of days off and was headed for Oklahoma. Where I was going was only a couple of hours away. Yet I figured it might take some time to run down the people I needed to see.

Milly was curious what I was up to but I wasn't ready to tell her. When she asked what I'd be doing, I told her I was going fishing. She pointed out that normally requires at least a pole and a line. I told her I was fishing for something else and I got to see her roll her eyes for the first time. I told her she did that well and she threw up her hands and shook her head.

"I'll tell you when I get back," I promised. "I may be chasing a will-o'-the-whisp. I'd rather look foolish after the fact."

"So you're fishing for *ignis fatuus*," she said. "Well, I guess you won't need a line and pole, after all. Not a regular one."

"*Ignis fatuus*?" I asked.

"Yes," she said, smiling. "You're not the only one who can read a dictionary, John Stone. I had a high school teacher who liked to spout Latin. He thought he was a wit, too, and he was half right."

"You never cease to amaze me, Miss Milly," I told her in my broadest Southern accent."

"Good!" she declared. "You need it!" Then she gave me a farewell kiss that made me an hour late getting away.

❧

The first place I headed was Fulger County, Oklahoma,

where I talked to my counterpart there. Before I saw the sheriff, however, I stopped by the County Clerk's office and made sure my information was right. The lady I talked to there was the same one I talked with over the phone. She seemed a little miffed at my asking her to check again until I told her it was a personal matter. When I told her it involved the lady I hoped to marry, she smiled. "Maybe she's just putting you off, Sheriff," she teased. Are you sure she'd accept?"

"I hope so," I confessed. "I just need to know whether or not to propose. I hope you'll keep our names out of it if anyone asks."

"Of course, I will," she smiled and I knew I'd given her a pearl without price for the county telegraph. She knew our names would mean nothing to her compatriots, but our story would generate lively speculation.

The story I gave the sheriff was different and I pulled no punches. I told him I was there on behalf of a lady who had married a drunken crook who beat her and stole her egg money to buy liquor. I told him I suspected that the marriage was not a legal fact and that I needed to check it out. I also gave him the information I had from Milly and when I was done, he nodded.

"Not to speak ill of the dead, but Brother James was a little casual about record keeping at times. Rumor has it that he had a drinking problem, too, but people didn't seem to mind. He was a good man and the rotgut didn't turn him mean. Whenever I came across him three sheets to the wind, I always took his car keys and carried him home."

The sheriff chuckled. "I kind of hated to because his wife was a tough cookie. You could hear her tearing into him a block away sometimes, and especially when he was drunk. She was some bigwig with the temperance people, and I guess she thought he disgraced her. Truth is, she did that good enough on her own. She didn't hesitate to tangle with a bootlegger if she saw him on the street. Talk about live entertainment."

"It sounds like the reverend is dead," I observed.

"Yes, sir, he's five years in the grave. No, wait. Damn! It's been almost ten years since he passed. I can look it up if you need the date."

"No need," I said. "What about his church? They might have a record."

"Not much use checking with them." Again he smiled. "They're the kind of the independent gospel folk who believe in letting the Lord keep the records. They don't even require a marriage license to do a wedding. Without it being recorded, it comes under common law. You live together and call yourself man and wife in Oklahoma, and you're, by God, married! Did the lady and her husband ever live in this state?"

I shook my head. "They've always lived in Texas."

"Well, you people do things different down there," he observed, shaking his head. "It makes things confusing."

"You got that right!" I told him.

I got an early start the next day and visited all four of the surrounding counties. The result was the same. There had been no marriage between Oliver Bates and Millicent, Mildred, or Milly Brown, both from Texas, on or about the date Milly had given me.

I also checked the archives of every small town newspaper in the area. All of the editors who had been there back in the day knew Brother Ruben James. Every last one of them had favorable things to say about the man and a dozen stories attesting to what a good man he was. His only fault, and most of the editors mentioned it, was a fondness for liquid spirits and a tendency to be forgetful when he was in his cups. "I wish every drunk was like him," one of the long term editors told me. "We wouldn't need so damned many jails and prisons if they were."

I took an extra day getting home, first letting Milly know I'd be a day late. I used the day to do the same search in every county surrounding the one where Milly was raised. The result was the same. There were no records of any marriage between Milly and Oliver Bates for months on either side of their anniversary, either in the county courthouses or in the local newspapers.

When I got home late that afternoon, the kids were out of school. There was something at school we needed to attend that evening, so we had to wait until the next morning to catch up with each other. Even then, the talk had to wait until we showed one other just how much we missed being together.

We were sitting at the kitchen table in my place when I told Milly about the results of my search. When I did, she reached out and touched my face. "You dear, sweet man," she said, her eyes soft and warm. "I wish you had told me first. I could have saved you some trouble." She picked up her family bible and opened it at the front. "I thought that might be what you were up to, so I brought this along today."

Milly's bible was designed for family records, and in the appropriate place was a filled in certificate certifying the holy matrimony of Oliver Bates and Milly Brown. At the bottom of the page there was a rambling signature written in the same hand that filled in the blanks. It read, "Brother Ruben James" and gave the name of a small town in Oklahoma. It was one of a multitude of small towns I had never heard of before.

"Is this Brother James' signature?" I asked.

Milly shook her head. "No, my daddy is who filled that in. Brother James and Oliver were sharing a bottle of rum." The way she said this was very matter-of-fact.

"I don't see your signature or Oliver's," I pointed out.

"No, Daddy filled all that in later on. Nothing was signed the day we got married.

A wave of relief washed over me. "I'd have to ask the judge, but this is not a legally binding document, Milly. You're not married to Oliver and you never were."

A stubborn look came over Milly's face. "That doesn't matter, John. I made some solemn promises and I need to keep them."

"Would that include obliging Oliver if he asked to sleep with you?" I asked. The moment the words were out of my mouth I desperately wished I could call them back. "No!" I said, throwing up my hands. "Don't answer, Milly! I didn't mean that. Please forget I said it!"

Milly looked at me sadly. "How can I, John? It's a fair question I have to face and the answer is 'yes.' It breaks my heart to say that, but it is." The she got up and held up her hands when I reached for her. "Now now, John, please. I need to be with myself for a while. Please don't stop me."

I have never experienced anything more heartbreaking than watching Milly Bates walk out of my house and drive away. I

didn't know if she would ever come back and I felt lost. I didn't
how I could stand going through life without her.

TEN

Brother Travis

Things were different between us when Milly showed up to pick up the kids the next morning. The kids were aware of this and, of course, they had to fight with one another to distract us. I didn't understand that at the time, but that's what was going on. I had to be very stern with them and afterwards, by myself, I felt like a real jerk. When I picked them up from school that afternoon, they were all right and I treated us to an ice cream cone at the drive-in.

I was just about to start the car and leave when Mary Alice dropped her bomb. "Are you and Mama Milly splitting up?" she asked. I looked at her and saw she was trying not to cry.

"I certainly hope not," I said. "She just needs a little time to think."

"You and her aren't married, are you?" Louis asked.

"No. We'd like to be but we can't right now."

"Is that why you don't stay all night?" Mary Alice asked. Her fear had given way to curiosity.

"That's part of it," I told them. "To be honest, a big part is because we didn't want to embarrass you kids."

"We can hear everything, you know," Mary Alice informed me. "We used to listen to Mama and Papa, too." Louis looked mortified when she told me this.

I couldn't think of a thing to say, so I kept my mouth shut. Yet, Mary Alice was not done. "We know what's going on," she informed me with a smile. "We watch the animals all the time. It's funny what they do." She began to mimic some of the sounds and motions the livestock made and her brother laughed.

Then Louis, emboldened by Mary Alice, asked the toughest question. "Are you and Mama Milly going to have a baby?"

I first impulse was to tell them in no uncertain terms that

it was none of their business. Seeing the fear in Louis' eyes, I realized that I was glaring at him. That was the last thing I wanted to do. I also realized it was their business. We were a family. What Milly and I did affected them greatly. I forced myself to calm down and told them, "We haven't talked about that." At that moment it also occurred to me that Milly and I had done nothing to prevent it. I was surprised how much the idea that she might be carrying our child pleased me.

Milly was not at the house when I got there, so I opened a couple of cartons of chili from the freezer and heated them while the kids set the table. I noticed they had set a place for Milly and I tried to be cheerful, but it fell flat. All of us missed her and supper was dismal with her gone.

When we were done eating, we all pitched in cleaning up, though we didn't clear Milly's place. I told the kids I needed to go and make sure Milly as all right, and they wanted to come along, too. I started to tell them to stay home, but I changed my mind. They had as much a stake in what was going on than I did, maybe even more. I hate to admit it, but it occurred to me that Milly was a lot more likely to say "no" to me than she was to them.

There was a car in front of Milly's place when we got there. At first I thought it might be Milly's brother, Sammy Ray Brown, but it was a different car than he had driven there before. The first one was a big dark Buick but this one was a snazzy little Studebaker Golden Hawk, and the three of us paused for a moment to admire it. "Wow!" Louis said, almost reverently. "I've never seen a car like that."

The front door to Milly's place opened and she came out, followed by a tall slender man. I knew this must be her oldest brother, Travis, and he could have been her twin. Not only did they look alike, but I could see it in the way he moved. Milly had told me about him after Sammy's visit. Like her, he took after their mother in disposition, and after high school he had gone into the Navy. He had always made very good grades and stayed out of trouble, and he moved up quickly as an enlisted man. He was invited to take screening exams and scored high enough that the Navy sent him to college. On completion of his engineering degree, he was commissioned as an officer. She thought he probably meant to make it a career.

Milly had also told me that Travis came to see her whenever he could, which was not that often, and wrote to her at least a couple of times a month. She also told me he had little use for Oliver but tolerated him for her sake, and that her brothers had grown apart since leaving home. "They are like night and day," she said sadly. "Sammy resents Travis because he's everything Sammy would like to be. He's like Daddy that way. He just doesn't seem to have what it takes make something more of himself." Unlike his brother, Travis didn't drink.

I'd never met Travis before, but I was glad to see the effect he had on Milly. She smiled at us warmly when she introduced him to the children, and then put her arm around my waist affectionately when she introduced him to me. "This is my special friend, John Stone," she said, smiling. "He's the sheriff and we cause a lot of talk."

There was no doubt in my mind that Travis understood the exact nature of our relationship or that he approved. "It's about time Milly had a good man in her life," he told me, shaking my hand warmly. "She wrote me about you and I had you checked out." He smiled at my surprise. "I'm in naval intelligence, if you can believe there is such a thing. The Coasties speak very well of you, as does the West Virginia Highway Patrol."

"Did they tell you how seasick I used to get?"

Travis nodded. "Oh, yeah, but I wasn't going to mention that. That's why I'm not a line officer. On a ship I'm upchuck Charlie." The kids laughed when he said this. They took to him right away. "Why don't you and I stretch our legs?"

"Can I go?" Louis asked.

Travis reached in his pocket and pulled out a set of car keys. Handing them to the boy, he said, "Tell you what, Louis. Why don't you ask Sis to give you a ride in my car? Would you like that?"

Louis couldn't believe his ears. "You want Mary Alice to drive?"

Travis laughed. "Actually, I was talking about my sister, your Aunt Milly."

The boy laughed. "We call her Mama Milly." He handed the keys to Milly and two minutes later, they were gone.

"You're going to spoil her for driving that old heap she has," I pointed out.

"I hope so," Travis said. "Let's cut to the chase, John."

"You want to know my intentions toward your sister."

"I need to hear it from you. I know what Milly thinks they are."

"It's simple," I told him. "We'd be married tomorrow if I could talk her into leaving Ollie. And I'd shoot myself before I laid a hand on her." I explained the situation, including the results of my research in Oklahoma. Nor did I hide the fact of her abuse from Oliver.

"That sounds like Sis," he said. "When she makes a promise, she's worse than a damn mule." He looked at me. "Did she tell you we had one of those growing up? At least, we did until Mama died." He was quiet for a moment. "It's good I don't live nearby. I might have a hard time keeping my hands off the bastard if I saw the bruises."

I nodded. "I know what you mean. I have to let my deputy handle Ollie when he's in custody."

"So he's really not her husband?"

"Not as far as I can tell. I haven't talked to the judge about it, but even if she was, I think he'd grant an annulment in a heart beat."

"On what grounds?" Travis asked.

I realized my mistake. "Travis, I shouldn't have put it that way. I think you need to hear anything to do with that from Milly, and I think it would be better if you didn't ask at all. Just the failure to record the marriage in Oklahoma should be enough. I don't think that certificate in the front of her Bible is worth much, legally. Your dad is who filled it out and signed it. There were no witnesses, no records kept, and everyone tied to it is dead, except for Milly and Oliver."

Travis looked at me intently. "You mean Oliver never...?"

I held up my hands. "I mean you need to hear anything about that from Milly. I really am sorry I even alluded to it."

"That son-of-a-bitch!" he declared. "I wondered why they

never had kids." Then he looked at me and said, "I'm glad you were her first, John. Thanks for telling me. Even if things don't work out between you, I'm glad of that."

"I don't even want to think about things not working out," I told him. "If that turns out to be what she really wants, I'll have to accept it and go on. I just can't imagine how."

A cloud of dust appeared at the gate and a sleek golden shape emerged out of it. I laughed. "Now I'm going to have to get her one of those," I said.

"She's worth it, John. She may even let you drive it once in a while."

⁓

Travis stayed for three days. He insisted on staying at my place with the kids while Milly and I stayed at hers, and that evening was wonderful. We were in each other's arms before Travis' car was out of the driveway, and afterwards we moved out to the rocking chairs and talked.

I told Milly about my conversation with Travis. "I didn't use these words, but what I tried to tell him is that I want you in my life, regardless of how it needs to be. I want you to be my wife and to bear my children, but if it can't be that, then I'll just have to accept it. I will never push you to do anything you don't see is right, no matter how I feel. So if you need to officially be Mrs. Oliver Bates, so be it. I just want you in my life." After a moment, I added, "So do the kids," and chuckled.

"What's so funny?" she asked, and I told her about my conversation with Louis and Mary Alice. Her face was flushed but she laughed when I described the noises and movements Mary Alice made. Then I told her about Louis' question and she was aghast. "What did you tell him?"

"I almost told him it was none of his business, but I realized it was. I mean, you and I are their parents in their eyes. We're all they have."

"Well, what did you say?"

"I told them we hadn't talked about it. Then I had the thought that we had not done anything to prevent it, either. I couldn't remember your ever having a time of the month, either."

"Oh, I have. You just never knew about it," she answered.

"I'm afraid I'm a little late this time," she added. "It's nothing to worry about. Sometimes it happens."

"So what do we do about it?" I asked.

"Why don't we just let nature take its course?" There was an unmistakable look in her eye.

I ran my hand over her cheek, then kissed her tenderly. "I'm afraid I'm feeling sort of natural right now."

"That's funny, so am I, John. I may even whoop and holler and do funny things." She smiled when she said this and I thought she was kidding. Which only shows how wrong a man can be.

❧

The next day I stopped by my place and carried the kids to school. When I got to the office, Cheryl told me the judge needed to see me. It turned out he had some papers that needed to be served and I wondered why he hadn't called the constable. Then I saw that the constable was one of the people to be served. Seeing the question in my eyes, the judge said, "He knows the papers are coming, so you won't have a hard time finding him. It's that wife of his. She is apparently determined to live in Austin. She is equally determined to be unencumbered."

There was no mistaking what the judge thought of this. Beulah Jarvis was half her husband's age and she made no bones about how boring she found life in Live Oak. Why she had married Leland was a source of unending speculation along the gossip telegraph. Leland was one of the kindest men I know, though he could be rough as a cob, too. He was also one of the homeliest men in the county. He was half a head shorter than Beulah, stocky and going bald.

What was not commonly known was that Leland was the sole heir of one of the most successful oilmen in Texas, and I think Beulah may have known this. I think she just got tired of waiting for Leland's uncle to die and figured her prospects were better in Austin. I wondered if she understood the competition there would be greater, too. I thought not. Beulah might be clever but she was certainly not very smart. Despite her discontent, Leland thought the world of her and treated her right. Once the inheritance was in his hands, she could probably have talked him into maintaining a place for her in Austin.

The judge asked me how things were going with the children and I told him about Travis' visit. I also told him about my failure to find any record of marriage between Oliver and Milly and the circumstances of her marriage. "You're right about the family Bible," he told me. "It won't stand up in court, particularly with the elder Mr. Brown dead. I suppose that Mrs. Bates is laboring under the misapprehension that she is obligated to honor the promises she was forced to make. Do you know, John, if their union was ever consummated?"

"I am very reluctant to answer that question, Judge. I'm not refusing, but I'm trying to honor her confidence in me."

"Then I won't order you to break it," he replied, smiling. "Just between thee and me and the doorknob, I believe you've told me what I want to know. Unless there is something of which neither of us is aware, I don't see that she would have any trouble getting relief from this court if she requests it."

"Now, if I could just convince her," I said and his honor nodded in sympathy.

⁂

Like a plugged nickel, Sammy showed up the day before Travis left. Travis had parked his Golden Hawk in the barn to keep the birds from fertilizing it, and I had parked in the back of the house. Travis and I were visiting in the living room and Sammy was almost to the door before we noticed him and Travis stepped out on the porch to meet him. I decided to stay inside for the moment.

"Hello, Sammy," Travis said. "I hear you're living around here now." Neither of the brothers offered a hand to the other.

"Travis," Sammy answered. "It's been a while, hasn't it?" From the way he said it, I could almost hear the afterthought. It had not been long enough for him.

"You're looking prosperous," Travis observed. "You seem to be doing well tending bar. Or are you still stealing cars?" He looked at the Buick pointedly and smiled, but there was no humor in his eyes.

This touched a nerve but Sammy kept cool. "It comes with the job," he said easily. "I'm the assistant manager now."

"One of three, I hear," Travis answered. "What do you need?"

"Why do you think I need something?" Sammy asked. "I came out to see Milly. Is she around?"

"You only show up when you need something, Sammy. Is your boss still looking for Nancy Hiller?"

"Who's he hell is that?" Sammy asked.

"You never were a very good liar," Travis replied.

"Not near as good as you?" Sammy sneered. When Travis glared at him, Sammy added, "What are you going to do, older brother, whip my ass?"

"If I had a mind to, that gun you're toting wouldn't do you a damn bit of good." Travis responded and I decided it was time to intervene.

"That's enough," I said, stepping out onto the porch. Sammy was startled to see me. "You gentlemen need to stand down. Milly's not here, Sammy. Maybe you need to head on down the road and try later."

Sammy started to say something but decided against it. He turned and stalked off, slamming the door of the Buick and churning up a cloud of dust as he peeled out up the drive. "I'm sorry about that," Travis said, watching Sammy tear off down the road. "My brother and I seem to bring out the worst in each other, John."

"Brothers can do that," I answered. "It took me and my younger brother a long time to get used to each other. At least, that's what Mama says. By the time we were in school I remember us being pretty good friends. We still had our moments, but mostly we liked each other. We still do."

"Here comes Milly," Travis told me. I looked up the drive and saw her old heap headed our way. She seemed to be in a hurry. "You've got to get her a better car, John," Travis told me.

"I had a devil of a time getting her to take that one," I replied and he laughed.

When Milly stopped in front of the house and got out, she looked worried. "I just passed Sammy on the road. He looked upset."

"That's one way of putting it," Travis told her. He shrugged. "We got in the usual fight five minutes after he got here. I wish

I could say I'm sad he left."

Milly looked at me, her eyes demanding an explanation. All I could do was shrug but I could see that wasn't good enough. When he saw this, Travis smiled. "It wasn't John's fault, Milly. I'm sorry. I think I probably started it. Sammy rubs me the wrong way. If he wasn't your brother, I'd beat the devil out of him."

I thought he might or might not, depending on how good Sammy was with the pistol he was packing. I started to point out that Sammy had a chip on his shoulder, too, but I kept my mouth shut. This was family business and I was the outsider.

Milly knew me too well and caught me. "What?" she demanded.

"My impression is that Sammy wasn't happy to see Travis, either," I told her. "He was carrying a pistol, too. I thought for a minute he was going to pull it."

When I told her this, Milly looked like I'd slapped her. Yet, she didn't blame me, either. "I'm glad you were here, John. You probably kept it from getting out of hand." Travis nodded when she said this. "Did Sammy tell you what he wanted?" she asked me, then looked at Travis.

"He never had a chance," Travis told her. "I'm afraid I jumped on him the minute I saw him."

Milly looked at me and I nodded. Then she burst into tears and threw herself into my arms. Travis decided it was time to make a tactical retreat, and once Milly calmed down, I suggested we sit in the shade a while. There was a bench under the big live oak in front of the house and I led her there. "Would you like me to bring you a glass of ice tea, love?" I asked and she nodded. When I went to get it, I noticed Travis was not in the house. I looked out the kitchen window and saw him out by the woodshed, splitting wood with a fury.

"I wish my brothers got along," Milly told me. "Travis was Sammy's hero until Oliver started paying attention to him. He'd give Sammy liquor and Daddy didn't stop it. That was when Sammy was about thirteen and Daddy said it was time that Sammy learned to drink like a man. Travis wouldn't touch it and he tried to get his brother to stop. He even tried to talk to

Daddy about it but all that got him was a beating. He didn't fight back, but when Daddy stopped, Travis told him that was the last time he would allow it. He told Daddy that if he ever tried to strike him or me again, he'd give him the worst beating he ever had. Travis was sixteen then and bigger than Daddy, and Daddy believed him."

"I'm so sorry, Milly," I told her. "I'm sorry you had to live through that and I'm sorry to say I don't think you can fix it. Maybe you need to let your brothers go."

"I think I need to go see Sammy, John," she told me. "Will you take me there?"

※

Two days later I was pleasantly surprised to discover how gracious Sammy Brown could be on his own turf. Gaylord Smith had taught him well, and the three of us had dinner in one of the private dining rooms the Roadhouse offered. Sammy showed us to our table and excused himself. When he did, I whispered in Milly's ear. "Don't look startled," I told her. "Everything we say is being recorded."

Milly was quick on the uptake. She smiled like I had whispered a sweet intimacy and patted my cheek. "Thank you, John," she said. "That's sweet."

Sammy was back a minute later with a bottle of wine and we both accepted a glass. "Oh, goodness, this is potent," Milly said when she took a sip. "Would you mind terribly if I had iced tea with our supper, Sammy? This is going to my head and I want to enjoy our food."

"Of course, Sis," Sammy said and pushed a button on the wall. A minute later a waitress came in with three glasses of iced tea. Maybe there was a prearranged signal for tea, but I took this as confirmation we were being overheard and probably tape recorded.

The food we were served was excellent and I enjoyed listening to Milly and Sammy catch up. That didn't take long and when they began telling family stories, the conversation really took off. Yet, I had the sense from Sammy that this was just to build trust. The real purpose of his second visit to Milly's would not be evident until I was not around. It was clear to me that Sammy considered me an interloper and that he would have preferred that Oliver be there in my place. Even so, he never alluded to this, even when Milly excused herself for a visit to the powder room.

"So what do you want to know, Sammy?" I asked when Milly left the room. "All I can tell you about Nancy Hiller is what I told your boss. I really have not heard word one from her or about her since she left."

"I want to know where you fit in the picture," he told me. All pretense of grace vanished when he said this. "She is a married woman."

I decided to lay it out for him. "I haven't been able to confirm that," I replied. "There is no record of your sister's marriage to Ollie either in Texas or in Oklahoma. Not that I can find." This surprised him but he didn't respond.

I continued. "At the moment, I've been appointed guardian to two children whose parents were killed in the twister we had a while back. I hired Milly to be my housekeeper so the kids would have a decent home. She also helps them with their homework and I provided her with an old car so she can do her job."

Milly came in just as I was finishing up and I stood and held her chair for her. Sammy blinked and jumped to his feet when I did. "Thank you, John," Milly said. Turning to her brother she said, "Oliver would never allow me to work outside our home, but he's been in jail for months now and I had to do something to pay the bills. I enjoy the children, Sammy, just like I enjoyed being with you after Mama died. It's a way I can be useful."

Sammy didn't like this but he nodded. "There's been all kinds of talk about you and the sheriff, Sis. People are saying you're living together."

"I can see how they might think that," Milly nodded. "It isn't true. John and I have become very dear friends. He rescued us when we had the tornado." She told him how the kids had run to her for shelter and how I had chopped away the tree that imprisoned them. "We could have died in there before anyone came looking," she told him. "He's also helped keep things going since Oliver has been gone. I don't think I could have managed as well on my own."

"You could have come to me," Sammy told her.

"Sammy, I had no idea you were anywhere nearby," she answered. "You never let me know and neither did Oliver. I don't understand why. Did I do something to offend you?" Sammy glanced at me and started to say something, but she interrupted him. "No, Sammy, don't lie to me. I know you must have been around at least a year or two. John and I only became close friends last summer."

Sammy nodded but didn't answer her. "Well, I'm trying to make up for that," he replied. "We have some good cobbler if you'd like dessert."

It was clear the subject was closed as far as Sammy was concerned. Milly didn't like it but she didn't push, either. Over dessert the two of them traded more family stories, and I sensed a vast ocean of sadness between the two. Then Sammy got called away for something urgent, whether for real or not, and he excused himself. A few minutes later a hostess brought us his regrets that he wouldn't be able to rejoin us. She also brought us a bag of food for the kids and we took our leave.

Milly sat close by me on the way home. Out of habit, I drove slowly to stretch out the time we had alone. After we had driven a while in comfortable silence, she said, "It's so sad. Sammy is smart and he's obviously capable if he was promoted to assistant manager. Yet, he doesn't really try to build an honest life. The sad thing is that he and Travis really aren't that different, either. Though both of them will deny it. The difference is that Travis takes on life's challenges and works to overcome them. Sammy looks for the easier way."

I nodded. "What Sammy doesn't understand is that the way Travis approaches life is actually easier. At least, that's what I think. It's hard work being a crook."

We were silent again. Then Milly spoke up. "Travis really likes you, John. He said you're the best thing that's happened to me in a long time, and I agree. He thinks I should dump Oliver and accept your proposal. He told me not to let you get away."

"Rest your mind on that, Milly. I meant what I said. I'm not going anywhere. Unless it's with you, of course. Is there somewhere else you'd like to live?"

"Colorado or Wyoming," she told me without a pause. "I could almost be talked into running away with you to go there."

"You say the word and we're gone," I assured her.

"I said 'almost,' sweet man," she reminded me.

"Why buy the pig?" I said without thinking. I intended to say it lightly but there was a raw edge to my voice I didn't like.

"What does that mean?" she asked, concerned.

I shook my head. "I don't know why I said that. It was something someone once told me. It doesn't apply to us."

"It was a woman who said it, wasn't it? It hurt you very deeply, too."

I tried to answer but I didn't trust my voice. I nodded.

"It was the married lady, wasn't it? The one you didn't know was married." Again, all I could do was nod.

"I overheard a married man say something like that," she told me. "He was talking about a woman he was seeing secretly. The man he was with asked him if he intended to leave his wife and marry the other woman. He said, 'Shoot, no! Why buy the cow if you're getting free milk?'"

Milly looked at me, her wonderful eyes full of compassion. "Only, she said something else, didn't she?"

I nodded and Milly thought a few moments. "Oh!" she said suddenly, frowning. "That's awful, John! Why buy the pig if you're getting free sausage? I hope you know that's not how I see things."

"I do, Milly. I know it's not. It just slipped out."

"Like a stinky poot at a prayer meeting?" When she saw the look on my face, she laughed. "I wish I had a picture," she said. "I told you I know all the words, John. I just save them for the right occasion. I thought you needed a little silliness and there's nothing more silly than a poot."

I chuckled. "Well, at least you called it a poot."

"Yes, but that's only a polite way of talking about a fart," she said sweetly. "Do you mind it when I use earthy language? It's not really cussing."

"It's not?"

"No, cussing is just another word for cursing. A curse is like asking God to damn something or telling someone to rot in hell. Earthy language is just using common words to describe things. It's being vulgar in the original sense of the word."

I just shook my head in wonder. "Well, just because I didn't get to college doesn't mean I can't read," she told me. "I looked up vulgar once and it just means common. For a thousand years the Bible was in Latin and was called the Vulgate. Try running that by your Sunday school class!"

I laughed. "This is not a conversation I ever imagined having with you."

"Oh, it's not me." She paused. "No, that's not quite right. That's not Miss Milly you're having this conversation with. It's with that wonderful woman who comes out whenever you're around. Now are you going to step on it and get us on home, or am I going to have to drag you behind those bushes up there?"

ELEVEN

Foul Play

It must have been two weeks after our dinner with Sammy that someone showed up at the office one day asking to see the sheriff. I was having coffee with Buzz and the constable at Polly's Coffee Pot when Cheryl tracked me down. Polly Green is a local institution. She seemed old to me when I grew up, which meant she was at least thirty, and she has been divorced four times. After her first husband, Billy Edgar left town after cleaning out their bank account and taking the librarian with him, Polly went back to her maiden name. She even had it legally changed when she filed for divorce, adding grist to the gossip mill, and she has kept it ever since. This is understandable since all her former husbands were Ollie's drinking buddies. Yet, she finally got it right. Her current has been around a dozen years or more. He doesn't drink and has no use for Oliver Bates or the crowd he drinks with.

When I got Cheryl's call, I wasted no time getting back to the courthouse. There was an older couple named Barker waiting in my office. They were from Canton, Ohio, where they owned and operated a furniture store, and they were in Texas looking for their son. He was a music student who was supposed to start his second year at a private university in Ft. Worth that fall. Yet he had failed to show up for registration in September. When the school had called his parents a week later, they, in turn, called the Cowtown police and reported their son was missing.

Randall Barker told me that at first the Ft. Worth police had not taken their son's absence that seriously. The detective assigned to the case told them that it was not at all unusual for young men to disappear for a while. The most common reason, he told them, was a young woman, and he predicted the missing son would show up sooner or later. Not satisfied with this, they decided to look for their son, Jeremy, on their own.

"Frankly, Sheriff, I think the Ft. Worth police didn't want to be bothered," Ellen, the mother, told me. "I think they were busy with what they thought were more important cases. Not even our chief of police in Canton could get them to do much. So here we are."

I nodded. "I'll do everything I can to help you, but I'm not sure why you came to me. I don't have much influence in Cowtown."

"Cowtown?" Randall asked.

"Sorry, Ft. Worth," I told them. "Cowtown is how it's known in Texas."

"Somehow that seems appropriate from what we've seen," Ellen replied. "The police there didn't seem very professional. Canton is not all that big but at least our police know their jobs."

"There are some very good people in the Ft. Worth Police Department," I assured them. "I'm sorry you weren't assigned to one of them. Why did you come to me?"

"Oh," Randall said. "I guess we didn't tell you. Jeremy stayed in Texas this last summer. He wrote and told us he found a job at a resort near Live Oak."

I couldn't think of a resort anywhere nearby. "Did he happen to mention the name of the place?"

"Yes," Ellen Barker told me. "It was called the Roadhouse Restaurant and Resort. Jeremy was hired as a pianist, but he had to work as a waiter, too. He didn't like that, but jobs for musicians are hard to find."

"Did you talk to anyone out there?" I asked, knowing the answer even as I spoke.

"Only over the phone," Randall replied. "I talked with one of the assistant managers. He told me he had no memory of anyone named Jeremy Barker ever working there. He told me he would check with the personnel office and call me back. He never did."

"Do you remember the assistant manager's name?"

"Yes, I wrote it down. It was someone named George. That was his last name. His first name was Lyman."

I nodded, relieved that it hadn't been Sammy Brown. The

last thing I wanted to do was arrest Milly's younger brother. Not that I wouldn't hesitate to bring him in with just cause. "Did Jeremy mention the name of any of his coworkers?" I asked.

"Yes, he was friends to a young man named Roger and to a young woman named Nancy. He apparently worked with them a great deal, especially Nancy."

"I don't suppose he mentioned their last names, did he?"

"Yes, he did. Roger's last name was Peyton. I remember it because of the book. I understand there is a town named that in Texas, too." Ellen's expression clearly told us what she thought about that.

"What about Nancy? Did he mention her last name?"

Randall shook his head but Ellen replied. "Yes, he did, but I don't recall just what it was. It sounded made up to me."

"Nancy Hiller?" I asked.

Ellen nodded. "Yes, that's it. Nancy Hiller."

It didn't sound made up to me. I wondered what she'd think about Sally Jones but I didn't ask. They had enough on their plate as it was. "What did he tell you about her?"

"Not much. Just that she was kind to him. Not like some of the others. I told him to watch out, she might be a gold digger."

I noticed that her husband was surprised when she said this and I made a mental note to talk to him about it when his wife wasn't around. "I don't suppose he ever sent you a picture of her, did he?"

"Yes, he did, and I even brought it along." She dug through her purse and took out a snapshot taken near a body of water. There was a dock in the background with motor boats tied up to it, and the brush and trees looked like those that grew in Rayburn County. There was no doubt the young woman was Nancy Hiller and she was standing next to a tall, slender young man with dark hair and dark horn-rim glasses. He was clean shaven and didn't look old enough to be in college.

"Is this your son?" I asked.

"Yes, that's Jeremy. Do you recognize the young woman, Sheriff?"

"Yes, I do. It's Nancy Hiller. Did Jeremy mention where she was from?"

Ellen shook her head vaguely and her husband spoke up. "He did once when he and I talked on the phone. It was a strange sounding name. I couldn't pronounce it right but he said it was not too far from Dallas."

That narrowed it down to a couple of dozen places. This would take a lot of time on the phone, not a prospect I relished. Then it occurred to me I could ask Cheryl to do This. She really liked doing "real" police work and she didn't mind using the telephone, either. My asking her to stay late at the office when I interviewed Nancy had thrilled her.

The Barkers didn't have a lot more to tell me. Nor was I surprised when Randall asked to have a word with me when they were leaving. Ellen didn't like this, but she didn't voice any objection. "I'll wait for you in the car," is what she said. Yet her tone told me she meant, "Just you wait, buster!" Her husband made no response except a shrug, which I suspect added fuel to the fire she'd use to rake him over live coals.

When we were alone, Randall made sure the door was closed before he spoke. "I didn't want to say this in front of my wife, Sheriff, but my son is...different. He's got lots of girls who are his friends, but he doesn't have a girl friend. He never has and Ellen is blind to this. She doesn't want to see it because it means she will never, ever have grandchildren. Am I being clear?"

"Are you telling me your son is queer?" I asked.

"That's a harsh way of putting it, but, yes, I am." Randall looked like he expected me to punch him.

"I didn't intend to be harsh, Mr. Barker. I just needed to be clear and that was the least judgmental way I know of putting it. I guess the proper term is homosexual."

"Among themselves they call it being gay."

"All right, let's use that. One syllable is better than five. Thank you for telling me about this, too. This puts a whole new light on his disappearance. It means that he may have gone somewhere with a gay friend, or alone to some place where he doesn't have to worry about being beaten up for being gay."

"I think he would have called me and let me know what he was doing and why," Randall said.

"The two of you talked about this?" I asked.

"Yes, I know it's usually the other way around. It's the mother who is more accepting and the father who has problems with it." He sighed. "That must make you wonder about me." He seemed to expect a reply but I simply waited.

"I used to be a musician," Randall told me. "There are a lot of gay men in music and most other musicians accept it as a person's choice. In some ways, they're a pretty tolerant group. So I learned to simply accept it."

"What was your instrument?" I asked. Nor was I chasing a rabbit. Barker was wound up tight as a drum and I needed him to relax.

"Mostly piano. I fooled around with guitar and clarinet, but there's more demand for a piano player. That's how I made my way through college. Sometimes I wish I had followed my heart and stayed with music. That's where Jeremy gets it, from me. When he was little we used to do improv together on the piano." He sighed, tears in his eyes. "He's probably dead, isn't he, Sheriff? Somebody killed him for being gay."

"You don't know that," I replied. "There is a chance he may be dead, but that's no reason to give up hope."

I thought a moment, then added, "You may be selling your wife short, too. You're a better judge of that than I, but she might be more accepting if you brought Jeremy's preference out in the open, at least, between the two of you."

"I've tried," he answered simply. "Numerous times. She simply won't talk about it. I think she's afraid talking about it will make it real. That would mean no grandchildren."

So would Jeremy's death, I thought, but didn't say it.

❧

I sat in my office a long time, thinking about Jeremy Barker. Despite my brave words to his father, I suspected the young man was dead. There were a number of ways this might have happened, but there were two scenarios that seemed most likely to me. Birds of a feather tend to recognize one another, and one possibility had Jeremy making an unwanted advance on someone he thought was giving off the right signals. It might even be someone who was gay and did not wish to acknowledge it. The point is, the killer may have lashed out in anger, overreacting and killing Jeremy in a fit of rage.

The second scenario involved a suspect who knew he was gay and kept this tightly under control. Then, either being drunk or unable to control his craving, the killer either seduced Jeremy or allowed himself to be seduced. Once the deed was done, the killer found himself overcome with shame and remorse, and he blamed the young man for causing it. So he killed Jeremy, either to hide his dark secret, or in a fit of outrage.

There were other scenarios that were about as likely, but I knew these two would be where I would start if Jeremy was found dead. I also knew I would have to take the initiative and that tackling this case could cost me my job in the next election, if not before. I decided that two heads were better than one, even if mine was a goat head, and I called the judge. I told him I needed his counsel in a case that popped up out of nowhere. I added that I wanted his counsel as a wise friend and not as the district judge.

"This intrigues me, John," he said. "I assume it is not something to be discussed over the telephone, so why don't you pick us up something to eat at Polly's and we'll have lunch in my chambers." Then he chuckled. "There are so many secrets in my chambers that I suspect they'll need to hire a sin-eater with a big appetite when I die."

Judge White listened carefully while I outlined what the Barkers had told me. Then I outlined the probable scenarios and how I was thinking of approaching the case. He nodded when I was done and sat at his desk quietly for a long while, playing with an ornate letter opener. As I watched him, I wondered if he'd ever been tempted to stab someone with it. I decided he probably had and began to wonder who it might be. I was considering Emory, the prosecutor, when I heard the judge sigh and clear his throat. I gave him my full attention.

"This is a political snake-pit, John," he told me. "I can't see a good outcome if you let it be known that the young man was... different. I hate euphemisms, but I think it may be called for in this instance. So if this turns out to be homicide, you may need to deflect prurient interest by letting it be known you are pursuing a more acceptable motive. You know how to conduct your investigation far better than I, but you might let Clint Farley know you're looking at fraud or blackmail as a possible motive. Privately you might let it drop to someone like Cheryl that you're taking a hard look at gambling debts and cheating at cards."

I smiled. "That should keep the pot boiling. I don't think anyone I talk to out at the Roadhouse will broadcast the questions I'm asking."

"However, we're getting the cart before the horse. You need to make sure a homicide has actually occurred, first and foremost. Until then, it would be better to treat this as a simple missing person's case. I agree that the Hiller woman is your most promising line of inquiry. Even if all she has is hearsay, it may at least tell you where you need to dig."

❧

The search for Nancy Hiller took a while. The reason is that I was the only peace officer in our department trained to investigate and there were no funds to hire more help. Cheryl could do part of the phone work, but to get the lowdown, I needed to talk directly with other officers. Nor could I justify hiring anyone else to do this if this was a straight forward case of a missing college student. So I ended up taking charge of the investigation, and I had to balance it out with everything else I had to do. This meant long hours and less time spent with Milly, but I always tried to make it home for supper. I also made sure to take the kids to school most mornings and to keep Sunday as a family day. Somehow, we made it work.

The first thing I needed to do was to get the word out I was looking for Nancy Hiller. So I sent out an all points bulletin, giving both her name and her alias, Sarah or Sally Jones, a detailed description, and what I knew of her work history. I added that she was wanted for questioning in a missing person case, and gave a cross reference to the APB I was sending out for Jeremy Allan Barker. This done, I headed for the train depot to talk to Clive Jastrow, the station agent.

Clive was busy, as usual, but he was happy to take a few minutes to visit. He's a short, wiry little cuss who is strong as a mule. I've seen him casually toss around large sacks that bigger men could barely pick up, and I was there one time when a big, loud drunk tried to push Clive around. Clive touched the man three times and we had to help the poor fellow into a car so someone else could drive him home. Word got around quickly and Clive Jastrow rarely had to show his strength.

When I asked Clive about Nancy Hiller and showed him her picture, he remembered her clearly. "I may be getting old, but I'm not blind, Sheriff," he chuckled. "She was a real looker and she seemed nervous. She bought a ticket to Odessa, but I happened to see her on the eastbound that afternoon. So she got off somewhere and headed back this way. I'd guess it was Abilene, though it could have been Odessa if the eastbound was running late. She wanted for something?"

"No," I told him. "I just need to ask her a few questions. A friend of hers has turned up missing and his parents need to know where he is. You know how it is with kids these days."

"You think the two of them had something going?" Clive grinned. "He looks a little young for her, but who knows?"

"I think they were just friends. They worked together and he might have told her something about where he was going."

"That must have been out at the Roadhouse, where they worked," Clive told me. "One of their men was asking about her, too. I can't recall his name right now but he was pretty anxious to see her. Think he was the reason she was leaving town?"

I shook my head. "I don't know. You remember what he looked like?"

Clive had a good head for detail and who he described was Sammy Brown. When I mention Sammy's name, Clive nodded. "That's him," he told me. "He had a nice set of wheels, too. It was a late model Buick. Dark colored and shiny." He shook his head. "I didn't care for the duck's butt haircut, either. He must have used a quart of gear oil to get it slicked down."

"That would have been Sammy Brown, all right," I informed him. "Did you happen to mention her coming back through to Sammy?"

"No, I figured he was the reason she was nervous. He sure wanted to see her. He must have asked me four times if I was sure she was headed west. Finally, I told him it was the only way the passenger train coming through that time of day runs, and there wasn't any place the engineer could turn around between here and El Paso."

"Well, at the risk of sounding like Sammy, are you sure it was her you saw headed east that afternoon?"

"I'd swear it in court!" he declared.

"That's good enough for me," I answered. "But if you don't mind, I'd like you to keep our talk between the two of us. That fellow is not good news. I'd appreciate it if you'd let me know if you see or hear anything else about Nancy Hiller or Jeremy Barker, either."

"Sure thing, Sheriff. You think someone might have done away with him?" Clive asked. He had an odd expression of his face when he asked me and it wasn't until later that day that I figured out what it was. Life can be dull in a small town and Clive craved excitement. It was important for him to be in the know, and not only for himself. He was hungry for exciting tidbits he could dole out to his cronies and a murder was at the top of the list.

"No. I'm sure he'll turn up sooner or later. You know how kids that are. He probably wandered off somewhere and it hasn't occurred to him that his parents might be worried."

When I said this, Clive looked like a kid who had just dropped his ice cream on the sidewalk. He didn't cry but he looked like he felt like it.

※

The next day I called the railroad office and asked for the name of the conductor for the train Nancy took. It turned out he lived in Odessa and was due back through on the afternoon train. I made arrangements to board the train in Live Oak and they agreed to drop me off in Ashtown, less than an hour down the track. There wasn't much left there but the church outhouse and a section house, and I made arrangements for Buzz to drive the patrol car there and carry me home.

It turned out that the train conductor was Henry Rose, someone I'd known growing up near Live Oak. His son, Harley, had played tackle when I was quarterback of our high school team and we used to hang around together. Harley had never left Rutherford County and managed a filling station and garage in Bole's Well. We didn't see each other very often, but every once in a while I'd stop by and treat him to a milk shake at the drive-in. His wife was a very strict Baptist who didn't believe in drinking beer.

Henry told me that Harley had been lucky when the twister passed through, leaving the garage and station untouched. However, it had put a serious dent in his repair business and the owner was thinking of selling the place. Henry hoped his son would buy the place, but he and his wife were talking about moving to Pecos. "That twister put the fear of God in his wife," Henry told me. "She wants to move to where they don't have to worry about them."

Our conversation took the first half of a forty minute ride, but Henry didn't have much to add to what Clive told me. "Yes, I recognized her," Henry said. "She's a pretty one, but the reason I remember is that she got off the train in Abilene. Then she got on the eastbound that evening and bought her a ticket to Weatherford. She bought it from me, not from the station agent, and I saw her get off the train when we got there. She was met by an older woman. They looked a lot alike and I'd guess it was her mother, or maybe an aunt. They seemed glad to see each other, too. Nancy didn't have anything but the bag she was carrying and the agent told me later that they left the station right away."

I asked for the station agent's name and Henry wrote it out for me. He looked in his book and added the telephone number for the station. "Mike's a good guy," Henry told. "He's lived around Weatherford all his life. I wouldn't be surprised if he knew the older woman's name."

❧

As it turned out, Mike Paulson knew a lot more than the older woman's name. He and she were distant kin, and while he spelled out the exact relationship for me, I'm not sure I really understood it. More helpful was the information that the older woman, May Harrison, was Nancy's aunt, her mother's sister. May and her husband, Harald, lived in a tiny community about twenty miles north of Weatherford.

Even though Nancy had been raised in Ft. Worth, she had spent enough time with her relatives near Weatherford to develop a reputation as a "wild one," as Mike put it. "Now part of that was pure jealousy," he added. "No, let's say most of it was. She was prettier and smarter than all the rest of them and they resented her for it. When she took a shine to some young man, she didn't care who his girlfriend was, either, and she seemed to attract a lot of young men." He shrugged. "Of course, that's been six or eight years ago. I haven't heard anything since."

When I asked for the address, Paulson not only looked it up, but he also told me how to find the house. "It's the last one on the road to the north side of the lake. It's set back off the road where you can't see it, but there's a mailbox with their name on it by the road. You shouldn't have much problem finding it."

When people tell me that, I always wonder, but Mike's directions were accurate. I drove straight to the place but when I got there, no one seemed to be at home. Then I wandered around to the back and found Harald busy sharpening a hoe in a tool shed. He was friendly enough, even when I told him I was there to talk to Nancy. "I don't think they'll be long," he told me. "Let me get us some iced tea."

We visited in Harald's shop for about half an hour before the women returned home. Actually, it might be more accurate to say I listened while Harald rattled on about everything under the sun. That was all right with me. I never learned much when my mouth was going and Harald finally got to something of immediate interest. He was talking about the family by then, and he confirmed a lot Nancy had told me about her mother and dad. He also lamented her mother's plunge into hard core religion. "May's sister, Annie, used to be the life of the party," he said. "Since she got saved she's been a pain in the neck. We used to have all kinds of fun at family gatherings, but now it's like a funeral if she comes. You don't dare say nothing without her taking exception, and she's got chapter and verse to prove it. I don't blame Nancy for moving out. One look from Annie could sour fresh milk!"

Nancy and May got back from the store just then, and May stuck her head out the door to ask why the sheriff's car was parked in front of the house. "Well, gosh, May," Harald laughed. "Maybe all your crimes are catching up with you."

May laughed, too, and Harald led me into the house. When we got there, Nancy was in the kitchen and she didn't look too happy to see me. "What's wrong?" May asked when she saw Nancy's face. "Are you in any kind of trouble, sweetheart?"

"No, she's not," I assured May. "A friend of hers has disappeared and I need to ask her some questions."

"A friend of hers? Who's that?"

"Gosh, sakes, May!" Harald declared. "Let the man ask his own questions." May just waved him off.

"Jeremy Barker is a friend of yours, isn't he?" I asked Nancy. She nodded without reply, frowning. "His parents came to visit me last week," I told her. "Jeremy never showed up for college registration and they're worried."

"Well, I should hope so!" May declared.

"Maybe Nancy and I need to talk privately," I suggested. "Why don't we do it in the patrol car?"

Nancy nodded again and led me out of the house. "Why come to me?" she asked when we were settled in the cruiser.

I showed her the picture Jeremy and her together. "He sent this to his parents," I said. "They also told me he worked at the Roadhouse. Were you simply friends or was there something more?"

"If they find out I've talked to you, they'll kill me."

"Nobody will learn it from me," I assured her. "Who are you talking about?"

"Mr. Smith, the manager. He'll come looking for me."

"He already is," I informed her. When I did, her face turned white. "He came to me and then he sent Sammy Brown to talk to Milly Bates. I told him you took off for Minnesota."

"Minnesota?" Despite the gravity of the situation, she laughed. "Why in the world would I go there? What's in Minnesota?"

"He asked me the same thing. I told him tons of snow and lots of dumb Swedes." I paused. "Look, Nancy, I really am on your side. You've had some tough breaks but you've also brought a lot of your trouble on yourself. I'm willing to do everything

I can to help you change that, but you've got to help me, too."

Nancy looked at me a long time. Then I saw her come to a decision. "All right, Sheriff. What do you need to know?"

"What I need to know is the unvarnished truth. Mostly, I want facts but I also want to know what you think, even if you don't know for sure. Just make it clear which is which."

"That's most of what I have to tell you, what I think. I have very few facts I know for sure."

"Fair enough. Let's start with the facts you know. What was Jeremy's job at the Roadhouse?"

"They hired him for a musician," she told me. "He had a couple of sets every night, but they made him fill in as a waiter when he wasn't making music. He was pretty good at that. At least, he told me he made pretty good tips and that's harder for a guy to do."

"Was he ever a card dealer?"

"No. I never saw him work the back room as a waiter, either." She frowned and stopped speaking.

"What are you thinking?" I asked.

"I hate to tell you this part," she said. "You know that as a waitress I was expected to entertain customers in the lake cabins if they wanted. That's what happened to the guy I was with that night you came out. Only he had a heart attack."

"He apparently had a heart attack," I corrected. "The doctor hasn't signed off on the death certificate. The manner of death is undetermined."

"You mean you think someone might have killed him?"

I nodded. "I think that may be why they're trying so hard to find you. They want to make sure you don't talk."

"But I don't know anything!" Nancy declared. "All I know is that I was with him and we did what men and women do when they're naked. Then, when he got up off the bed, he grabbed his chest and fell over. That's all I know."

"Had you ever been with him before?"

"Yes, twice. And it was just the same except for him having a heart attack."

"Do you know if they took pictures?"

"God, I hope not! I guess they could have. He always wanted

the lights left on. He told me it was because he liked to look at me. I never thought of pictures."

"So they could have been blackmailing him," I said. "Did he pay you?"

She gave me a long, searching look. "If I tell you he did, I could go to jail."

"I'm not looking to put you in jail, Nancy. I do need to know."

"Let's put it this way. He always left me a present. Not that I got to keep it, but that's what he always said. 'Here, darling. Here's a little present to buy yourself some flowers.'"

"Was this before or after?"

"The first two times it was after. The night he died, he laid a twenty on the table. 'Just so I don't forget,' is what he told me. I kept that one." She frowned. "I thought you were going to ask me about Jeremy."

"That was my next question. Jeremy worked as a waiter between sets. Was he required to entertain customers, too?"

"The only women I ever saw there came with a man," she told me. The look on her fact told me she was being evasive. She also knew I was aware of this.

"That's not what I asked, Nancy," I said gently. "I know this isn't fun but I need to know if Jeremy entertained customers the way you did. Men customers."

She glared at me. "Jeremy was a sweet loving man!"

"Nancy, this could be why he was killed. Now tell me what you know."

She shrugged. "All right, I guess it can't hurt him if he's dead. Some of the men wanted Jeremy to entertain them and they paid him for it. At least, that's what he said. He said being paid really made him feel dirty."

This raised a possibility I had not considered. "Nancy, I need you to answer this next question without thinking about it, yes or no. Do you think Jeremy may have killed himself because he was...different?"

She answered by nodding and bursting into tears. As much as I hated to do it, I pressed on. "Do you think his killing himself is as likely as someone else killing him?"

"No," she told me. "I don't think Jeremy killed himself. I think he would have left me a note. I think somebody killed him to keep their dirty little secret."

"That would mean that Gaylord Smith and Sammy Brown would have helped cover it up, wouldn't it?"

"That's what I think," she told me. "I think they got rid of the body and if they find me, that's what will happen to me, too."

Nancy looked so miserable it was all I could do not to take her in my arms and comfort her.

"Not on my watch!" I declared. "Do you have any idea where they might have hidden the body?"

"What about the lake?" she asked. "It's supposed to be deep in places."

"That seems pretty obvious. Where else would you look if you were in my shoes?"

"I don't know. I guess they could have buried him. They've got plenty of room for that." I nodded. County records showed the Homestead owned over five hundred acres of land, most of it perfect for hiding a body.

"Have they built anything new recently?"

"Nothing but the new trap range," she told me. "You know, where they shoot at clay pigeons and stuff. They build a shed and a trap thrower for that."

"What about a stock pond? Have they had one of those cleaned out recently?"

"I don't know, but they had a man here with a bull dozer and some other heavy equipment. I was told they're going to build a new garage, but I haven't seen it."

We talked for another half hour or so but Nancy didn't add much to what she already told me. I thanked her for talking to me. Then I added, "I don't think you should stay here any longer. I don't think it's safe for you or for your aunt and uncle. I found you and that means Gaylord Smith can, too. How are you fixed for money?"

"I have about five hundred dollars saved up," she told me. "I used to send Aunt May a little money from time to time and she put it aside for me."

"You ever been to Colorado?" I asked. She shook her head.

"I know some people near Denver who will help you get settled. Why don't you pack your bag? I'll drive you somewhere to catch a bus to Denver or wherever else you want to go."

❧

The young woman I dropped off in Jacksboro that evening looked nothing like the one who worked at the Roadhouse. Nancy had done what I told her to do, making herself as homely as she could. She was wearing a bland print dress cut to make her look dowdy, old lady's shoes that looked like they came from Buster Brown, and a dark scarf that hid her hair. Her fingernails were stripped of polish, she wore no lipstick or makeup, and she had on socks instead of stockings. She also had on a pair glasses she rarely wore, and when she saw herself in the mirror when May and I were done, she scowled. "I look like the wrath of God!" she declared.

"That's the point," I told her. "Nobody will recognize you as Nancy Hiller. You can change back once you get settled, but do it slowly. I'd suggest changing the way you do your hair, too."

"So what am I going to do for a living? I don't want to do what I was doing. That's a dead end."

"It's up to you. I'd suggest something out of the public eye, like a bookkeeper or a librarian. The main thing is to stay out of the circles you traveled in before. Or you could go to business school, even to college if you want. The thing is, you don't have to be in any hurry deciding. Take your time and think things through."

I handed her a list of things she needed to do to establish a new identity. At the top of the list was a new Social Security number. "Whoever you work for is going to want that," I told her. "Don't use the one you have now."

Nancy smiled. "I never got one, Sheriff," she told me. "I never needed it. What about a name?"

"Use something you can remember easily. Just avoid using the same initials or the same sound."

"I guess Mae West is out," she murmured. It was good to see her having fun. The idea of becoming someone new appealed to her. "What if I need to get in touch with you?" she asked.

"You can call me at the office. Just use a pay phone if you

do and don't leave a message with Cheryl. Tell her you're my cousin, Agnes."

"Agnes?" she laughed. "That sounds like a nun! Sister Agnes. I'm not even Catholic." She sobered. "I wonder if they'd take me?" Then she shook her head. "No, I'm too rotten for that. All right, I'll say Agnes is calling."

"You're not rotten, Nancy. You just made some bad choices."

She looked me in the eye a long time. "Do you really mean that?" she asked.

I nodded. "Yes, I do. I see a lot of rotten people in my work and you're not one. Rotten eggs don't love other people and it's pretty obvious you loved Jeremy."

We visited about other things after that and had an enjoyable dinner at the cafe across from the bus stop. The more we talked, the more animated she became about her new life. It was good to see her excited, but when the bus for Wichita Falls arrived she looked sad. Just before she boarded, she threw her arms around my neck and hugged me close. I could feel her young, warm body pressed tight against my own and I felt my body betray my heart in response. She pulled me close and held me a long while, then kissed me on the cheek and whispered in my ear. "Good bye, John Stone. It's too bad you're already taken."

"Good bye, Sister Agnes," I told her gently, trying to hide what I was feeling with a jest. Yet she saw right through it and there were tears in her eyes when she got on the bus. On the way home I had to remind myself sternly that there was someone else I wanted to marry, and that Milly was all the woman I'd ever need. I almost convinced myself that was true, but over the years, at the oddest moments, I could swear I caught the scent of Nancy's rich, womanly smell. At those moments, it was all I could do to suppress the vivid image of us in one another's arms.

TWELVE

Body of Evidence

I went directly to see the judge when I got back from talking to Nancy Hiller. He and Emory were working late that evening, and I caught them just as they were about to leave. The judge agreed that we had reasonable grounds for a search warrant for the Roadhouse and he promised to word it broadly enough to allow us to search the entire property. Given the size of the property, he granted us two weeks in which to execute the warrant and conduct the search.

Just to be certain, I asked him to wait until I formally requested the warrant to date it. "I want to use cadaver dogs, Judge," I explained. Emory was excited by this idea. Good dogs play well before a jury. "From what I've read, cadaver dogs can detect even a bare skeleton in deep water, but they need to be trained for this. The man I want to bring in is from east Texas. Everyone I've talked to says he's the best but the soonest he can be available is ten days from now. At the moment, he's working for the FBI down in Georgia."

"I gather you don't hold being from east Texas against him," the judge said dryly.

"No, sir, I don't. Or the fact he's working for the FBI." Emory laughed when I said that and the judge smiled. He, himself, grew up around Beaumont, a somewhat unreconstructed coastal city in east Texas. Nor was the judge's opinion of the Bureau that high, either.

People from up north don't understand the distinctions we make here in the Lone Star State. Unlike the area of Texas lying west of a line drawn from Denton to Waco, and down to San Antonio and across to Houston, east Texas is part of the deep South. Where the largest minority group in western Texas are Hispanic, the biggest minority in eastern Texas are black folk, and this has had a profound effect on the history of these areas.

Each speaks a different language and follows different customs, and each identifies with a different region.

West Texas is part of the American Southwest, the native habitat of cattlemen. The icon of the Southwest is the all American cowboy, personified more in Will Rogers than Gene Autry or Roy Rogers. The song that best captures the spirit of this vast, beautiful area is "Drifting Along with the Tumbling Tumbleweeds."

By contrast, the deep South is the habitat of the plantation owner and the proud but poverty stricken share-cropper. The icon is the rebel warrior of what is referred to as either "the war between the states" or, as the judge likes to say, tongue in cheek, "the late war of northern aggression." This icon of the rebel is personified in the gentleman warrior, Robert Edward Lee and the song that catches the spirit of the region is "Dixie."

After I left the courthouse, I dreaded going home. I hadn't done anything but I felt like I'd betrayed Milly. It was well after nine by the time I arrived and a front passing through had turned the sky dark, which fed my mood. Yet Milly was delighted to see me, as were the kids, who were already dressed for bed.

Milly was pretty attuned to my feelings by then and she sensed the contretemps within my soul. When the kids were asleep, she joined me on the porch swing, snuggling close under my arm. "What's wrong, John?" she murmured, so quietly I could barely hear.

"I'm not sure I even want to look at it," I answered her, kissing the top of her head. "Sometimes I just don't like myself very well, Milly."

Milly waited patiently for a long time before she pushed gently. "I understand that feeling," she said. "My greatest fault is that I find myself thinking very unkind things about people sometimes. I tell myself there's a reason why they're that way but that doesn't always help. I don't suppose your not liking yourself had to do with some other woman, did it?"

"Why do you ask that?"

"I can smell her on you, silly man," she answered, sniffing my chest. "She doesn't wear perfume, does she?" It was more an observation than a question.

"She wasn't at the moment." I explained going to see Harald and May Harrison, looking for Nancy Hiller. I told her about our conversations and about getting Nancy out of town so Gaylord Smith couldn't find her. Then I told her about saying goodbye and Nancy hugging me. "I don't know why I responded that way. There wasn't anything going on before that, at least not that I was aware."

"Oh, there was," Milly told me. "I know why she hugged you the way she did and I know why you responded the way you did, too, John Paul." I looked down and I saw Milly was trying not to laugh.

"Well, would you care to explain?" I tried to not sound as exasperated as I felt.

"She was in heat, dear man. She wanted your baby and you responded the way the good Lord intended. Like right now." She touched me firmly in a sensitive place and there was no denying the result. I gasped and she giggled.

"Now," she added, getting up and taking my hand. "If you care to follow me inside, kind sir, I'm going to show you why you chose to come home."

Show me she did, and more than once. She stayed over until morning and I'm pretty sure that was the night we conceived Simon. As a wise man once pointed out, when the good Lord and a woman decide there needs to be a baby, a man doesn't stand a chance.

⋇

I got a call from the dog man a few days later. He told me he had finished up with the FBI sooner than expected and could be in Live Oak in three days. We arrived at a price for his services and I offered to send him a letter of intent. "That won't be necessary, Sheriff," he told me. "One of the guys in the FBI used to work with you in West Virginia. He said you're a man of good character, despite being from Texas."

I chuckled. "That had to be John Foley. Did he tell you we were partners?"

"He did. He also said you used to like to fish."

"That's right, I told him. I still do. I'm afraid I don't get out much these days."

"Well, where you are is one reason I agreed to come for just one day's work. Why don't you take me fishing on Lake Texoma when we're done with the search?"

"You're on," I told him. "Rain or shine. I'll borrow a boat and get us a guide."

When I told Milly about the conversation that evening over supper, the kids wanted to come along with us. They were really disappointed when I told them they couldn't. So I had to promise to take them out, too.

"You ever been fishing?" I asked Milly.

"Not since my mama died," she told me, smiling. "We used to go a lot before then. It was one of my favorite things, especially when we were in Colorado."

❧

The dog man arrived three days later and I was surprised when I met him. For one thing, he was much older than I thought. Then, too, over the phone his deep, strong voice led me to expect a large man. Even so, Orville Walser turned out to be a slender man of medium height. His hair was snow white, though the lines in his face were not deeply etched, and when he spoke his voice was almost music. He liked to talk, too, and he was one of the most cheerful men I ever met.

"We have a choice, John," he told me later when we were out fishing. "We can live on the sunny side of the street or we can be miserable. I always thought it was better to be positive, even when it was hard to see the good. The work we do can get pretty grim, but we're not the ones who caused it. Our job is setting things as right as we can, and I find a lot of joy and satisfaction in that."

Just about then a big one took his bait and a few minutes later he hauled in a huge stripped bass. "See what I mean?" he asked when he was done reeling it in. "It's a rainy day but there's a lot of beauty to be seen and a lot of joy there for the taking."

When he was working, however, Walser was a different man. All his attention was focused on his dog, Rosalind, and he spoke mostly to her, giving her encouragement. "She's trained to sit down when she finds something underground," he told us before we started. "On the water, she'll start whining if she smells something."

The first places we looked, of course, were where the land had been disturbed. None of the new construction sites yielded anything, but Rosalind started tugging at her leash when we passed a large flower bed against one side of the main building. Orville let her lead and a few moments later she sat down in the middle of the bed.

"Looks like we found something," Walser told me and a couple of men I brought along began to dig. When they did, the door to one side of the flower bed opened and Gaylord Smith appeared.

"Hey! What are you doing?" Smith demanded.

"We're digging for a body," I told him.

"You can't dig there! You have any idea how much it cost to plant those roses?"

"We have a warrant," I reminded him. "We can dig wherever we want. You can bag up the plants we take up when we're done. We'll stack them over on one side."

The dig went quickly. Buzz and I alternated with the two men on the shovels and in less than an hour we were four feet down. Then one of the shovels turned up a rib and some cloth, and we began to work with whisk brooms and garden trowels. An hour later we had a corpse and I had the dirt underneath it bagged for screening.

There wasn't much doubt this was a homicide, either. There was a neat hole in the victim's forehead and another, much larger one, in the back of the skull. The hole in the forehead looked to me to be the same size as a .38 slug, and it was in the wrong place for a suicide.

"All right," I told Buzz. "You guard the body until the van gets here. Orville and I are going to look around some more."

The first thing Orville did was to check the rest of the flower bed but Rosalind found nothing. We spent the next three hours looking through the woods near every trail we found leading into them. There was nothing there so we sequestered a boat from the docks and began to search the lake. This took us into the afternoon and it was getting late when Rosalind leaned over the side of the boat and started to whine.

"Did she find something?" I asked.

Orville shook his head and grinned. "No, that whine means she needs to crap." Sure enough, when we arrived at the dock, Rosalind leapt out and squatted ten feet from the shore. Then she peed before turning around and jumping back in the boat. It had taken her less than two minutes.

"Anybody else?" I asked, getting out to do my business, too. Orville shook his head. Unlike Rosalind, I stepped into the woods.

We were just about done searching the lake when Rosalind once again leaned over the side of the boat and began to whine. This time I could tell the difference. Her whine sounded more like a moan, and once we had gone back and forth over the site a couple of times, Orville dropped a marker in the water. It was made from a piece of heavy fishing twine about twenty feet long. This had a big lead sinker on one end and a large cork float on the other. Once he made sure the sinker was on the bottom, Orville shortened the twine below the float until about two or three feet extended over the water. When he let go and the float bobbed gently. We were in about fifteen feet of water.

It was getting very late in the afternoon by then, but Walser dropped anchor and began to drag the lake with a special set of hooks made just for this purpose. The first few tries caught nothing, but then the drag hooked something. Orville tugged on the line gently and bubbles broke the surface. When they did, Rosalind began to moan again, this time more loudly.

"Bingo!" Walser said, his face somber. "It's not just an old tire, either." Sure enough, the drag had snared a tangle of rusted barbed wire wrapped around the rib cage, arms, and pelvis of a skeleton.

Buzz had joined us by then and I asked him how he felt about spending the night in a boat. He agreed and asked if he was allowed to fish. "Just be sure not to throw anything you snare back," I told him and Orville chuckled.

"What are you going to be doing?" Buzz asked me.

"I'm going to be arranging for a diver," I said. "Then I'll be back to spell you."

"No need of that, Sheriff," Orville interjected. "Find me a

line and a pole and I'll keep the kid company all night. Might not be nothing but turtles in this pond, but if there's a fish left, I'll find it."

Getting a diver out to the lake turned out to be easier than I expected. I knew the owner of a sporting goods store in Ft. Worth, and called him for a referral. He volunteered to be there bright and early the next morning. When I asked him what he charged, he laughed. "Are you kidding, Sheriff? Half the divers I know would give their eye teeth to be part of an official investigation. That's bragging rights not many have. I'll be bringing one of my diving buddies with me, too."

"You need more than one diver?" I asked.

"It's best. One guy can get in trouble by himself. It's much safer with two. It won't cost you anything, either. How long has it been since it's rained?"

"A couple of weeks," I told him. "Why?"

"Good. Most of the silt will be settled by now. Makes it easier to see."

❧

The underwater search the next day was a success. The diver's buddy turned out to be his grown son, who I recognized from visiting the store. The store owner brought his own boat, too, along with an underwater vacuum that allowed us to screen the slurry it pumped from the bottom. Using this, we were able to recover most of the skeleton. While the divers worked, Orville and I searched the rest of the lake. Rosalind did discover another site but there was nothing there the divers could find.

"It could be a pioneer grave," Orville told me. "We turned up a whole bunch of Indian bones out of the Red River last year. The river changed course and cut through a burial ground along the bank. We found six skulls."

I called off searching the grounds about two that afternoon. Gaylord Smith pitched a hissy fit when we moved the search inside, but there was nothing he could do. The warrant covered both the grounds and any buildings and I called in three members of our county posse to help. All of them were retired lawmen and they were glad for something useful to do. They were probably more thorough than they needed to be, but I wasn't about to put a damper on their excitement.

I have to admit they weren't the only ones having fun. After we were through searching, I enjoyed cuffing Gaylord Smith and taking him in as a material witness. When he objected, I explained that he was, after all, the manager, and that there was a homicide victim buried beneath his prize roses. I went on to point out that he had personally attempted to keep us from searching the flower bed, and that there were still questions about the death of Maynard Gentry.

"He died of a heart attack!" Smith declared.

"The medical examiner is still not sure of that," I replied. "You have to admit, Mr. Smith, that Maynard died under suspicious circumstances. The woman he was with wasn't his wife and she told me he was paying her for sex."

"All you have is her unsubstantiated word for that."

"That's all I need. There have been illegal activities at your place of business and you're the man in charge. You have information we need."

"I'm not telling you a damned thing!"

"Suits me," I told him. "You can be our guest as long as you want. There's no bail for a material witness."

Aside from the two bodies, our search didn't come up with much. There was lots of evidence of card games, but nothing to show that the wealth of cards, chips, and gaming equipment we found was actually used for gambling. We did find the financial books, which I took with us to photograph, but I knew I would have a hard chance justifying it in court. The official reason I gave for sequestering the books was to see if there was any mention of Jeremy Barker in them. What I was hoping to find when we looked them over was pay-dirt. It was also possible we might come up with evidence of tax evasion we could turn over to the IRS.

The only other thing we found of much value to the investigation was an old leather suitcase tucked behind some boxes in a storeroom. It was full of clothing and one of the sweaters in it had a tag with Jeremy's name sewn into an side seam. There were also four pair of blue dungarees and three dress shirts with the initials JAB written in unseen places. This was probably with a ballpoint pen from the appearance of the ink. Even though there was nothing remarkable about the suitcase or its contents, I took it along as evidence, too. It could help establish that Jeremy Barker had, indeed, worked at the Roadhouse.

⁂

Normally, I would have kept working on the case the next two days, but there was very little I could do until I had more information. The books I sequestered went to Granger Woods, an accountant who had retired home to Live Oak after thirty years as an auditor with the IRS. Like the owner of the sporting goods store, he refused compensation, and for the same kind of reason.

"They don't tell you how deadly dull retirement can be," he complained. "The wife has all kinds of things to do, what with the garden club and her sewing circle and the church ladies. What am I going to do, sit around the courthouse square all day? Or play dominoes? I help a few folks during tax season, but there isn't much for me to do the rest of the year."

Nor was there much information available right away from the two bodies we recovered. Dr. Pettigrew did a quick preliminary examination but suggested we send both bodies to the state laboratory in Austin for a full work-up. "We just don't have the equipment or the competence to tell you more than the cause of death, which is quite obvious. Assuming the skull your divers found belongs to the wired skeleton, both of your victims died of a gunshot wound to the head and I would rule out suicide for obvious reasons. As far as identifying the victims, that will probably have to be done with dental records. The state is better equipped for that than we are."

It was almost noon by the time I was done getting all this lined up. Nor was there anything pressing on my calendar. So Orville and I headed for Lake Texoma. When we got there, none of the guides I called wanted to go out. It looked like rain and they weren't too enthusiastic about getting wet. Yet, when I told Orville, it didn't faze him a bit. "Shoot, John, some of the best fishing I ever had was in the rain." Then he grinned. "It weeds out the panty-waists. I bet we have the lake to ourselves."

"I don't know where the honey spots are," I told him. "That's why I wanted to hire a guide."

"That don't matter. Between me and Rosalind, we'll find the fish."

I thought Orville was spinning me a whopper, but it turned out he was right. When we got on the water, Rosalind was as excited as a pup, and it wasn't long before she began to make a sound I hadn't heard before. When she did, Orville dropped a marker and had me make a couple of wide passes over the spot with our lines out to either side of the boat. On the second pass Orville hooked a keeper, and on the third pass, we both did.

"See!" Orville laughed. "You thought I was pulling your leg." He pulled in the marker. "You want to bet a nickel we can't find another spot just as good?"

I was glad I didn't take the bet. We found four sweet spots that afternoon and got our limit long before sundown. Since he had a job in Oklahoma starting in a couple of days, I asked Orville if he'd like to stay over to fish the next day, too. I told him the kids would like to come along and he was agreeable. "Kids can't catch the fishing bug too young," he said, and that evening we had him to supper out at the house.

At my suggestion, Walser brought Rosalind along for the kids to meet. Yet, he was surprised by me allowing her in the house. "A lot of folks don't hold with dogs in the house," he told us over dinner. "Not me. To me, she's just like one of the kids."

"She's wonderful," Milly replied, reaching out and patting the large head intently focused on the table. Then she picked up a small piece of cornbread. "May I give her a treat?"

"Sure," Orville told her. "I spoil her rotten. Just hold the bread in the palm of your hand so she won't nip your fingers."

Milly did as Orville said and Rosalind gently took the cornbread. The kids were fascinated by this and wanted to try it, too. Walser nodded and the two of them fed the dog several large pieces of cornbread.

"That's probably enough," Orville told them. "I don't want her to get so fat she gets lazy."

The kids stopped feeding Rosalind but stood by her side

petting her. Rosalind rewarded Louis with a lap on the nose, and both kids giggled. "Well, John," Milly said, smiling. "It looks like there needs to be an addition to the family."

"Just be careful what you pick," Orville told her. He went on to describe what to look for picking the best pup out of a litter, and what breeds made the best family dogs. "I don't hold with this pure breed stuff," he told us. "I've seen too many sorry dogs with fine pedigrees. I got Rosalind as a pup from the pound. She's the best dog I ever had, and that's been a few."

"We used to have cats," Milly said. When she did, Rosalind's ears perked up and she stared at Milly.

"Oops, you said the 'c' word," Orville laughed. "Rosalind thinks the good Lord put feline critters in this world for her to chase. Not that she wants to hurt them. She just wants to play. She doesn't understand why kitties don't like dog games." He reached for his wallet and pulled out a folded photograph. It showed Rosalind with a yellow tiger cat. "That's Rosalind and her best buddy. She grew up with him but we lost him last spring. I never heard of it before but he died of feline leukemia."

Orville turned to the kids. "That's the bad thing about having dogs and kittens. They don't live as long as we do and it hurts to lose them."

Mary Alice nodded. "We lost our mama and papa in a tornado," she told him. "Is it like that?"

Walser nodded. "Yes, but losing your folks is worse," he told them. "At least, it was for me. They were old and getting feeble, too, but it was still bad. Still, I'd do it all over again if I had the chance. It would be worth it." He looked at Milly. "I didn't mean to talk about this at dinner, Mrs. Stone. I hope it didn't upset you."

"It's Mrs. Bates but please call me Milly. We talk about most things with the kids. It helps us appreciate the blessings all the more. We try to stay on the sunny side, even when we get sad."

"You know that song?" Orville asked.

"Of course." Milly began to sing and Orville joined in. He had a wonderful tenor and their voices harmonized well. The kids and I sat and listened, mesmerized. When they finished, Mary Alice asked if they could sing Clementine and the kids and I joined in, too. By the time we finished we were laughing so hard we couldn't sing.

Milly asked the kids to help her clear the table and serve dessert. When they left the room, Orville looked at me and said, "You're a very lucky man, John. You have a wonderful family."

"Yes, I do," I told him. "It seems to be coming together. The kids lost their parents in that big tornado that came through a while back, and we seem to get along pretty well. I couldn't do it without Milly, though. She's the one who holds it all together."

"I take it she's a widow?"

"It's a complicated situation," I replied. "She's my housekeeper, but she's like an second mother to the kids." Just then Louis came in with two bowls of cobbler and I was saved from having to say anything more. I knew I had piqued Orville's curiosity but it wasn't really any of his business. That didn't keep him from thinking and I saw him chewing over what he'd learned. I knew he wanted to know more but he was too much a gentleman to pry. Nor did I try to explain when I drove him back to his hotel that evening. I wasn't even sure I understood what was happening, myself.

⚡

Over the next few weeks summer finally gave way to fall and the weather became cooler. The first fishing trip with the kids turned out so well that we started going out every time we could. We never caught as many fish as we did with Orville, but we caught enough and the four of us had a wonderful time. I was glad to see Milly putting on a little more weight, too, though she complained her clothes didn't fit as well. She laughed when I told her she looked better with them off and she even let me buy her some new dresses when the two of us took a shopping trip to Cowtown. I had to insist that she accept them when she saw the prices and I had to threaten to go into the ladies department to buy her undergarments if she didn't. I also had to insist she buy enough to last all week.

"Blast it, woman!" I declared, feigning mock exasperation. "I don't want the county thinking I'm a cheapskate. I can't have my housekeeper traipsing around the county bursting out of her dress. Think of the talk it would cause!"

"Beast!" she answered, laughing and startling the prim looking sales clerk. "I know what you're up to. You just want to take them off me!"

The clerk sneezed and excused herself, scurrying away with her handkerchief over her nose. "I can't believe I just said that!" Milly declared, blushing. "I embarrassed that poor clerk. Who is this woman, John?"

"Relax, sweetheart," I assured her. "She wasn't sneezing. She was trying very hard to keep from laughing. She thinks we're newly weds."

"I guess we are, aren't we?" she said, coming into my arms.

"I certainly hope so," I told her, holding her close. "I don't know what I'd do without you."

"You could always look up Nancy!" she laughed. Feeling my body tense, she looked up and saw my face. Her smile faded. "Oh, John, forgive me," she said softly. "I was only teasing. What's wrong?"

"What's wrong is that you're carrying my child. That means that Ollie's name is going to be on his birth certificate. Or hers. That bothers me. A whole lot."

Milly looked like I'd slapped her. "I don't know for sure I am carrying, but I certainly won't let that happen. We've got lots of time."

"No, we don't, Milly. It may be too late, already."

"What do you mean?" There was fear in her eyes. I hated seeing it there.

"I checked the law. It's up to the judge. Most judges won't allow a divorce to be final until after the baby is born. Not in Texas."

"You told me my marriage to Oliver was not a legal marriage."

"It wasn't but you've lived together all these years as man and wife. That means either you or Oliver can claim it's a legal informal marriage."

"Informal? Don't you mean common law, Sheriff?" There was fire in her eye and an edge to Milly's voice she had never used with me before.

"Milly, this is John Stone, the man who loves you with all his heart. Please don't talk to me like that. I didn't do anything to deserve it."

I could see she was not convinced. Nor did I think there was anything I could say to make things better. "I'm not going to fight with you, Milly. I'm sorry I said anything. I thought you needed to know. I'll wait for you at the car." The odd thing was I wasn't really angry. What I felt was hurt and incredibly sad.

I had no more than sat down in the car than Milly was right there beside me with her arms around my neck. "Oh, John, please forgive me. I don't know what's the matter with me. My emotions are all over the place."

I kissed her gently. "I don't know either, Milly. What I've heard is that this happens when women are carrying. Maybe it's time to visit the doctor to find out for sure."

She began to cry. "Please don't ever leave me, John," she said, her voice muffled against my chest. "Even if I'm a horrible witch."

"Of course, I won't, sugar," I assured her. "I may need to be with myself for a bit from time to time, maybe, but I'm not about to leave you. I've been looking for you all my life."

I glanced in the back seat. It was empty. "Where are your new clothes?" I asked.

"I couldn't carry them out without paying for them," she reminded me. She wiped away her tears.

I opened the car door. "I guess we better go take care of that. I won't have you running around the countryside with nothing on."

"Not even if it's just us?" she asked, smiling. "You could be Tarzan."

"If I tried to yodel like Tarzan, half the county would die laughing."

"Especially if I swung by your vine," she said, then blushed furiously, both hands over her mouth. "Tell me I didn't just say that!" she said.

"You didn't," I assured her. "It was that pregnant lady."

"Well, she would know, wouldn't she?"

❧

We had a wonderful time finishing up our shopping. On the way home, Milly was quiet and I wondered what she was thinking. When we got to the driveway at my place, she told me. "I've made a decision, John Paul. I'm going to tell Oliver I'm leaving him."

"Are you sure, Milly? I don't want you to do anything you think is wrong. What we have now is the important thing."

"Yes, it's time. I'm sorry it took me so long, but I'm sure. The only question is when to tell him, now or when he gets out of jail."

"It would be safer to do it now," I said. "You don't even have to talk to him. We can serve him the papers in jail."

"No, he needs to hear it from me," she said. Can you arrange for me to see him tomorrow? We need to be alone."

"Yes, but I'd rather you have bars between you when you do. We don't have any other prisoners so I'll have the jailer bring you up to the cells."

"Thank you," she told me. "I'm sure Oliver will be very angry. This will give him time to cool off. When is he due to be released?"

"I'll have to check. I know it's after the first of next month. I think it's the middle of the month, right before Christmas." We always tried to release prisoners then. This lets everyone have time for family, especially the jailer.

"Good, that will give us a nice time at Thanksgiving. I think I may need to stay at your place after he's released. Will that cause too much talk?"

"I don't care if it does," I told her. "I can always find another job. Maybe even in Colorado or Wyoming." Milly smiled when I said that.

⁂

Not much ever developed with the homicide case that fall. It never got off the ground, though the state lab confirmed that the body found in the lake was that of Jeremy Barker. This was done comparing his dental chart to the skull we found in the lake. Even if the rest of the skeleton was not his, we knew he was dead and how he had died. Yet we weren't able to single out a suspect. By the time Thanksgiving rolled around the case was dead in the water and the other victim had not been identified. It seemed unlikely she ever would be.

This didn't mean I didn't know who committed these murders. I was certain the decision to kill the victims had been made by Gaylord Smith or his bosses. Who had actually pulled the trigger would probably never be known, although I thought there was a good likelihood that it was Sammy Brown. However, we never recovered the bullets that passed through the victims' skulls, either, and there was no other physical evidence linking anyone to the bodies. The state lab was able to identify the wire that was used to wrap Jeremy's body, but it was a common brand widely used in the northern and western parts of the state.

Even so, there was a clear link between the two bodies. The woman buried in the flower bed was wearing a man's dress shirt and there was a tag sewn in it with Jeremy's name. Yet no one at the Roadhouse was willing to identify anyone but Sally Jones as a friend of Jeremy's. It was clear to me that most of the people we questioned were hiding something but we had nothing we could use to break down their denial. Even if they wanted to talk, they were too scared and I couldn't blame them. Two of their coworkers had been killed quickly and efficiently.

There had been no new developments in the death of Maynard Gentry, either. We did not have any hard evidence to justify a court order to exhume his body, and the family refused to allow it. The county commissioners kicked up a fuss over the cost of these investigations and refused to allocate more funds. Yet, I was sure it was not the money that concerned them. There was only one of them I believed was clean and I think the rest were afraid of the potential fall-out of digging too deeply into what was going on at the Roadhouse.

This decision almost lost us Dr. Pettigrew as our county medical examiner and I had to work hard at keeping him on board. "How can they do this?" he asked. "The potassium levels in Mr. Gentry's blood were far over normal. That's what caused his heart attack, Sheriff. All we need is the opportunity to prove it. Can't we get a court order?"

I nodded. "We probably could. I think the judge would take your word for it. The thing is, we don't have anyone to charge. Even with results from the state lab, I don't think we would have a case."

The doctor thought about this a moment. "I see what you mean. Why precipitate an uproar if we can't accomplish something?"

"That's right. What I've learned around here is to pick my battles. Sooner or later the bastards will trip themselves. Then we can kick up as much dust as we want."

A positive note in all of this was a short letter I got from Nancy Hiller just before Thanksgiving. There was no return address and the postmark was smeared beyond deciphering. It was also sent to the office. The plain white envelope it came in was addressed to me as "Sheriff John Stone" and was typed. The envelope was also marked "Personal," and the word was underlined.

The single sheet of notebook paper inside was written in a beautiful hand. After thanking me for all I had done for her, Nancy wrote that she had passed her GED and was working as a receptionist. She was also in night school, studying to become a bookkeeper, and hoped to eventually work her way through college. She added that if I needed to get in touch with her for any reason, I needed to leave a message with her aunt May. She signed the letter, "Love, N."

I was touched by the letter, and disturbed, too. Nancy had taken a risk writing me, though not that great a risk doing it the way she had. Yet, she could not count on the postmark being smeared, and Cheryl would have been curious about a letter from out-of-state. Even though she had been sternly instructed not to do so, she might even mention it to one of her gossip cronies. I was sure that Gaylord Smith was too smooth an operator not to be wired into the gossip network, and I was just as sure he was well enough connected to arrange for Nancy to have a fatal "accident" wherever she was.

What disturbed me most, however, was my response to the letter. I was all right until the closing, interested in a detached sort of way. Yet when I saw the way she signed the letter, I could feel her wonderful body pressed close to mine and I could smell her womanly scent. It was as if she was in my arms again and the image of us in one another's arms was as vivid as ever.

"Damnation!" I muttered, apparently more loudly than I

intended. When I walked out of the office a couple of minutes later Cheryl asked me if something was wrong.

"No," I assured her. "I was hoping for better information. I can't seem to get any traction with the Roadhouse murders."

"Traction?" Cheryl asked, puzzled.

"You know what I mean. It's like driving on ice." I got a blank look that told me that Cheryl had never experienced being in a car spinning out of control after a winter storm.

THIRTEEN

Christmas Presents

Our first Thanksgiving together was wonderful, and the kids made it even better. Louis and I completed my annual custom that morning and delivered Thanksgiving dinner to needy people. Most of these were older folk without families, but some of them were poor families Louis knew. I was surprised to learn that his father and mother had done much the same thing in the Hispanic community, and it meant a lot to Louis to continue their good work. As I thought about this later, it occurred to me I shouldn't have been that surprised. From what I've seen, the poor are far more generous with the little they than the wealthy with their vast resources.

When we got done delivering food, Louis and I headed for home. It was about one o'clock then and we were both hungry after smelling the food we delivered all morning. It was Louis who spotted the little gold car first. "Look!" he said as I turned into the drive. "Uncle Travis is here!"

I was glad to see Travis and was surprised when he introduced Katherine Tedrow, his companion. Like Milly, she was tall and slender, with olive skin and dark eyes, and her raven hair fell to her shoulders. "Call me Kate," she replied. "I hope we're not intruding."

"Of course, you're not," Milly assured her. She looked at her brother. "It's always good to see Travis and any friend of his is welcome."

"Oh, she's more than a friend," Travis answered, reaching for Kate's left hand and raising it so we could see the ring on her fourth finger. "In a moment of madness, she agreed to marry me. I told her we had to have my big sister's approval."

"Oh, Kate!" Milly said and hugged the younger woman. "How wonderful!"

Then she introduced me. "This is my special man, John

Stone. He's been pestering me to marry him and I've finally decided to do it."

"So you've left Oliver," Travis said. "I wondered when you weren't at the house." He turned and offered me his hand and I shook it dumbly. I was stunned at the news and must have shown it. He laughed. "I gather Sissy just sprang this on you. Get used to it. She's always done that."

"She's full of surprises," I said, taking my beloved in my arms and kissing her thoroughly. Travis and the kids clapped. "Now I have one," I added, reaching in my pocket and taking out a small box. When Milly saw it, she blanched and I thought she was going to faint. Then she recovered and her face turned bright red as I slipped the ring on her finger. It was a perfect fit.

"Travis, I'm leaving Oliver," she clarified. She looked down at the ring on her finger. "I haven't told him yet and I really shouldn't wear this now." Then she grinned. "I'm going to, anyway, and people can just talk!"

"I'm Mary Alice," my daughter said. "That's my brother Luís."

"*Buenas dias,* Mary Alice," Kate said, offering her hand. *"Me gusta encantada."*

"*Y yo tambien!*" Mary Alice responded, delighted. *"El es mi hermano, Luíz."*

Louis blushed furiously when Kate offered him her hand. "You're beautiful!" he stammered in English.

Kate smiled and gave him a hug. "And you, Luís, are a gallant *caballero.*" She kissed the top of his head and he grinned, his face as red as a rooster.

"These are our children," I said, offering Kate my hand. "Congratulations."

"To you, too, John. You're getting a wonderful brother-in-law."

"Nothing about this family is usual," Travis tried to explain to his bride to be.

"Not since John Paul led me astray," Milly added, smiling. "Or maybe it was me leading him. Oh, well, the important thing is that we're all together and we all love each other. Welcome to our crazy family, Kate."

I've never had a Thanksgiving so good as that one. We've

never had a bad one since, but that one set the bar very high. Kate fitted in like she'd always been there and insisted on helping clean up afterwards. Conversation around the table was lively and when dinner was done we ended up singing "Sunny Side of the Street" at Mary Alice's request. Then Travis asked Milly to sing a Thanksgiving hymn she knew by heart. It was one their mother had sung and Milly had apparently taught it to the kids because they chimed in on the chorus. It begins, "We plow the fields and scatter good seed," and we have sung it at Thanksgiving ever since. I was pleasantly surprised that Kate had a beautiful voice, too. She asked if we could sing "Amazing Grace" and her contralto and Milly's mezzo-soprano blended so well they sounded like one.

After dinner the rest of us cleaned up while Milly and Kate visited in the living room. It was a cool day, so I built a fire in the fireplace and we spent most of the afternoon visiting. Kate turned out to be a pediatrician with the Public Health Service and Milly told me later that she asked Milly when she was due. "It wasn't if, but when I was due," Milly fretted when we were alone. "I didn't think I was showing. Is it that obvious?"

"Not at all," I assured her. "She's a doctor and I imagine she's seen lots of women with child."

"With child? Since when are we being so delicate, lover man? You knocked me up higher than a kite!"

"I guess that means we don't have to worry about you swallowing a pumpkin seed," I said, nuzzling her neck.

"As if we ever did," she responded, giving me a kiss that shivered my timbers.

The visit from Travis and Kate was our first Christmas present that year. The second came in early December when the judge approved my adoption of Mary Alice and Louis on a permanent basis. This was much sooner than I expected and I was surprised when the judge called me in to tell me. As a matter of fact, it was a surprise to all of us and I had no idea why the judge acted when he did.

When I asked him about it, the judge shook his head sadly. "I'm afraid the sins of my youth have caught up with me,

Johnny," he told me. "I haven't smoked or allowed tobacco use in my court in thirty years, but I became habituated to cigars when I was in law school. Now Dr. Pettigrew tells me I have lung cancer and it's spread. I don't have a lot of time left and I wanted to get this done."

I was shocked. I knew the judge's color hadn't been good lately and that he'd lost some weight, but I thought it was kidney stones. He's had trouble with those from time to time over the years. "Are you sure?" I asked, but I knew it was a foolish question. Pettigrew was no fool and he wouldn't diagnose something until he was quite sure what it was.

"Yes," the judge told me. "Dr. Pettigrew insisted I get a second opinion and he gave me the name of a specialist in Dallas. That's where I was last week." He chuckled dryly. "You might say I lost my final appeal. They tell me I have six months, but I may have to step down much sooner."

"I assume this is confidential," I replied.

"Yes. I don't mind Miss Milly knowing, but I don't want to be a lame duck." He smiled again. "At least, I don't have to stand for reelection or worry about retiring."

The kids knew adoption was in the works, of course, and they wanted it to happen. Yet, when it did, they were a bit subdued. "They're happy about it, John," Milly explained to me when I mentioned it. "Remember, it's not been long since they lost their parents. This reminds them of what they've lost and that bothers them. It always will, but right now it's worse. So they're happy and sad at the same time and it gets confusing."

That made a lot of sense to me. I knew Milly must be speaking from experience. It occurred to me that this was what she was going through, too. I had always thought you were either happy or you were sad, and the idea of being both at the same time was unsettling. Then I realized that Milly had been going through this all her life, and I understood even better just how strong a person she must be.

I also realized I was going through the same thing. There was lots of joy in my life those days, but knowing the judge was dying cast a pall over everything. My own dad was killed in the

Pacific in the war. I was just turned six then and my memories of him were not that clear.

Though my mother eventually remarried, it was the judge who reached out to me. He helped me grow into the man I am, teaching me the manly things I needed to know like how to shoot and handle firearms safely. He also taught me how to fish and the name of every plant in the county, and he taught me to be a man of my word. He was just a lawyer then, of course, with no family of his own, and I even suggested to my mother that he might make a good husband. She laughed when I said this and she told me she didn't think the judge was interested in marriage.

Even so, my mother had always included the judge in family celebrations like Thanksgiving and Christmas, even after she married my step-dad. I continued the tradition when I moved back to Live Oak, and I now understood why he had declined my invitation to join us this year. It took me a while to sort out how I felt about this, too. The judge had lived well past his three score and ten, so he'd had a good run. What I had trouble with was imagining a world without him. Even with Milly and the kids there to fill the empty places in my soul, I felt lost.

❧

Not long after that, Milly told Oliver that she was leaving him. She went to see him alone, but I was watching through a spy hole in the jailer's apartment. It was put there so he could keep an unseen eye on the prisoners and there were several concealed microphones near the cells. So I listened to their conversation through a speaker next to it. Milly knew I would be watching and listening in, and she told me it gave her courage to do what her heart desired. What I didn't tell her was that I made a recording of the conversation. Nor do I know why I didn't say anything about it to her.

Oliver didn't even bother getting up from his bunk when the jailer led Milly into the corridor outside the cells. "Good morning, Oliver," she said but he didn't even look at her.

"I came here today to tell you I am leaving you, Oliver," she told him. "I will be filing for a divorce later today and I wanted you to know."

Oliver glanced her way then, but there was no indication he had heard what she told him. "Do you understand what I'm telling you, Oliver?" she asked and he shrugged. I wondered if he really believed her.

Milly must have had the same doubts, so she spelled it out for him. "When you get out of jail this time I will not be here to take you home. You will have to find your own way and I will be gone when you get there. All I will be taking with me are my own personal things."

"The land stays with me," Oliver glared at her when he said this. He apparently thought she was bluffing and I understand why he did. Their history told him she would always excuse what he did and still be there when he needed her.

"Of course, it does," Milly answered. "It was your inheritance, not mine. I will be taking my chickens, too."

"Good. I hate the filthy things. What about the rest of the stock?"

"I have sold them off and will give you your half," she told him. "You won't have to take care of them when you get out. The jailer will have your money."

"Good riddance," Oliver growled. "You and the rest of the damned animals." He turned away from Milly and lay down on the bunk with his face to the wall. I think he still didn't get it and I wondered if he ever would.

"Good bye, Oliver," she told him. "I wish you all the best."

There was still no answer and when Milly turned around, there were tears in her eyes. I realized then just how much she actually cared for the man, despite all his abuse. I felt like marching into his cell and beating some sense into him, but I had to laugh at myself. Coming to his senses was the last thing I wanted Oliver to do at that point, though I doubted it would do him any good with Milly. Travis was right. Once she made up her mind, no mule was any match for her. There would be no turning back.

Milly was quiet going home that evening. I know she was cut to pieces inside but by the time we ate supper, she seemed like her normal, cheerful self. I think the kids had a lot to do with it. They were thrilled when they learned she would be moving in and they wanted to help her pack. When I looked at Milly, she nodded. "All right," I said. "We'll all help. The hardest thing will be moving the chickens, but we'll let Mary Alice do that. She likes them so much." Louis laughed when I said this and Milly smiled.

"What?" Mary Alice exclaimed, indignant. Then she realized I was only kidding. "All right," she smiled sweetly. "As long as Louis cleans up after the pigs." When she said this, he made a terrible face and pinched his nose.

"You don't have to worry about any of that," Milly told them. "I've already sold the pigs and the rest of the stock. Someone will be coming to get them. We'll all do the chickens at night. They'll be easier then."

"Yeah, but then you can't see where you're stepping," Mary Alice protested. "Why don't we just eat them?"

"All of them at once?" Milly asked, smiling. "We'll still have to go into the pen to catch them."

"Why?" Louis asked. "Our papa used to take his .22 out in the yards and shoot the head off the one he wanted to eat."

"Grand mama used to wring their necks and pop off their heads," Mary Alice added, twirling her hand to demonstrate.

"Do you really want to have chickens?" I asked Milly. "You don't have to if you don't want to. You're gainfully employed now."

"Oh, my," she said. The idea floored her. "I've always had chickens. What would I do without them?"

"How much are they worth?" I asked. "If you had to buy them."

"Ten dollars, maybe," she said.

I took out my wallet and handed her a bill. "There," I said. "They're mine now."

Milly stood there confused, holding the bill. "We still have to move them."

"No, we don't," I told her.

"What are you going to do with them?" Milly asked.

"I'll give them to Clint and Mary. I'll let them come pick them up. They've been good neighbors and that will definitely give them something to talk about."

I could tell that Milly was still trying to comprehend the thought of not having chickens. She never noticed I'd handed her a twenty dollar bill. The next morning she asked me where it came from. I told her it was from the chicken fairy.

⁂

True to her word, Milly had Oliver served with divorce papers the next day. This was like dropping a tub of bloody guts into a pool of sharks. The gossip telegraph went into overdrive at the news. Divorce was uncommon in rural areas back then and the word, itself, was often whispered. This was something outrageous that Hollywood people did, and maybe a few city folk, too. Our community was familiar with annulments. This was what happened when under aged high school kids ran off to Oklahoma and got married. It was scandalous but it didn't carry the same freight of shame that divorce did. People who got divorced were considered immoral, and Milly had always been held up as a paragon of virtue. With the act of having Oliver served, her reputation evaporated like early morning mist in a strong morning sun.

Or, maybe I'm being too harsh. There were a lot of good people who stood by her, even the pastor at the Methodist church. He made a point of preaching about what a marriage was supposed to be, and while he didn't mention Milly and Oliver by name, everyone knew who he was talking about. They also knew about Oliver's abuse and his alcoholism, and the pastor spoke about both. He described them as cancers that destroyed what God intended in marriage, and he pointed out that "until death do us part" included marriages that die. He also reminded the good folk that not all marriages are made in Heaven, and that divorces sometimes were.

This was radical teaching for the time. It cost the congregation a few members, but I heard the treasurer say that those who left hardly ever contributed much, either of their time or their money. "We're way better off without them, Sheriff," Granger told me. "The way most of us look at it, you saved Milly a world of grief."

"It was her decision," I assured him. "I'm damned glad she made it the way she did, but it was completely up to her."

The treasurer fixed me with a look he must have used to good effect when he was with the IRS. "That's right, John, but you gave her the option. I, for one, am grateful to you for that. Milly is a saint in my book. She sat with my mother before she died, and she made my mother's last year bearable."

"She's been a real blessing to me and the kids, too," I told him.

"That's another thing I respect you and her for, taking in the kids. A lot of people don't care for Mexicans. I personally think they're better people than a lot of white trash I could name." I knew he was referring to Oliver, among others.

"I didn't have much choice, Granger. They didn't have any family left."

He grinned. "Yeah, right. To quote Harry Truman, 'horse manure!'"

❧

Oliver was released just before Christmas that year. As I recall, Christmas fell on a Wednesday and he was released the Saturday before. We let him go at ten that morning and by noon he was falling down drunk at Randall's. So was Horace Springer and they got into a fight the way they always did. Yet they were too drunk to do much damage to each other and Tony tossed them out. He told me later that they drove off together in Horace's beat up old truck.

Where they headed was to Neville's to replenish their supply of booze. Neville told me that Horace was passed out by the time they got to his place and Oliver was driving. He said that Oliver told him he was celebrating his freedom. He had lots of money from Milly's sale of the livestock, and he bought three gallons of white lightning. Unlike regular whiskey, moonshine ran about a hundred and eighty proof, ninety percent alcohol.

At first, Neville thought Oliver meant liberation from jail and enforced sobriety. "Then he started cussing Miss Milly," Neville said. "He told me he was glad to be getting shed of her. That dumb bastard. He didn't have the brains God gave a striped jackass! She was the best thing that ever happened to him and he drank it away!

Yeah, I thought, with you helping out every step of the way, one jug at a time. Yet I didn't say it. I didn't see how it would do much good. Neville would deny he had in any part in the poor choices Oliver made. That might be true in the strictest sense, but selling Oliver liquor was like selling a pyromaniac matches and gasoline. The result was predictable from the get-go and damned near certain.

What happened after Oliver left Neville's was all too predictable, as well. Horace never woke up while they were at Neville's, and the last Neville saw of them was when Oliver turned onto the county road from Neville's driveway. Eight miles down the road, Oliver was driving way too fast and missed a bad turn near the river. The truck went out of control and struck an enormous live oak at the bottom of the rise. This time Oliver's luck ran out. His neck was broken in the crash and he never felt the flames that burned the truck to a rusty pile of iron. Horace was not so lucky, though he did not die in the fire, either. The collision threw him out of the truck and into the river, where he drowned. Even then he might have survived, but Horace Springer had never learned to swim. As we put it together, the cold water sobered him up instantly. Then he panicked and never saw the tree limb he could have grabbed to pull himself to safety.

The road Oliver was driving didn't carry much traffic and it was the middle of the next morning before the wreck was discovered. This was on Sunday morning and I was in church when Buzz came to tell me. The service was just over and I was talking to Granger when Buzz found me. All he knew was that there had been a truck wreck and someone was killed.

I asked Granger to spread the news and went to find Milly and the kids. I told her what Buzz told me, that there had been a bad truck crash and I had to go. When she asked who it was, I told her it was Horace Springer's truck but that someone else had been driving. We didn't know who it was. Nor did I have any idea it might be Oliver driving. I thought they were too much at odds to be drinking buddies.

Word had gotten out and there was a crowd waiting for us when Buzz and I got to the crash site. The body behind the wheel was burned too badly for identification. Someone said they thought it was Oliver Bates, but another bystander took exception. "Oliver Bates with Horace Springer? You must be drinking. They hate each other."

"Yeah, but I saw them together last night when they left Randall's," the first man said. Horace was driving and they was sharing a bottle. I seen them, myself!"

"Sure it wasn't you drinking?" the second man said and the first man flushed.

"Hey!" I hollered and they both looked at me. "You two want to fuss, then move it down the road," Then I spoke in a gentler voice. "Right now I could use some help recovering the bodies." The two men glared at each other but neither left. Helping out with a car wreck was clearly more exciting than settling their differences. That could wait.

With the help of those two and a couple of other bystanders, we managed to get the remains out of the truck. The two men who had been arguing helped Buzz break Horace out of the brush where his body lodged in the river and to drag him up on the shore. There was no doubt he was dead or who he was. It was cool the night before and he had been in the water long enough for his body to shed all its heat. He was colder than a catfish, but he had not been in the water long enough to bloat.

The charred body in the truck was a whole different matter. The face was too badly burned to make out distinct features and not much was left of the clothes. We did find what we thought was a billfold but that didn't help. It looked like a large lump of charcoal, too charred to open without crumbling. Then we got lucky. Buzz found a pocket knife and some coins on the floor of the truck, along with a set of keys. The keys were distorted by the heat of the fire, but there was a stainless steel disk on the ring. It was about the size of a half dollar and there was a shamrock stamped on one side of the disk. On the other was a phone number I recognized. It was the number for Oliver and Milly's place.

"Anybody know Oliver Bates' phone number?" I asked, holding up the disk for the crowd to see.

"No, but I recognize that medallion," one of the men said. "That's Oliver's good luck piece."

"Didn't work too good, did it?" another man pointed out and the group laughed. "I think I recognize it, too. Is that a shamrock on the back?" I told him it was. "Look on the other side, Sheriff," he told me. "Ollie had his initials scratched on it."

I looked and, sure enough, there were three initials crudely engraved in the disk. I read them off to the crowd. "Says, 'ORB.' Anybody know what the R stands for?"

"Rotgut!" someone hollered and the group laughed again.

"Thanks," I said, putting the disk into my shirt pocket. "I'll check it out. He looks about the right size to be Ollie."

"That looks like his pocket knife, too," Buzz pointed out. "Or what's left of it."

The county ambulance arrived about then and we loaded both bodies. I told the driver to take them to the hospital and asked him to notify Dr. Pettigrew. Then Buzz and I began to reconstruct the crash, and I made sure to take plenty of pictures. Once that was done, I asked Buzz to drop me at the house. On the way there I told him he also needed to go by Horace Springer's place and let his wife know what had happened. "She's probably already heard about it by now, but we need to let her know officially. I'll notify Milly."

"Did you see all that glass on the floor of the truck?" Buzz asked me.

"I did. It looked like a couple of gallon jugs broke. Maybe three." The fire had been so intense some of it had melted.

"What do you make of it?"

"I think it must have been moonshine Ollie got from Neville. That's what made the fire so hot. You saw how burned the body was. Neville's moonshine is almost pure alcohol."

"Crispy critter," Buzz nodded. "Think he felt anything?"

I shook my head. "I hope not. I think he was probably killed when the truck hit the tree. I don't see how he could still be alive the way the front end was smashed."

Buzz nodded. "I hope so, too. Nobody deserves to be burned to death like that." He glanced at me to see if I agreed.

"Yeah," I said. "Not even Adolph Hitler."

"I don't know if I'd go that far," Buzz replied. Then he shrugged. "He's probably burning in Hell, anyway." I didn't even bother to answer. Who gets to heaven or not is definitely not up to me.

❧

When I got home, I found Milly and the kids sitting at the dinner table. I was dreading giving her the news, but it must have been written all across my face. "It was Oliver, wasn't it?" she asked. The kids were looking at me and I could see they were scared.

"Yes, Milly, it was. He was driving Horace Springer's truck. They were both killed." I showed her the ring of keys. "This is his, isn't it?"

"Yes, it is." She took it and looked at it. "This looks burned. Was there a fire?"

I nodded. "I don't think Oliver burned to death, though. He was driving pretty fast and drove headlong into a big live oak. I think he was killed instantly."

"Thank God he didn't hit someone else!" she declared. Then she burst into tears and I took her in my arms. A moment later I felt Louis and Mary Alice put their arms around her, too.

After a long while, Milly pulled back. "Where can I see him, John?"

"It's not something you want to see, Milly," I told her. "He was burned beyond recognition. We identified him from the key ring, and someone saw them together in Horace's truck in town. Ollie was driving. I think Dr. Pettigrew will have to use dental records to make positive identification."

"I really need to do this, John Paul," she told me. "I may be able to tell if it's Oliver. It's my duty."

"Then at least wait until we try everything else," I asked. "Believe you me, you don't want to see it. I wish I hadn't. It was horrible."

She looked at me gravely. "All right, John. As your wife to be, I'll respect your counsel. Tomorrow I'll need to make funeral arrangements. Will you come with me? It may not look good, but I want you there."

"Do we have to come, too?" Mary Alice asked. "I hate funeral homes."

"No, sweetheart," Milly answered, touching Mary Alice's

cheek. "You don't have to come, but it's not going to be at the funeral home. It's going to be a very simple memorial service at the church."

"I want to come," Louis said, giving his sister a stern look. "I'm part of your family, too."

"Yes, Luís, you are," Milly said, hugging him and reaching out for Mary Alice. "Both of you. But you two need to go to school tomorrow."

*

Oliver was identified fairly quickly once he got to the hospital. The dentist he used to extract teeth gone bad lived in Live Oak, and the dental records were a match. Dr. Pettigrew was also able to identify Ollie's blood as AB negative, a type he shared with only one percent of the American population. This, together with dental records and the evidence I gathered from Neville and other sources, confirmed that the charred corpse was Oliver Roy Bates. This meant that Milly never had to view the charred corpse, something for which she later told me she was grateful.

Then Milly did something that added fuel to the gossip fire. She decided to have Oliver's remains cremated. When people asked why, she told them it seemed right to do it that way. "Oliver didn't like the idea of being buried," she told people. "He told me once that he wanted his ashes scattered in an appropriate place."

This led to a lot of speculation about what she meant by appropriate. When the lead gossip inquired what appropriate meant, Milly pretended to misunderstand. She gave her the dictionary meaning, suitable or proper under the circumstances. When the harridan allowed that was not exactly what she meant, Milly said, "Oh, I'm sorry. Silly me. Oliver always loved that farm so I think it's fitting for me to scatter his ashes there. Don't you think?"

This decision to cremate what was left of Oliver also gave rise to some rough humor among the crowd at Randall's. Tony assured me this was directed at Oliver, not Milly. Nor was it easy to keep from joining in. I was in the judge's office when I overheard one lawyer tell another that by all rights, the crematorium should give Milly a discount since their job was already half done. His companion quipped that he'd really be burned up about it if they didn't. He went on to point out that Oliver had urned his rest.

What I couldn't mention, of course, even to Milly, was what I really thought about the whole thing. Oliver may not have intended it that way, but by getting drunk and killing himself when he did, he gave Milly and me a real Christmas present. I truly believe Oliver was trying to drink himself out of this world, but that he had failed until that day. It may not be very charitable, but I guess you could say the forty-eleventh time was the charm for Oliver Bates. I was grateful he was gone without killing someone else and that Milly didn't have to go through the stress of divorce.

⁂

Since Christmas was so close upon us, Milly decided to have Oliver's memorial service on the Saturday following Christmas day. It turned out to be one of the coldest days we had that winter, and I think most folks were grateful there wasn't a burial following the service. Nor was there a coffin, only a small square box that would eventually hold Oliver's remains for a while. Our medical examiner had not released them and the remains would not be available for a few weeks. We were waiting for test results from the state lab in Austin and the nearest crematorium was in Ft. Worth. The lab tests were a formality but Dr. Pettigrew was being cautious. Considering the strange things he'd seen since coming to Rutherford County, I can't blame him.

Since Milly intended to scatter Oliver's ashes, the funeral director explained that what we got back from the crematorium would not be ashes. The cremains, as he called them, were tiny pieces of very dry bone, some of them so fine they resembled dust or talcum powder. Everything else had been consumed in the burning. He had gone on to suggest one of the urns he had in stock, but Milly insisted on a plain pine box. We ended up having it made by a local cabinet maker.

It seemed odd planning a memorial service with only a box, too. All the ones I've been to had a picture of the deceased next to the urn. The problem was that Milly didn't have a decent picture of Oliver. The best ones available were mug shots and

Milly snorted when I suggested one of those. "I'm trying to be reverent, John Paul," she told me with mock severity. The effect was ruined by her attempt to remain solemn. "I could use a little help, you know."

"I understand," I said solemnly. "Maybe you could put a black ribbon around the box. A bow would be nice, too." Louis, who was listening to us laughed but Mary Alice rolled her eyes.

"I know, dear," Milly told her, smiling. "The menfolk are hopeless but they have their good points, too."

Louis asked if he could see one of Oliver's mug shots and I brought one home the next day. He disappeared for a while but an hour later he brought out a pencil drawing of Oliver and handed it to Milly. "My goodness, Louis!" she gasped. "That's wonderful. I had no idea you could draw like that."

She handed me the drawing and I saw what she meant. Somehow, without ever meeting him, Louis had captured the character of Oliver with some very simple lines. What struck me was the haunting eyes in the drawing. Looking at them up close, they were just well drawn eyes. Six feet away they revealed the despair so evident in Ollie when he didn't think anyone was looking. There was no sign of the tough guy front he assumed, only the middle aged man who drank to dull the pain of living each day without hope.

Even so, there was something else in the drawing, too. There was a hint of the man Oliver might have been if he hadn't become a drunk or if he had sobered up. I've known men who have done it, too, a number of them right here in Live Oak. Some of these men had been much worse off than Oliver and they now lived sober, sane, useful lives. I knew they would have bent over backwards to help Oliver put the plug in the jug and find sanity. All he had to do was allow them into his life and to accept their help.

I also know for a fact these men tried to get through to Oliver. Yet he had refused their help, time and again. He turned his face to the wall, just as he had with Milly, and he never allowed the man he might have been a chance. Now he was dead, not a year older than me.

"He's always drawn good pictures," Mary Alice informed us,

giving Louis a look that was pure vindication. "I've told him that but he doesn't believe me. What do I know? I'm only his sister."

Louis glared at his sister but Milly reached out and touched his cheek. "I'm so proud of you," she said. "You're going to grow into a wonderful man." When she hugged him, he stuck out his tongue at Mary Alice. Then he saw me watching and his eyes got wide, but my face gave me away. I felt it trying to grin.

"I've got a nice frame we can use down at the office," I told Milly. "It's not fancy but I think it will fit Louis' picture. It's your call, but I think we ought to use Lewis' drawing. It's better than any photo."

"I agree," she said, giving Louis another hug.

"I could use a hug, too," I told Mary Alice. Milly told me later that while she was hugging me, Mary Alice stuck her tongue out at her brother. She added that she and Travis used to do the same when their mother was alive.

FOURTEEN

Year's End

Because of Oliver's death, our Christmas celebration was muted that year. The judge joined us and he brought a couple of bottles of fine brandy. "I've been saving it for a special occasion," he told us. "I can't think of a better occasion than Christmas with this delightful family." Then he opened a paper sack he was carrying and took out an imported hot chocolate mix and a package of small marshmallows. "This is for you," he told Mary Alice and Louis. "You can have some after dinner."

"You're part of the family, too, sir," I assured him. "You were always like a father to me and the way I figure it, your court order made these kids your grandchildren."

"Oh, my," he replied, obviously touched but not trying to hide it. "I'm at a loss for words." Then he laughed and shook his finger in my face. "Don't you say it, either, young man. I know what you're thinking. It's not a first."

Travis and Kate were with us, too. After Thanksgiving they headed for the beach near Corpus Christi rather than returning to the East Coast. Travis was due back by Christmas but his commander granted him compassionate leave to extend his stay for Oliver's funeral. He was not due back until after the first of the year.

The only family missing that year was Sammy Brown, Milly's younger brother. We talked about inviting him but Milly thought it was a bad idea. "He's made his choice clear, John," she told me sadly. "It breaks my heart, but he's chosen not to be part of our family. We need to respect his decision."

I was just as glad, of course. Sammy had not bothered to call or come by since Oliver was killed, and he avoided me in town. Nor had he even sent Milly a note of condolence. I thought he might be at the funeral, but I doubted he would choose to sit with the rest of us or to sign the guest book. I certainly didn't miss him at our Christmas celebration.

The judge and Travis hit it off right away, which was no surprise. Over dinner the judge kept us entertained with funny stories from his days as a country lawyer, and Travis and Milly shared their memories of Christmas growing up in north Texas. When it came to me, I told the story of my grandpa getting his foot stuck in the milk bucket one year when my grandmother needed fresh milk to finish Christmas dinner. I happened to be there with him when it happened and the kids thought it was hilarious the way I aped him jumping up and down.

Kate was a good listener and hadn't said much. When we asked her for a story, she told us about delivering a beautiful baby boy one Christmas morning. She had got caught in a winter storm in a small town in West Virginia where she was visiting a cousin in the hospital. She was the only doctor in town and when she tried to leave the evening before, a state trooper ordered her to stay off the highway.

Kate paused and looked at me intently. "You know, John, he looked a lot like you. You don't have a brother in the West Virginia highway patrol, do you?"

Milly laughed when she asked this. "I thought you looked familiar," I said. "That was me. I thought I was going to have to arrest you to get you turned back. That was the worst storm in thirty years."

Kate laughed. "Talk about a small world. I was mad at you until I read the papers the day after Christmas. Four people were frozen to death in their cars that night on that highway while I slept in a nice warm bed at the hospital. I'm glad I finally got the chance to thank you."

"I imagine the child's mother was glad you were there to deliver him," the judge offered, nudging her back to the story.

"Oh, she was. There were complications and I had never delivered a baby before, but there was a nurse in the next town with lots of experience. They got her on the phone and she talked me through it. The mother and the baby were just fine. They wanted to name him after me but they couldn't think of a boy's name related on Katherine."

"So what did they name him?" Mary Alice asked.

"That was the interesting thing," Kate told her." There was a baby book there and they found a Hungarian name, Katóne. I looked it up later and it's a form of Jeremiah."

"Jeremiah?" Louis asked. "He was born on Christmas. Why didn't they just name him Jesús?"

"Makes perfect sense to me," the judge said, looking at the rest of us sternly. We all nodded our agreement, all of us but Mary Alice.

"Jesús?" she asked. "Come on, Louis! That doesn't sound a bit like Katherine."

The church was having a candlelight Christmas eve celebration, so about nine we bundled up and headed into town. The judge begged off. He looked really beat and I offered to drive him home. "No, Johnny," he told me. "You go on to church with your family. I'll be fine. It's just this damned cancer. It robs me of my natural strength. Thanks for a grand time," he added, kissing Milly on the cheek.

The church service that night was pretty much what we had every year, and everyone but Milly crowded into a pew near the front. The choir was doing some special music and she had to sit with them in the choir loft. They had a better overall view up there, but I enjoyed being in the middle of things. Then, at the last moment, the pastor came over and asked me to do part of the reading of the Christmas story. The reader had come down with a sore throat and I had filled in before. Thankfully, there weren't any throat twisting Hebrew words in my part.

I don't know if it was from having Milly and the kids in my life, or being part of the service, but that year the things seemed different. I seemed to understand what was being read in a way I never had and when we sang "Little Town of Bethlehem" during the Christmas story, my eyes started to leak. I'd never had that happen before but I couldn't wipe them away without calling attention to myself. I was up next and Milly told me later that night that my face seemed to shine as I read.

"I'm terrible," she confessed with a giggle. "When I saw your face like that I got all bothered. It was all I could do to behave myself until we got home."

"I wondered what got into you," I told her with a smile.

"After we turned in you seemed particularly inspired."

She chuckled. "You didn't seem to mind, John Paul." She paused. "Are you sure you don't mind me getting inspired like that?"

I was having trouble staying awake. "No, Milly, not a bit. As far as I'm concerned, you can get inspired like that anytime you want."

"Any time?" she asked. It was all I could do to nod and whisper, "Yes, any time."

"Good!" she said in her chipper voice. "How about right now?"

❧

I showed up at the office the day after Christmas, mostly to check the mail and to be seen. Louis came with me and we cruised around the county roads, stopping in to visit a bit with the people I keep an eye on when I can. These are mostly older folk who don't have family nearby and they seem to appreciate the visits.

One of the families I check on regularly are the Krauses, and Louis was quite taken with them. I didn't know how comfortable he would be but after the first little bit, he was fine. He had no trouble communicating with them and they seemed to really enjoy his company. We ended up staying a lot longer than I had intended, and we weren't out of the drive before Louis was peppering me with questions about the three older folk.

Morton walked us out to the cruiser when we were leaving. He handed me a clipping from the county paper and pointed to the obit for Oliver Bates. "You want to know what happened?" I asked and he nodded. I gave him the basic details and told him the memorial would be on Saturday. "Do you want to come to that?" I asked. "I'll find you a ride if you do."

Morton shook his head and with his hands outlined a ceramic jug, including the finger ring, and mimicked taking a drink. "Oliver brought you whiskey?" I asked and Morton nodded. "Are you getting low?" I asked and he nodded again. "All right," I told him. "I'll make sure you get some. You need it before New Year's?"

Morton shook his head and signaled that he had another

question. He pointed at Milly's name and drew a question mark on his palm with a finger. "Miss Milly's fine," I said. "She's going to be all right."

"She's my new mama," Louis said proudly.

Morton looked surprised and I told Louis he needed to explain how that had come to pass. So Louis told him about the storm and how he and his sister lost their parents. He went on to tell him how I had rescued them from the cellar and adopted them, and that Milly had come to live at our house.

"She's our house keeper," I interjected, but Morton just grinned and shook his head when I told him this. He wasn't fooled for a moment but he didn't seem to think it was wrong, either. He held out his hand and shook mine like he was offering me his congratulations. Then he gave me the A-OK sign.

"Are you and Mama Milly going to get married now?" Louis asked on the way home.

"Just as soon as we can," I assured him. "Just as soon as we can."

"Good," he said. "Then you can have some babies."

❧

Oliver's memorial service was plain and simple. It was held at the Methodist Church and I was surprised how many people turned out. I think this was mostly for Milly, but there were also a number of men there who had not darkened the doorway of a church in many years. Some of these were Oliver's drinking buddies and a number of them were well on their way to being drunk.

Nor am I sure just why these men were there. Maybe it was because they had nothing to do and it was an occasion to get drunk. Or maybe it was simply because they knew Oliver and came to pay their respects. I knew there was no love lost between Oliver and Morris Acker, but he was there, too. After the service I asked him why he came and he told me it was to see where we buried Oliver. "So I can come back later and piss on his grave," he added.

"Oh," I answered. "He's not being buried, Morris. His ashes are being scattered on his land." I almost laughed seeing the look on his face when I told him this.

While I really hadn't expected any trouble at the service, I believe in being prepared. So I had asked Buzz to wear his uniform to the service. Since I would be sitting with Milly and her family, I wore my best suit with a white shirt and tie. I knew the pastor didn't like the idea of guns in the church, and Milly didn't, either. So neither Buzz and I were armed except with a few small packets of mixed pepper we could fling into the faces of attackers or rowdies.

This was an idea I picked up from a fellow trooper who served in Japan and I used a mixture of finely ground cayenne and black pepper. The Japanese call it *metzubishi* and it works wonders. There's nothing like a fit of sneezing and temporary blindness to divert a belligerent drunk or break up a bar fight. Nowadays police carry pepper spray, which is more accurate, but this was ten years before that was around. We had to make up our own, but they worked very well.

There were also people from other congregations at the memorial service. This didn't surprise me since Milly was so active in community organizations. With me sitting at her side, along with the kids, I was sure this would hurt Milly's reputation even more, but she insisted. "We have nothing to hide, John Paul," she told me. "At this point, trying to hide being together would only add fuel to the fire. I'm not ashamed of who we are and I don't believe you are, either. People will think what they want to think, regardless what we do."

The only thing that concerned me was the upcoming election. Yet that was many months down the road and I was serious about what I told the judge. The the welfare of Milly and the kids came first. So if Mrs. Grundy the gossip queen decided to climb the miff tree because of us, that was her privilege. Once we were married, talk would die down, and if worse came to worse, I could always get a job as a policeman in Cowtown or Abilene.

As I said, the memorial service was plain and simple. We began by singing all the verses of "Amazing Grace" and then the pastor called us together with a prayer. The pastor had asked me to read the famous passage from Isaiah about binding up the brokenhearted and setting the captives free. Then, at Milly's request, Kate sang "Precious Lord Take My Hand" a cappella. This is a hymn that always made a lot of sense to me and by the time Kate was done, I felt chill bumps on my neck.

That was just for openers. The pastor got up and read his sermon text from Luke. It was the story of the prodigal sons, or, as the pastor pointed out, the waiting father. He pointed out that all the father wanted was his two sons safely at home and sharing his joy in their being home. He went on to remind us that the father had set no conditions on the younger prodigal's return, and that he had left the celebration to seek out the older prodigal who was angry with his brother and his father.

Then the pastor socked it to us, as people were beginning to say. He pointed out that we were forbidden to judge one another, and for a good reason. None of us are wise enough or intelligent enough or loving enough to sit in judgment of anyone, including ourselves. We are commanded to leave all judgment to God, and when we do that, we are happier and our lives are more peaceful. This included Oliver, who was created in God's own image and whom God loved as much as he did anyone else in this world. As broken and sinful as Oliver might appear to us, he was still the beloved son of a heavenly father who only wanted him safe at home.

There were some prayers after that and a pastoral blessing. Then we trooped out singing the final hymn, "Joyful, joyful, we adore thee." As we did, I spotted Sammy in the last pew and our eyes met. What I saw in his eyes told me there was no love lost between us as far as he was concerned. Nor did he come forward to greet Milly at the main door. I happened to be standing outside by then and caught a glimpse of him slipping out the side door.

I was just as glad I didn't have to deal with Sammy Brown just then. By the time the service was over I felt like I'd been lifted up, cast down, and wrung through the mill. I found myself so moved by the service that I wondered if my days as a lawman were coming to an end.

Nor was this a new thought. With a family to protect, it had occurred to me that it might be a good idea to get into a lower risk profession. My children had already lost one father and they didn't need to lose another. The same could be said for Milly, too. Having lost one husband to alcoholism, she didn't need to lose another to a stray bullet or a high speed crash in pursuit of a criminal.

Of course, Milly sensed that I was troubled, and that night after we turned in, she asked me about it. When I explained my dilemma, she told me, "John, I accepted that risk before we ever were together. There is no way you can protect us from life. It just happens the way it does, and the best we can do is to keep from taking unnecessary chances. That's all I ask."

"Thank you," I told her. "Thank you for being the wonderful person you are and for letting me share your life."

"Well, I have something in mind, speaking of sharing. Right now, I'm too tired and so are you. So, if you don't mind, I'd like to just be held for a while."

❦

Five days later, one year ended and a new one began. Travis and Kay headed back to the east coast after the memorial service and the day after New Year's, Milly and I drove down to Waco with the kids to get a marriage license. Three days later, the judge quietly joined us as husband and wife in his chambers, with Dee and his wife for our witnesses and our kids watching. The judge was surprised when I asked him to do this but he agreed when I told him a child was on the way. At our request, the judge also made Milly the alternate guardian of our children.

"All this is somewhat irregular," he told us. "However, it is perfectly legal, in my opinion, and I won't have to deal with any consequences. That's one of the few benefits of terminal illness. Even so, I would like to live long enough to see your new child." He smiled. "No, make that my newest grandchild."

We didn't broadcast the fact we were married, but we didn't try to hide it, either. Milly took off the engagement ring I had given her and put on a wide gold wedding band, and I began to wear a matching band, too. Oddly enough, no one asked me if I had committed matrimony, but word filtered around. People began to make references to Milly as "your wife" instead of calling her by name, and my failure to correct them was eloquent. I know a lot of people were curious but we didn't volunteer any information and they didn't ask. The county paper did print the public record of Mildred Brown Stone being appointed as alternate guardian for Luís Xavier and Maria Alicia Rodriguez y Degas, but it took a while for people to make the connection. Once they did, it wasn't news any more. It's hard to pull of being scandalized over last week's public notices.

Then, a few days after the first of February, a plain cardboard carton arrived at the funeral home. They called Milly to let her know Oliver's cremains had come in and I picked it up on the way home. The kids were curious about the contents and Milly opened the box to show them. Not that there was much to see. A sturdy plastic bag held the ash gray remains and Milly even opened the bag to let the kids feel the stuff. It surprised me that neither of them were creeped out about this, but Milly was very matter of fact about it.

"What are you going to do with them?" Mary Alice asked.

"I'm going to pour them out at Oliver's farm," Milly answered.

"Can we watch?" Louis asked.

"There's nothing to see," Milly answered. "Tomorrow I'm going to drive over to Oliver's farm and pour them out in a special place. Then the wind take them as it will. After that, your daddy and I are going to pick you up from school and get hamburgers at the drive-in."

"Cool!" Louis declared. "Can I order curly fries?"

"May I order curly fries," Mary Alice corrected him.

"Of course, you can," I told her and Louis grinned.

⁊⁊

Milly was very quiet the next morning as we drove over to Oliver's farm. Actually, it was her place now, or it would be when Oliver's estate was settled. Ollie had never bothered to make a will and there were no children from the marriage, so Milly got it all. She wanted to refuse to take it, but I insisted that she accept ownership. "You earned it, Milly," I told her. "You were a loyal wife to Ollie all those years he abused you, and it's yours by all rights."

"I don't want to live there ever again," she told me. "I want to forget those years and keeping it would be a constant reminder."

"Then sell it and put the money in a trust for yourself and

the kids," I told her. "It will go to good use that way and you don't even have to think about it. I would like you to have some money for yourself, anyway."

"Why, John? You give me all I need."

"So you won't feel beholden to me. Or always have to come to me if you want something."

"I am already beholden to you, John," she said. "You saved my life. I don't know how much longer I could have held on and Oliver would have killed me in a drunken rage, sooner or later. You've given me a child and two lovely children and a whole new life. I'll never be able to repay you for that."

"Milly!" I said sternly and she blinked. "You. Owe. Me. Nothing. I want you with me because you love me and want to be there. I never want you to feel beholden to me, never, ever!"

Milly smiled for the first time that morning. "Are you trying to get me all excited, John Paul?" The smile turned into a grin. "You know how I get when you act all stern and official!" She reached over and took a firm hold on me. "Now turn us around and get us back to the house. We can take care of Oliver later."

⁂

"It just gets better and better, doesn't it?" Milly was looking at me, bright eyed and wide awake. I was almost asleep. We were lying on our bed at the house, our clothes scattered where we had thrown them.

I wanted to agree but all I could manage were odd sounding moans. "You take a nap and I'll fix lunch," Milly said, kissing me lightly and jumping out of bed. It was incredible how beautiful she was right at the moment. Pregnancy had filled out her figure and given her skin a wonderful glow, and it was all there for me to admire. Nor did I ever tire of looking at her, and when she was finished dressing, I felt a little sad that she was done. Then I remembered I would see it all again that evening, and I dropped off to sleep with that happy thought.

Milly woke he an hour later. "We need to get going, John. Lunch is on the table but it's getting late if we're going to the farm." I noticed she didn't say Oliver's farm, which was good. She was beginning to claim the place.

When we got to the farm, Milly told me she wouldn't be

long. "I'm not sure I want you to see this, John," she added.

"What are you going to do?" I asked, but she shook her head and headed for the house with the cardboard box of remains.

This alarmed me and I went after her. When I opened the front door, I heard the back door close. I was there in a flash and as I went outside, I saw Milly opening the door to the outhouse. I almost stopped because she was so private about privy things, but she was having a hard time untying the string on the box and holding the door open, too. "Let me help you," I said. I handed her a pocket knife and held the door. When she looked at me I saw she was crying.

"These aren't sad tears," she said, slashing the string in two with one stroke. A moment later she slashed open the plastic bag, too.

I suddenly realized what she was doing. "Milly?" I asked as gently as I could. "Are you sure you want to do this?"

"Yes! I need to get him out of my mind!" She still didn't say Ollie's name. Taking the plastic bag out of the box, she flipped open the flap covering the hole. "I've been thinking about this ever since he died."

Milly paused and took a deep breath. Then she emptied the plastic bag through the hole. "Goodbye, Oliver Bates. I'm sorry I ever met you, but I hope you rest in peace." Then she closed the flap and threw herself into my arms, weeping.

I edged us away from the outhouse and closed the door, turning the wooden peg that kept it shut. Then I felt Milly pull back. "Thank you, my husband," she said, smiling. "You want to know something strange?"

"Sure," I said, wondering what could be stranger than what I just saw.

"That woman you bring out in me kept me from making a big mistake just now. Ever since the service for Oliver I thought about what I wanted to say to him right now. Mostly it was bad names I wanted to call him, awful things. Then, as I was about to dump him down the hole, she stopped me. She reminded me I had a part in all of it, too. I put up with it, which I never should have. So I didn't curse him like I wanted to. I would have been cursing myself, too."

I nodded. That made perfect sense to me. "I think you're right, Milly, but I'm not as forgiving as you. I think he's in the right place now. I hope you don't regret that."

"No, I think he's in the right place, too. He was a real shit!"

I was startled. I had never heard the word used so eloquently. Then Milly smiled and kissed me lightly. "There, now I've said it. It's our time now, John Paul, you and me and the kids. Let's keep this to ourselves."

I glanced at my watch and nodded. "Of course, but we better get a move on. I seem to remember someone making a promise about some curly fries."

FIFTEEN

Brandy Sloan

Things settled down for a while after that. Milly was able to hide carrying a child for a while, carefully letting out dresses and fitting them to her changing figure. Yet even the best tailoring couldn't keep up with the changes and she began to show more and more. Then one day she stopped. "That's enough!" she declared. "I'm tired of hiding. People are just going to have to accept the fact I'm carrying my husband's child. When it was conceived is none of their business."

It occurred to me that Milly might have to accept those facts, too, along with all the consequences that went with them. Once she did, other folk would either go along with her or not. Like what she did or not, Milly had done a world of good in Live Oak and she was one of the people who kept the community going. People knew it, too. It might slip their minds for a moment, but they knew. I didn't figure she needed their forgiveness, but I knew they'd give it, anyway.

Yet, I held my peace. I couldn't see any good that would come out of saying what I thought. When Milly craved my opinion, I felt sure she would ask. Even then, I'd need to be very careful what I said and how I said it. Milly was not normally prone to wild mood swings, but pregnancy was a whole new ball game. One moment she could be flying high, talking about all the things she wanted to do with our first born, and the next she could be in the deepest, darkest pit of despair, ashamed of the way she looked and blaming me for putting her in such a fix.

Lucky for us, not much was going on at the sheriff's office just then. So I was able to spend a lot more time with Milly and our kids than I might. Having Mary Alice around was a real blessing for us, too, particularly for Milly. Mary Alice took over most of the cooking and Louis and I took over the house keeping. At first Louis was a little put out at having to do what he saw as woman's work, but when he saw me jumping in cheerfully, he went along with it. We made a game out of it and had so much fun that Mary Alice got jealous. So Louis or I took a turn cooking once in a while and she pitched in on the cleaning. This worked well and Milly was always there to supervise. The result was that Louis and Mary Alice both turned into excellent cooks.

Then one afternoon I got a call at the house from Dr. Pettigrew, asking me to meet him at the hospital. When I asked him what it was about, he said he'd rather show me, but it was rather urgent. I realized he didn't want to talk about it over a party line and I told him I was on the way. Milly asked what was up, I told her I had no idea and promised to fill her in when I got home. It was late in the day and I told her I didn't know when that might be.

"Be careful, John Paul," she told me when I kissed her goodbye.

When I arrived at the hospital, there was an orderly waiting to take me directly to the good doctor. He led me through the emergency room and into a smaller room next to it. These days they call these Intensive Care Units, but back then this room did double duty for critical care and served as a second surgical area. It was equipped with everything available for life support and the treatment of trauma, and the bed was occupied by a heavily bandaged patient whose skin was an unhealthy gray and whose eyes were closed. The doctor told me the patient was a young woman who worked at the Roadhouse and he began showing me her injuries.

When I saw what had been done to this young woman, I found myself growing more and more angry and I didn't understand why at first. Then I realized that some of the injuries looked a lot like those I'd seen on Milly. Yet, this was much worse. I don't think there was a square foot of the young woman's body that had not been scraped, cut, or bruised, and the color of the bruises told me this had taken place some time before. "This didn't happen this afternoon, did it?" I asked, looking at the doctor for confirmation.

"No. From the color of the bruises and the formation of scabs, I'd say it occurred late yesterday afternoon at the latest. It could have been hours earlier."

"Who brought her in?"

"A couple of the people from the Roadhouse."

"What did they tell you?"

"The fellow I talked to claims she was kicked and trampled by a horse. When I asked for details, he said no one saw it happen. She was found lying in the corral with a bridle beside her, and the gate was open. His sidekick told me the same."

"Did either of them mention an oat bucket?" I asked. Using oats wasn't always done, but it was the easiest way I knew of getting a horse close enough to put on a bridle.

"No, and I didn't think to ask, either. I was concentrating on keeping her alive at the moment. I can tell you it was touch and go for a while."

I nodded. "There was something about this you didn't like, isn't there? That's why you called me."

Dr. Pettigrew nodded. "There are three things that didn't seem right. First of all, any of these injuries could have happened just like they said. That could be true of almost any combination of these injuries, too. However, all of them taken together seems very unlikely. The poor woman would have had to get up and be injured again two or three times for all of these to happen. Once she was down, I doubt the horse would continue to trample her. Not with an open gate. It would have run away once the woman was down."

That was a good point. Horses aren't normally that aggressive. "So you think someone beat her?" It was more of a statement than a question.

"Yes, I do. I think someone tried to kill her. That brings me to the second thing that didn't seem right. When I asked why the woman wasn't brought in sooner, the man who seemed to be in charge told me they were afraid to move her. I then asked why they hadn't sent someone to get me and he hemmed and hawed around. Finally, he said they thought she was about to die, and if she did, they wouldn't need me."

"That doesn't make a damned bit of sense to me," I told him.

"Nor does it to me. She could easily have died. So I called you." He shrugged. He was telling me he had done all he could.

Now the ball was in my hands.

"You said there were three things that didn't seem right," I reminded him.

"Yes, of course. The third inconsistency was how she was dressed. Most women wear slacks or dungarees when they ride these days, and down here they wear boots. This young lady was wearing a skirt and flats when they brought her in."

I nodded. It was a telling point. "Did they tell you who she is?" I asked.

"Names seem to be a very elusive commodity at the Roadhouse," the doctor said dryly. "At first the man in charge called her Annie, but the other one called her Cary and the man in charge started calling her that, too. He didn't seem very clear what her last name is."

"Did he give you his name?"

"Very reluctantly. Even so, I think what he gave me was an assumed name."

"What makes you think that?"

"Well, the other man with him called him Sammy and the surname he gave me was Brown. The first thing that came to my mind, of course, was the military sword belt. How many people do you know named Sam Brown, Sheriff?"

"Just one, and that's plenty," I told him. "He's my brother-in-law."

"I see," he replied, but clearly the good doctor did not.

Nor did I care to explain at the moment. "That won't stop me from arresting him," I assured him. "Not for a moment. Did you get a good look at Sammy's hands?"

"Yes, as a matter of fact. I was able to see them quite clearly, though I didn't examine them closely. They were not cut or scraped or bruised. He might have been able to protect his hands with the right kind of gloves, but I don't think he did. I knew he was hiding something but I didn't think that was it. It would be hard for him to inflict some of her injuries without bruising his own hands, even with gloves. He didn't seem that powerful a man, either, to tell you the truth."

I nodded. "You're probably right, but I'll have to check it out. A knife or a gun seems more his style."

"That was my impression. Of course, I may be wrong all the way around. Just about anyone in a rage can do incredible damage. Even a child."

"Do you think he might have used something else, like a club or a baseball bat?"

"I've seen a lot of truncheon and bat wounds," he told me. "Along with lots of other blunt instruments. I'm pretty sure this was done with his hands."

"So this was up close and personal," I murmured, talking to myself. "With lots of rage."

"Yes, a very sadistic and angry man did this."

"Could it have been two of them?"

The doctor nodded, anticipating my next question. "Yes, it might. However, I didn't see any bruises on the other man's hands, either."

"I guess they didn't hang around," I said. "Sammy and the other guy. There wasn't anyone in the waiting room."

A ghost of a smile crossed the doctor's face. "No, I don't expect they lingered. Once they heard I was calling you, they seemed anxious to get back to work. Brown told me they had to pick something up before some warehouse closed. It was about three o'clock then."

"I think I better check this out right away," I said. "Can you get pictures made of all her injuries?"

"I certainly will, Polaroid and film. Are you headed out to the Roadhouse?"

"That's the only place I know to start."

"Well, I think you need to take someone along with you," the doctor said. "These people are vicious. Give me five minutes and I'll have some Polaroids for you."

❧

It was dinner time by then and Buzz was glad for an excuse to get out of church that night. I could see his wife was not happy with either one of us, though she didn't say much. She had roped Buzz into calling Bingo for their fund raiser, and this was something he dreaded. It's always struck me odd how big strong men can go weak in the knees when you put a microphone in front of them. Buzz had a worse case than most.

"All you have to do is call out numbers," I told him when we were on our way. "It's not like making a speech."

"That's easy for you to say," he replied. "You're a politician."

"What!" I exclaimed, pretending to be deeply offended. "Wash out your mouth with kerosene, Buzz! Calling me a politician! Do I call you names?"

Buzz thought I was serious. "No, Sheriff, I'm sorry. That's not what I meant. What I was trying to say is that you have to give speeches to get elected."

"I'm just kidding," I assured him. "But have you ever heard me give a speech, Buzz?"

That stumped him and he sat there for a couple of minutes, trying to remember. His brow was knotted so hard I laughed. "Don't sprain your brain, Buzz. Ask the newspaper editor the next time you see him. I don't do speeches."

"I guess not," he told me. "I can't remember it if you ever did." Then another puzzled look crossed his face. "So how do you get elected if you don't give speeches?"

"I talk to people, Buzz. I listen to what they have to say and I help them out when I can. Even the people who don't care for me know I'm not just the sheriff for my supporters. I'll give anyone the benefit of the doubt."

Buzz nodded. "I've heard them say it, too." Seeing the question in my eyes, he grinned. "It's just like you say, John. It's amazing what people talk about without thinking who might be listening."

By then we were almost to the Roadhouse and I pulled over for a moment. "Buzz, I'm not looking for trouble this evening or expecting it. One of the things I'm looking for is a man, or men, whose hands look like they've been fighting, but I don't think their faces will be marked. So what I need you to do is to be my eyes and ears when I'm talking to somebody. I need you to keep very alert, too. If trouble happens, there won't be much warning. Got it?"

"I got it, Sheriff," he told me. "What's our code word?" This was a word we used to warn each other of danger in an emergency. Nor did we ever use the same code word twice. There were other words we used to designate less than critical situations, and these never change. The danger word was always different.

"I don't know. Why don't you pick it?" I suggested.

"Great! I've been thinking about it. Lets use '*Banzai!*'"

I looked at him and shook my head sadly. "You've been watching too many old war movies, Buzz."

"Well, then, let me think what else would be good."

"No, it's your pick and there's nothing wrong with *banzai*. That's the word tonight. Hopefully we won't have to use it."

It was clear to me that we were expected at the Roadhouse that evening. When I asked at the bar for Sammy Brown, the bartender picked up an extension phone and spoke to someone. I couldn't hear what he said but a minute later Gaylord Smith joined us. "Good evening, Sheriff," he greeted me, then nodded to Buzz. "Deputy." Buzz nodded back and looked around the rest of the room.

Turning back to me, Smith added, "I'm sorry you drove all the way out here for nothing, Sheriff. Sammy had to go to Ft. Worth this afternoon for supplies. That's where he went when he left the hospital."

"That's all right, Mr. Smith," I said. "I needed to talk to you, too. There seems to be some confusion about the name of the young woman he brought to the hospital. The names he gave were Annie and Cary, and he didn't seem to know her last name."

"Well, if you've seen her, you know that's understandable. The horse did a pretty good job of making her hard to recognize, and several of our younger women look very much alike. They seem to do that on purpose. But once we checked with our department heads, we discovered the only employee missing was Brandy Sloan."

"Is that her real name?" I asked. I noticed that Buzz was seemingly not paying any attention to our conversation and I was pleased. I had no doubt that he was taking in every word we said and he had a good memory for detail. I also knew he was doing exactly what I had asked, though he looked bored. When Buzz seems most laid back is when he is the most dangerous. I've seen him shrug and grin like a fool before taking down two larger opponents. He tells me he learned it from watching me.

"I wondered that when we hired her," Smith answered. "But she has a driver's license and a Social Security card in that name. One of my people checked her purse one night when she was working and she has a library card from Dallas under that name, too."

"I gather she was not aware you were looking in her purse," I replied.

"Oh, it's all perfectly legal, Sheriff. All we did was look, which all of our employment contracts allow us to do at any time. Those who don't accept that don't work here. We took nothing and we left nothing that had not been there before."

"So you don't trust your employees," I observed.

"With good reason, given our business. We handle a lot of cash and greed is to be expected. I'm sure you're familiar with the halo effect."

I'd heard it before but wanted to hear it from Smith. "Remind me," I asked him.

"It's very simple. When they know they are being watched, it's amazing how many of our employees have halos." He circled his thumbs and index fingers to make a halo over his head.

I chuckled. "I bet the warden in Huntsville would swear to that, too. So tell me about Brandy Sloan."

"She's new here. I'd have to check our records but I'd say she's only worked for us a couple of months now. Maybe longer, but not much. She is from a good family in Dallas and her legal name is Brandeis."

"I see why she goes by Brandy," I replied. "How old is she?"

"Twenty-two, according to her driver's license. One of our people called her high school and verified that she graduated four years ago." Smith seemed very pleased with himself giving me this information. I was sure that if I called the same school, the principal would verify that Brandeis Sloan had graduated four years before. The question in my mind was whether the young woman in the hospital was Brandy Sloan or someone using her identity. It happens all the time.

I nodded. "All right. I need to see her belongings and talk to the people who were her friends here."

"I'm afraid I can't help you there," Smith told me. "From what I've heard, Brandy tended to be a loner. She is friendly enough at work but after hours she keeps to herself. Or so I've been told."

I wondered why Smith was spinning this tale in such detail. "All right, then. I'll need to talk to her coworkers. We need to look at her things, too."

"I hate to be difficult, but do you have a warrant, Sheriff?" Smith asked with a frown.

"I don't need one," I replied. "The doctor says she may have been the victim of a crime, and that's all I need." I was certain that Gaylord Smith knew this as well as I did. I wondered why he was reluctant for us to go through Brandy's possessions. "Where is her locker?"

"I don't believe she had one yet. We normally don't assign them until someone has been here a while."

"All right, then, show us where she stayed."

⁓

There wasn't much for us to search when we got to the room Brandy shared with three other young women. Brandy had a suitcase and vanity case under her bed and the two lowest drawers in a tall dresser. The other three drawers belonged to Bunny Hooper, the young woman Smith sent with us to observe. When I asked, she told me she didn't know much about Brandy Sloan. "She kept to herself, you know," Bunny told me. "I mean, she was polite and nice enough, but she didn't have much to say. She seemed kind of shy, but she did all right waiting tables. Somebody told me she made good tips."

"What about entertaining clients down at the lake cabins?" I asked.

"Oh, I wouldn't know anything about that," Bunny answered, a little too quickly. "It wasn't any of my business. Even if it was, what I say is live and let live."

"That's very generous of you," I said dryly. "So you're not involved in that?"

When I asked, Bunny looked scared. "Oh, no, not me. The only way I know about it is what I've heard. You know, rumors."

"Are you sure you haven't heard any rumors about Brandy

working the cabins?" I asked. Bunny shook her head but I held up a warning hand. "Don't lie to me, Bunny," I told her sternly. "If I find out you've lied to me, you're going to be in big trouble. You understand."

"Yes, sir!" Bunny said but she didn't volunteer anything else.

"All right, then. You sit on your own bed and Buzz and I will take a look around." I nodded for Buzz to handle the dresser and I fetched the suitcase and vanity from under Brandy's bed. The suitcase was locked but it was easy to pick with a paper clip. I opened it wide on the bed and went through it quickly. It didn't hold much of any help to our investigation. There were a few personal photos, mostly snapshots, but there was a glamor shot done by a photographer in Dallas. "You know who this is?" I asked Bunny.

"Yes, sir, that's Brandy. It looks like her senior picture. She looks a lot older now."

"She looks a lot worse than that," I told her. I reached in my pocket and picked out a Polaroid shot taken at the hospital. Bunny blanched when she saw it. Buzz glanced at it and shook his head. I could tell it made him angry.

"I take it Brandy likes to ride horses," I said, putting away the photo.

"Who told you that?" Bunny asked. "Brandy won't go near the horses. She's scared to death of getting kicked or stepped on, or even bit. That happened to one of the girls last month."

"Oh, I must have heard it wrong then," I told her. "What does Brandy do when she isn't working?"

"She likes to read, a lot. When she isn't doing that, she likes to do crossword puzzles. She works the one in the paper every day and she gets books of them."

"So where are her books?" I asked.

"Gosh, I don't know. They were here yesterday." Bunny looked puzzled and I thought it was for real.

"Over here, Sheriff," Buzz said. He was standing next to a tall trash can. When I looked inside it, I saw a half dozen paperbacks and four or five crossword magazines. I picked a handful up and showed them to Bunny. "Are these her books?" I asked.

"Yes!" she said. Nor did I think she was faking the surprise in her voice, either. "Why in the world would anyone do that?"

"Do you think she threw them away?"

"No, why would she throw them away? She just got them in a couple of days ago. She belongs to some kind of book club. They swap books and when they're done with them, they send them back."

I looked through the titles and recognized the names of all the writers. One was John Steinbeck and another was Ursala LeGuin. John O'Hara was among them, too, along with Jane Austen and Oscar Wilde. None of the books were pulp fiction and once again I got the feeling that Brandeis Sloan was not who she claimed to be.

I salvaged the books from the trash bin and put them into an empty box I found in the closet. Looking at the label on the box, I saw it was from the book club and I decided to take the books with us. I thought Brandy Sloan would like to have them when she came to, if she did. Assuming she could still read. I knew from experience that head injuries can be tricky.

The vanity case held the usual things women carry in them. Or so Buzz told me and I bowed to his greater domestic experience. I did notice that the mirror fitted into the lid was fastened into place with small brass screws. I removed these and the mirror came out easily, revealing a plain white half size envelope taped to the back of the mirror. Inside were six items.

One of these was a driver's license issued to Anita Colombo at an address in Ft. Worth. I know most of the main streets in Cowtown but I didn't recognize the name of the street. I had no idea what part of the city it served but it would be easy enough to find out. The date of birth on the license put Anita at twenty-four, which was close enough.

There was also a Social Security card for Anita Colombo in the envelope, along with three family pictures. The young woman we knew as Brandy Sloan was in all three snapshots and she closely resembled the other people pictured. The father was much darker than the woman I assumed was his wife, and I pegged him as Italian. The mother, on the other hand, looked as Irish as Molly Malone, and I wondered how in the world the two of them had ever gotten together. It occurred to me that their family reunions must be quite a challenge.

The last item was a typewritten poem folded inside a half sheet of typing paper. It sounded vaguely familiar but what caught my attention was the handwritten note at the bottom and the signature. It said, "This is as much as I can remember of the words, but it's very close to the original. I hope you enjoy it and I look forward to seeing you soon." The note was signed, "Jeremy."

I showed Buzz the note and pointed to the signature. He looked at it a moment and then looked at me and nodded. I wondered if he was feeling as confused as I was. A connection between Jeremy Barker and Anita Colombo seemed very unlikely, but Jeremy is not that common a name. Nor was it very likely that this was a simple coincidence, if there is such a thing. It was also possible the two had met during Jeremy's first year at college, and equally possible that Anita had come to the Roadhouse looking for her friend. It was even more possible she had been mauled because she asked had too many questions.

One of Brandy's other roommates came in just then. "What are you doing here?" she demanded, angry. Then she saw our badges and was clearly frightened.

"Which drawers are yours?" I asked her but she only stared back at me.

"What's the matter with you?" Bunny asked and pointed to the bottom drawers of the only other dresser.

It didn't take me long to discover why Julie, the new girl, was so scared. I took the bottom drawer first and in ten seconds I was holding an expensive woman's blouse watch. I turned it over and saw engraving on the back. It read, "For Anita, our A+ student. Mama & Papa. May 23, 1954."

"Where did you get this?" I asked sternly, but Julie just stood there in shock.

"That's Brandy's watch!" Bunny declared. "I've seen her looking at it." She turned on Julie. "You stole it, didn't you?"

"I didn't mean to steal it," Julie stammered and Bunny snorted. "No, they told me she was going to die," Julie protested. "I only took it so they wouldn't. I wasn't stealing it. I was just keeping it safe." Her fear had given way to indignation.

"Who told you Brandy was going to die?" I demanded.

"Mr. Smith, the assistant manager," Julie replied. "He came here with Arnie and dumped her books."

"Sammy Brown?" I asked and Julie nodded.

"All right," I said. "I'm going to take your word for it, Julie." Bunny looked at me as if I was crazy. "And you!" I turned on Bunny. "You're not going to say a word about this to anyone, understand?"

"Yes, sir," Bunny said meekly.

"The same goes for you," I told Julie. "I'm going to take this with me to give to Brandy. She's going to be all right. But if Gaylord Smith finds out what went on here tonight, I don't think he's going to be very happy with either of you." I showed Julie the picture of Brandy. "That's what happened to her and it wasn't any horse."

Then I remembered something else. "Do either of you know where Brandy's locker is?"

Both young women shook their heads. "I don't think she had one," Bunny told me. "She always came back here to change."

"They only give to people who work here a long time," Julie added. "Brandy had only been here a few months."

"Can you remember about when she started?"

Julie shook her head but Bunny spoke up. "She started just before Halloween." She turned to Julie. "Don't you remember. She wore that cool witch outfit with the tall, pointed hat. She was there with Jeremy. He was Dracula."

I glanced at Buzz and he nodded, smiling. One of his favorite quotations was a Yogi Berra classic. I can't remember the exact words but it was something like this: "You can observe a lot by just watching."

We talked to a number of Brandy's coworkers and to her other two roommates, but none of them added much to what we gleaned from Bunny. We did discover that Brandy did have a locker, but there was nothing in it, not even a uniform. It looked like someone had thoroughly cleaned it out, and I suspected that we would not find a single fingerprint if we took the trouble to dust.

Just to be sure they didn't disappear, we took all of Brandy's possessions and locked them in the cruiser, along with the suitcase and the vanity case. I didn't think we had much chance of recovering anything more that night at the Roadhouse and I was tired of the place. It felt like we'd been wading in a cesspool of human corruption. I was ready to get going, and said as much, but Buzz said, "There's something else you need to see, Boss. I spotted something on our way out."

I followed Buzz back into the building and he went directly to a table we had passed near the back of the main room. There were three men seated at the table but Buzz addressed a burly fellow with black hair and a surly countenance. "Let's see your hands, Mike," Buzz said but the burly man only glared at him and kept his hands hidden under the table. Then he leaned forward slightly. His right arm moved back and his eyes shifted toward me.

"Banzai!" I shouted, drawing my pistol and shoving it in the man's face. When I did, Buzz turned the table over into the laps of the two other men and they went down. Mike glared at me and for a minute I thought I was going to have to fire. Out of the corner of my eye I could see a wicked looking knife in Mike's hand and I could see him debating trying to stab me.

Buzz grabbed Mike's knife arm with both hands and squeezed as he twisted it behind the man. It was dead quiet by then and the sound of Mike's wrist snapping filled the room. Even so, he never screamed in pain. He simply groaned and blanched, and the knife clattered to the floor where I grabbed it.

We had Mike in cuffs and were taking him to the cruiser by the time Smith showed up. "What's going on, Sheriff?" he demanded.

"Mike was about to stab me," I told him, showing him the ten inch Bowie knife Mike had been holding. "I damned near had to shoot him!" I was still feeling the adrenaline.

"Don't say a word!" Smith told Mike. "Keep your mouth shut and we'll have you out of jail by tomorrow morning." Turning to me, he added, "This man needs medical attention!"

"Good!" I snapped back at him. "That's exactly where I'm going to take him first."

꙳

I was very late getting home that night, but Milly was waiting up for me. I was still wired from the incident at the Roadhouse and it took me a long time to calm down enough to come to bed. I had come very close to killing a man and I had no doubt I would have done so had Mike tried to stab me. I had killed before in the line of duty and that was something I would carry with me to the grave. It had been a clean shooting in a firefight with a smuggler while I was in the Coast Guard and I was given a medal for it. Yet, it left three men dead and the memory haunted me. Sometimes we have no other choice, but there are still consequences.

I had never told Milly about the incident before, but I told her that night. I also told her how close I came to having to kill again, and how much this bothered me. She nodded and took my hand. "You carry an awful responsibility for the rest of us, John," she said gently. "I would hate to be in your shoes making that decision. I'm just glad it wasn't Sammy."

"Sammy's involved in it, Milly," I told her. "I may end up having to arrest him."

"I know," she said. "I just don't want you to have to shoot him. But if you do, don't hesitate on my account. Sammy has made his choices and you need to protect yourself. You have a wife and children."

I must have looked dumbfounded because she added, "I mean it, John Paul. It may sound cold and callous, but Sammy's not the sweet little brother I had growing up. He was taught better, and he knows better, but something went wrong. The brother I knew died somewhere along the way. So protect yourself, for my sake and the sake of our children."

We talked a while longer and then went to bed. I was surprised how strong my response was when Milly settled down next to me. Our lovemaking was a tempest, like we were trying to drive death from the room with our passion. Then I went out like a light and I slept until almost nine o'clock the next day. Milly took the kids to school without waking me and she called to let Cheryl know I would be running late.

The judge looked worn out when I brought Mike Simms before him late that morning. The lawyer Smith had sent tried to raise hell over me being so late getting to the courthouse, but the judge cut him off at the knees. When the lawyer tried to argue, the judge slammed his gavel down so hard it sounded like a shot. "You are out of order, sirrah!" the judge roared. "One more word and I'll hold you in contempt of court. You're wasting our time and only delaying the proceedings."

The lawyer opened him mouth, but the look in the judge's eye stopped him cold. He nodded and sat down, glaring at me while Emory presented the charges. "How do you wish to plea, Mr. Simms?" When the judge asked, his voice was calm.

"Not guilty," Mike said and the judge nodded.

"Very well," his honor said calmly. "This seems like an open and shut case. We will set the trial date for two weeks from Monday. Does that suit the defense?"

I was surprised when the defense lawyer agreed. "Thank you, Counselor," the judge said. "We're moving right along. What does the prosecution say about bail?"

Emory jumped to his feet. "Given the seriousness of the charges and the fact the defendant shows no visible means of support, we recommend no bail be granted, your honor." The defense lawyer raised Cain about that but in the end it was useless. Simms had a record for similar charges and I reported there was a fugitive warrant out for him from Louisiana. Even Simms' lawyer realized at that point there could be no bail.

"This Simms matter may be a difficult case," the judge warned me when I returned later to tell him about the assault of Brandy Sloan. "Quite frankly, Emory is out of his depth against a man like the one Smith brought in and I may have to recuse myself due to illness."

Seeing my look, the judge nodded. "Yes, John, the doctors tell me I don't have long now in this veil of tears, and I grow weaker each passing day. I am trying to get Emory to bring in a hotshot for second chair, and to allow aforesaid hotshot to carry most of the burden, but Emory has stars in his eyes. He doesn't understand he's David without a slingshot against Smith's Goliath."

The old man smiled. "I'm also trying to have a close colleague of mine sit in for me. Normally, I wouldn't consider the man. He is quite strict and quite fair, but he is also a judge who believes that, when in doubt, a judge should hang them all and let God sort the sheep from the goats."

I nodded. "Sounds like a winner to me. The other case, Simms beating Brandy Sloan, is looking stronger all the time. I doubt we will be able to find an eye witness willing to testify, but Dr. Pettigrew turned up some interesting evidence. When he looked at Mike Simms' hands, he found a chip from a tooth in one of the wounds. It's a perfect match to a piece missing from one of Brandy's teeth. He also thinks she will wake up in the next few days and may be able to testify against the man."

The judge nodded. "Keep digging, John. For now I suggest proceeding as if Brandeis Sloan will never be able to testify. I doubt she is out of danger yet."

"No," I told him. "She's not. She is still in critical condition. What the doctor's worried about right now is a blood clot going to her lungs or brain."

The judge shook his head sadly. "The things God's children do to one another. It's not the worst I've seen, John, but hopefully it's the worst I'll ever see again." He sighed. "Well, I'm told I'll be meeting the celestial Magistrate soon, face to face. And if it's allowed, I shall have some hard questions to put to the Court."

SIXTEEN

Building a Case

By the time I got back from court after we arraigned Mike Simms, Cheryl was already there. When she asked, I told her Milly was doing well. "You know she's expecting, don't you?" I asked. The moment I said it, I wondered why I bothered. I was certain the cat was long out of the bag, but nothing had been said in the office.

"No, Sheriff, how wonderful!" she answered, smiling brightly.

I wondered why Cheryl was lying. I was sure she not only knew Milly was pregnant, but that she had known for some time. I had not said anything to Cheryl up to then but Buzz had asked me about it weeks before. I allowed that I had, indeed, committed patrimony and he told me he'd heard this from Clint Farley. "Of course, I didn't let him know it was news to me." When he said this, Buzz gave me a reproachful look.

"Sorry, Buzz," I told him. "I should have told you. I had a lot on my mind."

The third best thing about Buzz is that he doesn't hold grudges. His best traits are being very loyal and knowing how to keep his mouth shut. He's very good at smiling and saying, "You need to talk to the Sheriff about that." For my part, I try to be very clear with Buzz what is, and is not, public information. Even though it was personal information, I was wrong not letting him know earlier. Once Clint Farley knew something, the news moved around our six county area at speeds approaching that of light.

Smith had given me the name of Brandy Sloan's high school the evening before, so I called there and asked to speak with the principal. After a long delay, I was shunted to a guidance counselor, instead, one who had a voice I could listen to for hours. Her name was Paula Wheeler and she explained why I was talking to her. "The principal is out of town today," she told me. "Since you're a law officer, we assumed it had to do with one of our students and I'm the one who's most familiar with them."

I explained that I was interested in knowing whether Brandeis Sloan had been a student there, and when she had graduated.

"Oh, that's easy," Paula told me. "I knew Brandy quite well. She was one of our star students and it must be at least three years since she graduated. Let me look that up to make sure." She was back a moment later. "No, actually, it was four years ago that she graduated. She was the salutatorian of her class."

That didn't sound quite right. I wondered how a young woman who had everything going for her had ended up working at the Roadhouse. "Any idea why she might be working at a private gambling resort?" I asked. "I would think she would have been a good candidate for college."

"A gambling resort? No, the Brandy Sloan I'm talking about got a full ride scholarship to the University of Texas. She was a brilliant student and went there to study astrophysics."

"That doesn't sound like the young woman I'm talking about. I suppose it could be a case of mistaken identity," I answered. I didn't think for a moment it was.

"Two young women from Dallas, the same age and named Brandeis?" she asked, as if she were reading my mind. "It doesn't sound likely, Sheriff."

"It could be someone else using her name," I answered. "Do you know where I can reach the Brandy Sloan you know?"

"Oh, of course. I assumed you knew, but you don't. Brandy was killed in a car accident in her second year at the University. She was coming back from the beach over spring break. It was a drunk driver and everyone in the car was killed. How odd that someone would be using her name. You'd think they would choose someone less...flamboyant."

"It is odd, which is why I need to check it out. The young woman I am talking about is anything but flamboyant."

I spent a while getting all the details the counselor could give. When I was done I assured her I'd let her know the outcome of my investigation. "Please don't tell anyone about this conversation," I asked. "I think it's quite likely that someone else assumed her identity and I don't want them to hear I'm looking into it."

"Mum's the word," Paula said. Then she added. "You know,

it's so sad, isn't it. Someone with all that potential. What a waste."

"Yes, it is sad and it doesn't make a bit of sense," I agreed. Then I added, "I see that a lot, you know, too much." I was thinking of Jeremy Barker.

"I imagine you must. I certainly do and I'm not on the front lines like you are. Tell me, Sheriff, would a personal question offend you?"

"Not as long as you don't expect a truthful answer," I quipped. "My first name is John but I don't answer to Jack."

Paula laughed. "This is not that personal. I was just wondering if you are married. I hope that's not out of line."

"Not at all," I told her. "But, alas, I am and it's terminal." I could still hear her laughing when she hung up.

I was surprised to see how long I had been on the phone with the school counselor. It brought to mind a story about Albert Einstein who pointed out the relativity of time with a wonderful analogy. He observed that an entire evening spent in the presence of a delightful woman seems like a few brief moments, while five seconds on a hot stove feels like eternity. Yet, what I had told Paula Wheeler was true. I was, and am, terminally married. Nor would I have it any other way.

It was almost noon but I decided to try calling Steve Mills, a friend on the Cowtown police force. He was about to head for lunch and I was lucky to catch him. After we went through the ritual of exchanging insults, we exchanged personal news and he whistled when he learned that I was married and had kids. "So another bastion of bachelorhood has fallen," he laughed. "How did you manage three kids in such a short time? You weren't married this time last year, were you?"

I explained the adoption and our subsequent marriage and he congratulated me. Then he said, "As pleasant as this is, John, I need to get going. Is there something I can do for you?"

I told him about the Anita Colombo driver's license and gave him the license number and the address in Ft. Worth. "Let me check the street directory," he said. "That's in a very good part of town." A moment later he came back. "Man, you hit a big one. I don't know if you're familiar with the Civello crime family, but Alfonso Colombo is a key man in their Cowtown operations. The family runs most of the organized crime in Texas and Colombo is the CPA who audits their business here in Ft. Worth. I'm sure he tells them how to cheat on taxes, too. The street address you gave me is his home and I'd guess Anita is his daughter. She sounds too young to be his wife."

"What about the Roadhouse here in Rutherford County? Is that one of their operations?"

"Let me check and get back to you," he said. "Assuming the Roadhouse is one of their joints, how does Anita connect with it? The mafia usually keep their daughters out of the family business."

"I don't know," I told him. "It looks like she's going under a false identity and working there, and someone almost beat her to death. Another employee."

"Well, if he did, he can kiss his sweet ass goodbye," Mills told me. "What do you figure she was doing there? It sounds like she was undercover, maybe, spying for her dad."

"Checking up on Gaylord Smith, probably," I replied. "She was a very shy, retiring girl who liked good books."

"Was? Is she dead?"

"She may be circling the drain," I told him. "I hope not. She seems like a sweet girl."

"Yeah, but the nut doesn't fall far from the tree," Steve reminded me.

"Or the apple from the horse," I quipped and he laughed.

"I'll have to remember that. That's a good one. Anything else I can do?"

I told him not and he told me he would get back to me about the crime family's connection to the Roadhouse. "Be careful with these scum bags, John," he added. "It sounds like Gaylord Smith is on the short list for Hemorrhoid of the Year and I imagine his crew is no better. I'd stay out of their way if you can. I'm sure they have you outgunned and if you bide your time, they'll probably kill each other off. I can almost guarantee Smith is history if he had anything to do with beating up Colombo's daughter."

"Well, that's one kind of justice," I answered.

"Yeah, but you know how it is, John. Sometimes rough

justice is the only kind of justice we're going to get."

⁂

I called the hospital after I hung up to see how Anita Colombo was doing. I was told they didn't have a patient by that name and I asked if the patient in the critical care room had died. "Oh, you must mean Brandy Sloan, Sheriff," the clerk told me. "She woke up for a while this morning but she drifts in and out. She's off the critical list. Also, the doctor left a message for you to call him at your convenience. That's how it reads, at your convenience, so it's probably not urgent."

Urgent or not, I called the good doctor. He seemed quite chipper that morning. "It looks like we pulled another one back from the grave," he told me. "Miss Sloan fades in and out, but she is aware where she is and why she's there. She also remembers what happened, which surprises me. I expected retrograde amnesia."

When he said this, I wondered why medical people always say retrograde amnesia. Is there an anterograde? I almost asked but it seemed like a stupid question. How could someone have future memory loss, except maybe a psychic? I almost laughed at the thought but I learned later that there is something called anterograde amnesia. It's the loss of the ability to form new memories and it happens all the time. The most common example is an alcoholic blackout.

I suddenly realized the doctor had stopped talking. "I beg your pardon, doctor," I told him. "I got to thinking about something you said and missed that last part."

"I'm glad to hear that," he told me, chuckling. "It happens to me all the time. What I said was that you can see Brandy any time you want, but try not to stress her too much. Her grip on reality is still tenuous."

"I'm afraid I need to confront her," I told him. "Her name is apparently not Brandeis Sloan. It's Anita Colombo and she's from Ft. Worth, not Dallas. You might want to make a note of that in her chart."

"Colombo? That sounds Italian. She looks more Irish to me, more Celtic."

"That's because her mother's Irish," I said. "I'd be willing to bet she's a red head, too. I found a picture Anita had hidden away. Brandeis Sloan was killed in a car crash a couple of years back. She was a much different person, too. Anita doesn't look like her at all."

There must have been something in my voice that alerted the doctor because he asked, "What is it you're not telling me, Sheriff?"

"Well, this is just between us right now, but there's a good chance Anita is the daughter of a big shot in the mafia."

"That doesn't surprise me. From what you've told me about the Roadhouse, it sounds like one of their outfits. Gambling, illegal liquor, and prostitution, not to mention dead bodies in the lake and buried in the flower garden."

"Normal mob family life," I responded.

"Have you talked to the Rangers yet?" he asked. The Texas Rangers were the elite division of the Department of Public Safety. They had a long and bloody history in south Texas and, from what I've read, there were large segments of the population that needed to be protected from the Rangers. At one time their motto was "one riot, one ranger."

"No, I'm sure they're aware of the situation. They probably think I'm on the take, too."

"All the more reason to grab the bull by the horns and call them," the doctor pointed out.

That made sense but I was reluctant to call from the office, or from any phone in town. Even if no one overheard a call, there were phone records too many people could get. I knew the Rangers had field offices and that there was one in Ft. Worth, so I decided to make a quick trip to Cowtown the following day. Using a pay phone outside the drive-in, I called Information for the number. Then I paid an extra quarter and had the operator dial the number. I identified myself and learned that one of the Rangers would be in the office the next afternoon. I made an appointment for three o'clock.

It was almost noon, so I went home to have lunch with my bride. When I told her what the doctor had said, and about setting up an appointment, she agreed. "I think that's a very good idea, John. Buzz is a good officer but there are only two of you. You need help, and outside help would be best. That way you won't put anyone local in danger, either. I can pick up the kids after school tomorrow."

We talked a while longer about other things, but when I got up to leave, she asked, "Just where do you think you're going, mister?"

"I thought I'd stop by the hospital and see Anita Colombo. Then I need to get back to the office."

"Not so fast, kemo sabe," she replied, giving me a saucy look. "The kids are in school and I have plans."

❧

Anita was asleep when I got to the hospital. I asked the nurse to call me when she woke up again and headed for the office. When I walked in, Cheryl looked at me and smiled in a knowing way. I don't know how women know these things, but most of them do. I wish they were as easy for us to read as we are for them, but that might ruin the fun.

I took care of a pile of paperwork Cheryl had set out for me and was just finishing up when the nurse called and told me Brandy was awake. I didn't waste any time getting there and I was glad to see that some of the bandages on her face had been taken away. "Hello, Anita," I greeted her. "I'm Sheriff John Stone. How are you feeling?"

"So you know my real name," she said. "Have you called my parents?"

"I wanted to make sure who you were first," I told her. "I'll call them when I get back to the office. Do the people at the Roadhouse know who you are?"

"No," she told me. "They think I'm Brandy Sloan. Do you have to call my parents? I'll be in big trouble if you do. My dad doesn't know I'm working here."

"You're of age, so it's your choice. If you were my daughter, I think I'd be even more upset if you didn't let me know."

"You don't understand," she said. "My dad...." She shook her head and stopped.

"Yes, Anita, I do understand. Your dad is Alfons Colombo. He's an important man in the Joe Civello family in Dallas. I believe the Roadhouse is one of their operations."

"Then you know he's not going to mess around if he hears about this. Somebody's going to die, and it may be me."

"No, I doubt that. Somebody else, maybe, but not his own daughter." Seeing the fear in her face, I said. "It's your choice, but he is going to find out, sooner or later. I think he'd rather hear it from you."

Anita didn't look convinced so I turned another direction. "Do you know who did this to you, Anita?"

"Please, call me Brandy. Yes, I know. It was Mike Simms. He's one of the bouncers at the Roadhouse."

"Do you know why he did?"

She nodded again. "I was asking too many questions about Jeremy Barker. He's the one who got me a job there and we were good friends. Then he disappeared. Mike asked me a lot of questions about him."

"How did you know Jeremy?"

"We went to school together in Ft. Worth. I'm a music major, too. We got to be very good friends and I didn't want to spend the summer with my parents. So I told them I was going to find myself a job. I just didn't bother to tell them where. My dad wants to run my life. He wants me to get married and have a lot of children."

"So you haven't been in touch with your parents at all since school let out?" She shook her head. "Not even your mother?"

"Well, her, sure. I called her a couple of times to let her know I was all right but I used a pay phone. I called when I knew my dad wouldn't be home and I swore her to secrecy."

I changed directions again. "So Mike Simms didn't know who you were?" She shook her head. "Did anyone else?"

"Only Jeremy and Nancy Hiller. She had a made up name, too, with a driver's license and all. She was the one who told Jeremy where to get mine. Then she disappeared and I asked around about her, too."

"Did Mike Simms mention her when he beat you?"

"Yes, he wanted to know where she was. I couldn't convince him I didn't know that, either. Do you have to ask me all these questions?"

"Yes, I do, but not right now." I debated with myself a

moment, then plunged on. "There is one thing you need to know. I'm afraid it's bad news, Brandy. Jeremy Barker is dead. Someone shot him."

Anita looked like she'd been punched in the stomach. Then she began to cry. "I knew it!" she sobbed. "I knew it!"

Then her grief turned into anger. "The bastards! Those dirty bastards! I may tell my dad after all! He'll make them pay."

"Do you know why they killed him?" I asked, but she shook her head. "How about Nancy? Did she know?"

Anita nodded. "She was going to tell me something but she disappeared before she could."

The doctor came in about then and asked to have a word with me. We went into the hall and he shut the door. "Do you have many more questions to ask, Sheriff? Miss Sloan has been through a lot. I don't want her to relapse."

"No, I've got all I need for now. She identified Mike Simms as her attacker. I will need to talk to her later on and get a sworn statement when she's stronger, but that can wait."

The doctor nodded and started to leave but I stopped him. "There are some things you need to know about your patient and her family," I told him. "Is there a quiet place where we can talk?"

※

I had no trouble finding the Texas Rangers' office the next afternoon. The officer I talked to was named Dillon Ramsey and he didn't offer a hand when we met. I got the impression he considered me a suspect, and our conversation confirmed it. Yet he seemed to thaw out a degree or two when I told him what all I knew about the Roadhouse and about my futile attempts to shut the place down.

"I take it you don't have much solid evidence for what you're saying," he observed at one point.

"No, I don't have any solid evidence. All I can give you are lots of informed guesses but no proof. If I had proof I'd have nailed the bastards a long time ago. Now the judge is dying and God only knows what the next one will be like. David Allen White is a righteous man but he won't be around long enough to do much more. We have one of their enforcers in jail for aggravated assault and the judge will throw the book at him. Other than that, we don't have a thing but two bodies."

Ramsey nodded. "Why are you coming to us now, Sheriff?"

"I can't get anywhere on my own. I thought I might, but the whole county political machine is against me. With the situation the way it is, only your people or the FBI stands much chance of nailing them. I have one innocent kid who was killed, a second body buried in the flower bed, and another young woman who was beaten within an inch of her life. I think there's a good chance the Roadhouse is run by the Civello crime family out of Dallas. They have the resources to buy high powered lawyers."

"And you've got no connection with them, yourself?"

"That's right. At least, not until recently. I got married a few weeks ago and one of my brothers-in-law, Sammy Brown, works for Gaylord Smith. He's an assistant manager at the Roadhouse, and I think he handles a lot of Smith's dirty work. He may have signed his death warrant doing it." I told him about the beating of Brandy Sloan. "Her real name is Anita Colombo and my information is that her dad's a higher up in the Civello crime family."

"So the problem is likely to resolve itself," the Ranger pointed out dryly.

"Yeah, one killing at a time. Look, I want them out of my county. I don't want somebody else getting caught in the crossfire if there's a gang purge. I'd do it myself if I could. The fact is, I'm outnumbered and outgunned. I believe that alone justifies my requesting your help."

"It does, but you realize there aren't that many of us. We cover the whole state and we have to set priorities just like you do in your county. I can't promise anything but to talk to my superiors."

"Fair enough. I appreciate it. I'd much rather deal with you all than the FBI."

"That may be who needs to handle this," Ramsey told me. "Since this is mob related, I'm sure federal crimes are involved. Again, this is not my decision. As much as I might like to ride into Dodge and kick ass, I go where I'm told."

Ramsey brought our interview to a conclusion not long after

that. He surprised me by offering his hand when I left. "Thanks for coming in," he told me. "We've had our eye on Rutherford County for a while now. It's good to get first hand information. We'll be in touch, one way or the other, but the fewer people who know about this interview, the better. I'm sorry to hear about Judge White, too. He's a good man. Call us if you get any evidence that will stand up in court."

"No chance of your putting someone in undercover?"

Ramsey smiled for the first time. "Put yourself in my place for a minute, Sheriff. Would you tell a local sheriff if you were sending someone in?"

"Yes, I would. Two minutes before the bust."

※

I thought about the last part of our conversation as I drove back to Live Oak. I couldn't read Dillon Ramsey well enough to tell if he was simply making a point about keeping an operation secure or if he was telling me something. It could be that the Rangers were already thinking of inserting someone undercover at the Roadhouse. He had told me that they had been keeping an eye on Rutherford County for some time. If so, what was their source of information, the Highway Patrol? Then it occurred to me that they already had someone there undercover and were playing their cards close to the vest.

I could understand this. Given what I knew about my fellow county sheriffs, I wouldn't endanger one of my undercover officers by letting the local man know. Most of the ones I knew were honest enough, but too many of them liked to talk. It would be all too easy for the information to fall into the wrong hands. The result would be a dead officer.

After a bit, I gave it up. There was no knowing what was what. So I thought about what I needed to do next. I figured trying to get anything from any of the Roadhouse employees would be a waste of time, though I did consider talking to Bunny again. She seemed to know a lot about everyone else's business and might let something drop. Yet, singling her out could put her in danger. Nor could I think of any way of interviewing her again without attracting the wrong kind of attention.

Then I remembered that I needed to talk to Granger about

the set of books I'd given him. We had talked about them several weeks before. "They look pretty straight forward to me," he said. "Not knowing where they came from, I would think they were the real books for a very successful business. As a matter of fact, that's what I do think. They look too good to be fake and I think you just got the goods on the Roadhouse. Their net profit margin is unbelievable. Suspicious soul that I am, it makes me wonder if they are paying taxes on all that. No way to know, of course, without seeing their tax returns."

"Couldn't we get that from the IRS?"

"It would take an Act of Congress." he told me. "What you could do, of course, is to give these books to the IRS and have them do the scut work. I can tell you who to send them to and I'd be glad to call ahead to be sure they got the right attention. This is a bird's nest on the ground for them and you might even get a finder's fee for your trouble."

"I don't care about a finder's fee. You can have that. I'd just like to nail the bastards."

"Then let me make a few phone calls," Granger said. "This is a not good time of the year to get it to them. They're gearing up for tax season and most of their resources are dedicated to that. Toward the end of the summer would be better, and there's no rush. Assuming I'm right, what you've got here is the taxman's equivalent of an atom bomb."

Recalling our conversation, I realized I had forgotten to tell Dillon Ramsey about having a copy of the Roadhouse's books. I also remembered something else Granger told me. "There are some things tucked away under consultant fees that bother me. They are cash payments to independent contractors for services rendered and whoever did it was quite creative. The expense categories are really ambiguous. One that comes to mind is 'workforce reduction.' What do you suppose that means?"

"Well, it sounds like a labor efficiency expert. Knowing whose books these are, it could be for bumping someone off."

"Exactly, and I suspect the equivalent entries on the tax returns read differently."

Remembering this, I stopped by Granger's house on my way

to the office. When I knocked, his wife came to the door. "Oh, Sheriff, Granger's been meaning to call you," she said. "He's in Austin this week at some kind of tax seminar. He asked me to bring the books you left by your office, but I'm afraid I forgot. I hope it wasn't important."

"No, Selina, it isn't that urgent. I should have called him earlier. It skipped my mind, too. I'll talk to him when he's back."

"Well, he said to tell you there were some other things about them he saw that he wanted to talk to you about. He should be back tomorrow night. Why don't you come by on Saturday morning?" She smiled. "Bring your lovely wife, too. We don't get to see as much of her now as we did before you all married."

"Let me check with her, first," I said. "I think we have something planned."

⁂

By the time I got to the office, Cheryl was just leaving. "The doctor called," she told me. "He would like to see you today, if possible. Other than that, there's nothing that won't wait until tomorrow."

I thanked Cheryl and dialed the doctor's office number. "Oh, he's still at the hospital, Sheriff," the receptionist told me. "He does want to see you right away. Shall I call him and let him know you're on the way?"

The same orderly as before was waiting for me when I walked into the main entrance. This time he led me down a hallway to a semi-private room. Nor was I surprised to find one of the beds occupied by Anita Colombo. There was no one in the other bed and the curtain separating them was pulled back.

The doctor was talking to Anita when I walked in and he turned and thanked me for coming. "I need your help getting Miss Colombo to allow me to call her parents. There is vital medical information I need to treat her, but she is adamant about not calling."

"I can imagine," I told him. "She and I have had a similar conversation." I turned to Anita and smiled. "Hello, kiddo. You're looking better. How do you feel?"

"I feel fine!" she told me. "I don't see why it's necessary to call my parents. It will only upset them."

"I've thought about that," I said. "When you were brought in, we were told you'd been in an accident. We were also given the wrong name and we couldn't contact them until we were sure who you were. You can say the doctor was concerned about amnesia. " I shrugged. "It's a stretch but I think it covers the bases." I turned to Pettigrew. "Can you live with that, doctor?"

"Yes, it is factual even though it's not the whole truth. However, at some point they will find out about the assault."

"And you know what will happen?" Anita said, close to tears. "My daddy will find out who did it and he'll make a phone call. Then that man who beat me up will be dead! And it will be all my fault."

"No!" I said gently but sternly. "You are not to blame, Anita. Mike Simms chose to attack you. You don't have to press charges if you decide not. When they learn who your dad is, the Roadhouse people will be happy to go along. So will Mike. We've got him on assaulting a law officer and attempted murder, and we can send him away for that. When he knows who your dad is, he'll probably plead guilty to what we have on him now. What you choose to tell your father is up to you." I looked at the doctor and he nodded.

Anita wavered but she finally nodded. "It's a good choice," I told her. "You'll need to give the doctor your home phone number."

"Maybe my dad won't be home yet," Anita said. Then she wrote a phone number on a scrap of paper an handed it to the doctor. He nodded and was gone.

"Now," I said. "You need to listen to me very carefully. At some point your dad will learn about the assault. You need to tell him the truth. What he chooses to do with it is not up to you. If he chooses to beat up Mike Simms, or even worse, that's up to him. It's his fault if that happens, not yours." I smiled. "Are you against marriage?"

"No, of course not. I want to have children."

"Then tell your Papa that. Tell him it's your choice who you marry, not his. Don't get angry and don't shout, even if he does. Just quietly insist it's got to be your way. He'll give in eventually, especially if you can get your mother on your side. I don't have to tell you how to do that. Just mention grand babies."

When I told Milly about this later that evening, she laughed. "My husband the genius," she told me. "You make me so proud to be your wife."

"I just hope it works," I told her.

સ

Cheryl was on the phone when I walked into the office about nine the next morning. "Wait a minute. Here he is now," she told whoever was on the other end. Covering the mouthpiece with her hand she said, "It's some detective from Ft. Worth." She seemed very excited giving me the news.

It was Steve Mills and he razzed me about keeping banker's hours. "What do you mean?" I lied outrageously. "I cleared two homicides on the way in!"

"Must have been road kill," Mike laughed.

"Actually, it was two armadillos. I guess I should have said 'dillocides.'" I heard Cheryl laugh from the other room. I had forgotten to shut the door. I decided not to.

"They must have been getting it on in the middle of the road."

"That was my take on it," I answered. "It's funny how they do that. You do know the real reason the chicken crossed the road, don't you?"

Steve confessed he didn't and I told him, "To show the armadillo it could be done."

"That one is bad," he said, chuckling. "I did some digging and you are right. One of my buddies who keeps an eye on organized crime tells me the Roadhouse is a Civello operation. He also had some interesting information about Gaylord Smith. It seems that's an alias. He is a real slime-ball from Chicago named Carmello Conti. He has a rap sheet as long as your arm, but only one felony conviction. Most of his arrests have been for the flesh trade, first as a pimp and later as a white slaver. That was where his one felony conviction came in, taking the hit for someone higher up. Since it was his first conviction, he got a light sentence and he was a model prisoner. He was out in two years and the Roadhouse was his reward."

"Well, I think he's about to get a black eye. I told you one of his heavies beat up Alfonso Colombo's daughter. Conti may not take the hit himself, but when Al finds out, he'll take some heat."

I no sooner hung up than I got another call. This was from a woman who wouldn't identify herself to Cheryl and I almost didn't take it. On the other hand, anonymous tips do come in from time to time, and I did. When I answered, the lady identified herself right off the bat. "This is Mrs. Alfonso Colombo," she told me. "You have my daughter there in the hospital." She spoke with a heavy Irish accent and the way she said this sounded like an accusation.

"She's a patient there, Mrs. Colombo. She's not in custody."

"So what happened to her?"

"Why don't you ask her?" I suggested. "She's awake now."

"All she gives me is some song and dance about an accident! Sure and it don't look like no accident to me, Sheriff!"

I suddenly realized the lady was in town. "Are you at the hospital?" I asked.

"Yes, of course! My daughter is hurt, isn't she? Where else would I be?"

"I'll be there in five minutes," I said. As I walked out of the office Cheryl looked up at me in question. "Our assault victim's mother," I told her. "She's in town."

"No kidding!" Cheryl said. "I could hardly understand her."

※

When I got to the hospital, I was surprised. Lucille Colombo's voice and intensity over the phone led me to expect a larger woman, despite the picture I'd seen. What I found was a small, slender firebrand with bright red hair and a disposition to go with it. Nor did she hesitate pouncing on me when I walked into Anita's room.

"What's going on here, Sheriff?" she demanded in a brogue you could cut with a knife.

"Your daughter seems to be recovering quickly," I told her. "She was very lucky."

"Haven't I looked at her wounds, man? 'Twas no accident that's putting her abed, is it?"

I decided enough was enough. "Woman, you'll not be talking

to me like that!" I roared back in a brogue as broad as hers and Anita's eyes grew wide as saucers. "You'll be showing me proper respect, you will!"

For a moment I thought Lucille Colombo would attack with her fists, but then she smiled. "Now where are you learning to talk like that, Sheriff?"

"At my grandfather's knee," I assured her. "He was a strong man. Now, to answer your question, I have my suspicions, myself." I lapsed into my normal voice. "Your daughter is worried about her father. She is afraid if she tells him the truth, he will make a phone call and a man will end up dead. She doesn't want to be responsible for that."

"Even if he deserves it?"

I nodded. "Even if he deserves it. You have a very tender hearted child. I would count it a blessing."

"Oh, you poor dear," Anita's mother said and hugged her daughter close. They cried a bit together. Then she looked at me grimly. "The man's got to suffer some consequences."

"He will," I assured her. "I'm going to see him alone this afternoon. I'm going to tell him whose child Anita is. Then I'm going to offer him a choice. He can plead guilty to assaulting an officer and take the maximum sentence. Or he can plead not guilty and I will have a talk with your husband. I think he will understand the consequences of that."

"What about the man who ordered her beaten?" Lucille wanted to know.

"I'm going to do something even worse to him," I told her. "He will be hurt and he will be held accountable by your husband."

"And what are you going to do to him?" Anita's mother wanted to know.

"You'll know when it happens. That's all I'm going to say. I assure you, he'll pay dearly." I looked at Anita. "This takes you off the hook, Anita. Can you live with this?"

Anita nodded and I turned to Lucille. "Is this acceptable to you, Mrs. Colombo?"

Lucille nodded. "How about you, Sheriff? How does this sit with you?"

I shrugged. "The way I look at it, justice is served. I doubt that I'll be able to make that strong a case, anyway, and it saves the county the cost of a couple of expensive trials."

I was a little worried when I went to the judge to warn him what I was up to. I was well aware I was playing fast and loose with the due process of law, but I need not have worried. "At one point, I would have raked you over the coals for something like this, John," he told me. "Facing death seems to have made me much more flexible. I agree that justice is well served in both cases, and if they became involved in the judicial process, justice might well be denied. The only thing that concerns me is that this not become a habit with you. So I will extract a promise for my cooperation. When I am gone, you will exercise great prudence in staying within the framework of the law when you do your job. I need your word on it."

SEVENTEEN

Transitions

There was a birth in our family in late May that year, 1958, and two funerals in June. The birth, of course, was the child Milly and I conceived long before we were formally married. The way we looked at things, we had become married in our hearts almost from the beginning. The baby arrived on Memorial Day, liberating Dr. Pettigrew from a dismal afternoon and evening with some distant relatives.

"I don't want you to get the wrong idea, Sheriff," he added and I knew he had something up his sleeve. "I actually like distant relatives. I wish all my relatives would be distant – and stay there!"

The birth of our child set the local gossip chain rattling, of course, as people counted the months on their fingers. It was known that the baby weighed in at over eight pounds, seven ounces, far too big to be premature. While I am sure various opinions were conveyed with great conviction, I was far too busy to pay them much mind. Someone once told me that it really isn't any of our business what other people think of us, and I agree. There is very little we can do to control what other people think, or what they say behind our backs. Our friends know better than to believe the evil spoken of us, and our enemies will never acknowledge our goodness. I prefer to let them choke on their own malice.

I didn't know it at the time, but Dr. Pettigrew was a little worried about Milly. She was a little old to be having her first child and it was clear she would have a large baby. As it turned out, she was in labor less than eight hours and the delivery was smooth and without complications. When he was done, Dr. Pettigrew said to me, "Your wife is an amazing woman, John. Toward the end, when most women are screaming their heads off, she was very calm and I heard her mumbling something.

Then I realized she was praying, not for herself, either, but for you and the kids and the baby who was arriving. I think that's what got her through. I wish they were all that easy."

Then it was over and Milly was holding our newborn son. Smiling at me, she said, "I would like to name our son Simon, after your grandfather, John Paul. Do you mind?"

"Of course not," I said. "Grandpa Simon was my favorite relative growing up. How did you know his name? I don't remember talking about him."

"We haven't. I was out to the graveyard one day and happened to see gravestone for a Simon Stone. Then I asked someone who might know and was told who he was." She chuckled. "They told me a lot more than I wanted to know, too. I think the name is beautiful. I like the way it sounds, Simon Stone."

"It kind of goes together, doesn't it?"

"I want to have him baptized right away, too," she told me. "Are you all right with that?"

"Yes, I am. Let's have Travis and Buzz for his godfathers."

"What about the judge?" Milly asked.

"The judge is his honorary grandfather," I said. "Would you mind calling him Simon David?"

"Yes, but I don't want to call him by a nickname."

I shrugged. "I don't know. After going through childbirth, it seems fitting to call him Big Sigh."

"You're terrible," she said, but she was smiling.

Things at the office slowed down after the high school graduation a week before the baby was born, and I was grateful for that. The strategy I mapped out with Anita and Granger Woods worked quite well and that pretty much wrapped things up with the Roadhouse cases. There were no arrests or convictions, but I was able to close the cases. When I went to visit Mike Simms, he remained surly until I explained to him whose daughter he had beaten. Tough as the man might be, he turned pale when the consequences sank in. Then I offered him the alternative and he jumped at it. The judge handed him a ten year sentence without a chance of parole, and Simms never turned a hair.

Even so, Mike never served but three months of his sentence. He was killed in a quarrel with another inmate in the prison bus transferring them between TDC units. As far as anyone could ascertain, there was no connection between Robbins, the prisoner who killed Mike, and the Civello family. Robbins was a machinist who had been sent down on a charge of vehicular manslaughter while intoxicated, and he successfully claimed self-defense in the fight with Mike. He was much smaller than Simms and all the other inmates on the bus swore that it was Mike who started the fight. Robbins had only hit Simms once, unintentionally landing a solid blow that connected with Mike's larynx. Simms was dead from asphyxia before they could get him to medical care.

Not long after that, Granger Woods turned the copy of the Roadhouse books I'd made over to some of his friends at the IRS. As he suspected, what we had turned out to be the real books and Carmello Conti, commonly known as Gaylord Smith, took the fall for the family. He was indicted of fourteen counts of income tax evasion. He was sent away for two years per count, but the federal judge in charge of his case had been burned by the Civello family. He ordered Carmello's sentences to be served in sequence. This meant Conti was looking at twenty-eight years in prison. Not that it mattered. Six months after starting his first sentence in a medium security federal prison, Carmello was found dead in the exercise yard. He had been stabbed through the heart with a shank made by sharpening the end of a toothbrush.

Nor was it hard to figure out why this happened or who ordered it. Alfonso Colombo had to do some fancy footwork to keep being taken down for the same charges. It took a young clerk in his office acknowledging that it was his fault for intentionally giving his boss the wrong figures. According to the clerk, it was Carmello Conti who ordered him to do this or be shot, and the prosecutor knew he was licked. Since it was his first offense, ever, the clerk was sentenced to two years, and three weeks after his release, married Anita Colombo. A grandson arrived on the scene less than a year later and Alfonso moved his son-in-law to the main office, where he put him in charge of auditing the family's legitimate business. Like many mobsters, Colombo craved respectability and he was determined that his daughter and grandson would have it.

I am sad to say we never made an arrest for the murder of Jeremy Barker, even though the case was eventually closed. I kept digging when I had a spare minute, but those didn't come too often after Simon was born. Mary Alice jumped into the care of her youngest brother, often beating Milly or me to the crib when Simon cried at night. I finally had to put down my foot with her. Even though she enjoyed taking care of Simon, I told her, the first priority was to go to school and get herself a good education. I unfortunately pointed out that she was still growing and needed her sleep.

Louis jumped in just then and said, "Yeah, she's growing fat!" I told him he was lucky she didn't have a frying pan in her hand when he said it.

"Yeah!" she said. "The big one!"

Ever the negotiator, Mary Alice did talk us into allowing her to take care of Simon on Friday and Saturday nights. This was a real gift to Milly and me and Louis nicked named his sister *mamacita*, which, literally translated, means little mother. They called my bride Mama Milly and myself, Papa John. Yet the way they said it sounded like one word, Papajon, and that's what Simon called me, too, almost from the start.

❧

The first funeral came in early June, not long after Simon arrived. The Honorable David Allen White, district judge of Rutherford County, died quietly in his sleep from complications related to his cancer. Yet, his mind was sharp to the end and he had been able to hold his namesake in his arms the day before. Dr. Pettigrew told me that looking forward to holding Simon was what kept the judge alive the last few weeks of his life.

The funeral was at the small Episcopal Church in Live Oak, and the building was packed. When we arrived, the funeral director asked the five of us to sit in the family area just behind the pall bearers, and the padre asked me if I would do the reading from the Old Testament. I said I would, but when I looked at the selection he wanted read, I almost came undone.

It was from the sixty-first chapter of Isaiah, the passage that talks about healing the broken hearted, setting the captives free, and comforting all who mourn.

I was grateful to the padre for giving me a little time to pull myself together before I had to read. Then, when the bell rang to start the service, Milly got up and walked to the back of the church. There she sang "Morning has Broken" a cappella while the funeral procession walked in behind the cross, bearing the plain casket the judge had requested. I had never heard her sing so well and by the time the song was done, there weren't many dry eyes in the house. Even the padre was having a hard time keeping his composure.

I know a lot of folk prefer spontaneous worship, but I felt a great comfort in the solemn opening ritual that ended with a prayer by the padre. After the prayer it was time for me to read and I managed to make it through somehow. I was surprised later on when a number of folk told me how well I'd done.

Someone else led us in reciting the twenty-third psalm. That was calming but I almost fell apart again when a piper marched in from the back of the church playing "Amazing Grace." He marched up to the casket, then kept step in place facing the casket as we sang all four verses. When we came to the last one, I thought the roof was going to go flying off the church. By the time the hymn done, I felt like I'd been put through a wringer.

I also found a lot of comfort in the padre's sermon that followed, and the rest of the service went well. Yet, the surprises weren't done. Once we were all gathered back at the parish hall, the padre called for our attention. As he slipped out of his robes, he told us that the judge had asked him for a personal favor. Then he nodded to the piper, who broke into a wild Irish reel, and the padre started dancing. A moment later Landon burst out of the crowd and joined the good father dancing while the crowd clapped in time and cheered. My feet were still twitching in time as we drove home. I couldn't think of a better send-off for a truly great man.

⁂

Even knowing it was coming, the death of the judge hit me hard. He had been such an important part of my life that I felt lost for months. I could accept his death in my mind, but not in my heart, and for a long time it was all I could do to finish the simplest tasks. I would catch myself staring off into the distance with no idea how I had come to be wherever I was, or why I was there.

It was Milly who gave me a way of coming to terms with the loss. She bought me a spiral notebook and a couple of pencils, and told me to write down every memory I had of the man. Then, at supper time, when we had talked about everything under the sun, she'd ask me to tell her and the kids a story about the judge. Most of these were very short, but they reminded me of how much goodness the judge brought into my life. I filled four notebooks and was working on the fifth when I stopped writing. Somewhere in the process, the sadness began to be displaced by the joy I remembered.

Telling these stories also had an unintended result that brought a lot of grace to our life as a family. I might ask the kids what they wanted to do next Saturday and one of them might say, "Why don't we (fill in the blank) like you and the judge did that time when you were growing up?" The blank might be anything from going to the state fair in Dallas to gathering pecans in the fall to going to the rodeo.

There were a few of these things we did more than once, like gathering pecans or wild plums, and they became regular things we did. Yet there were many others that were one time events. Going to the fireworks display at the Cotton Bowl on the Fourth of July was one of those things, as was driving down to Austin to see the capital building or watching the state legislature in session. Most of the time Milly and Simon went with us, but sometimes it was just us three. I think it was these kinds of adventures, along with our daily life together, that really made Louis and Mary Alice our children. It seemed to heal my grief, as well.

※

The second funeral that June was nothing but sad. Where there was joy mixed in with the sadness when we buried the judge, the second funeral held no joy. What made it so heart rending was how senseless the events were that led to it. For the man we buried on the last day of June in that year of our Lord, 1958, was none other than Samuel Ray Brown, Milly's youngest brother.

The way we found out about Sammy was through a phone call from the hospital in the wee hours of the morning. There had been a shooting at the Roadhouse, and while the clerk who called wasn't sure who all had been shot, one of the victims was asking for Milly Bates. Nor could the doctor or a nurse come to the phone to clarify. There was more than one victim and everyone was busy trying to keep them all alive.

I was reluctant to leave the kids by themselves, but Mary Alice had awoken when the phone rang. She insisted that she was perfectly capable of looking after the baby while we were gone. I was surprised when Milly agreed with her, pointing out that she, herself, had to take over at age sixteen when her mother died. She reminded me that Mary Alice had just turned sixteen and could call any of the neighbors if she needed help. She pointed out that our daughter could also drive either of our vehicles quite well, if necessary. I realized at that point that I was outnumbered and did what sensible men have done in such circumstances since the beginning of time. I agreed and Milly and I left for the hospital.

"I have a bad feeling about this, John," Milly told me as we drove in. I wasn't running the siren, but I did have my red emergency light going and was wasting no time. Normally it takes about fifteen minutes to get to town over the dirt roads we had to travel, but that day I made it in ten.

When I checked in with the emergency room clerk, she sent us down the hall to what was normally the recovery room for surgery and deliveries. This was a large open room with several screened treatment bays for gurneys. Only one of these was occupied just then and the doctor and two nurses were working on the patient.

The doctor was surprised when I stuck my head around the curtain. "Good!" he said. "Is your wife with you?"

Milly looked in just then and the doctor waved her over to the gurney. "This patient has been asking for you. He's drifting in and out of awareness."

Milly gasped when she saw who it was. "Sammy?" she asked.

I was right behind her. "It's her younger brother," I told the doctor.

"Milly?" Sammy said weakly. "Are you there?"

"Yes, Sammy, I am," she answered, taking his hand,

"I'm so cold," he told her. "Is John with you?"

"Yes, Sammy, I'm here, too," I answered, moving to the other side of the gurney.

"I don't think I'm going to make it," he said. "I need to get some things off my chest."

"Do you want me to call the padre?" I asked.

"No," he said. "I want to do the right thing. I've been covering up a murder. Two of them."

I felt a chill run down my spine. "Listen to me, Sam. I'm the sheriff. If you tell me, I'll have to do something about it. I may have to arrest you. If you tell the padre, no one else will ever know."

At that point, my brother-in-law smiled. "You're the strangest lawman I ever met. Every other one wanted to bust me."

"Let me call the padre, Sam," I said, nodding to the doctor. He nodded to the nurse and she left the room.

Sammy nodded. "You're the only one who ever called me that," he told me. "Except for my dad. Milly used to call me Toad." Then Sammy flinched and groaned. "I don't have time to wait," he told me, and he began to talk.

"It was Jeremy Barker they killed," he said. "He knew we were blackmailing Lew Tucker and he threatened to tell you."

This was bad. Lew was the chair of our board of county commissioners. "Who was doing the blackmailing?"

"Gaylord Smith. He had me take some pictures of Lew with Jeremy down at one of the lake cabins. They were doing it."

"Sam, I need you to be specific," I told him. I felt Milly looking at me but stayed focused on Sammy. "What were they doing?"

A look of distaste came over my brother-in-law's face. "You know, John, queer stuff. They both got naked and were.... I don't want my sister to hear this."

"It's all right, Sam," I told him. "I don't need specifics. They were having sex, weren't they?" Sammy nodded. "I need to hear you say yes or no, Sam," I told him.

"Yes, they were having sex the way queers do."

"And you were taking pictures?"

"Yes."

"What happened to the pictures?" I asked.

"Gaylord had me develop them," he told me. "He asked me to make two sets of prints. I made three. I gave two of them to Gaylord. I think he gave a set to Lew Tucker."

"So who actually killed Jeremy?" I asked.

"Mike Simms. I saw him do it. I also heard Gaylord tell him to kill Jeremy."

"What happened to the third set of prints?" I asked.

"I hid them at Oliver's place in...." He gasped and fell back, holding his belly. His face turned a ghastly pale green.

Just then I felt someone beside me. It was the Episcopal priest. "This man needs to make confession, Father," I told him.

The padre nodded and I took Milly's hand and led her from the room. She was weeping quietly and clung to me. Not more than three minutes later, the padre came out to where we were standing. "That was close," he said. "Thank God I got here when I did." Then he looked at my bride. "I'm sorry, Miss Milly. Your brother is dead. I did hear his confession. He repented and died in a state of grace."

Milly nodded dumbly. "Thank you, Father," she said.

"I'm glad I could be of help," he answered, shaking his head. "Is there anything I can do for either of you?"

Milly actually smiled. "No," she told him. "Thank you anyway, Father. I married my confessor."

⁂

I called Buzz from the hospital and asked him to get the cruiser and pick me up at the office in an hour. I told him about the Roadhouse shooting and told him I'd talk with his boss. Then I took my bride home,changed into a uniform shirt, and carried the kids to school. Milly told me she and Simon would pick them up that afternoon if I couldn't shake loose. "I know you have to go, John," she told me with a sad smile. "Don't worry about me. I'll be all right. I've survived worse and I have

Simon for company."

When I got to the office I called ahead and told Gaylord Smith of that we were coming. This was some time before he went to prison. I asked him to have the staff who had witnessed the shooting available for us to interview. It was only then that I was told there had been an attempted robbery and that Sammy was shot by one of the robbers. I told him we would be there right away.

"So he told you there had been a robbery?" Buzz asked when I told him what Smith had said. "You think that's horse apples or for real?"

I realized just then that my mind was still in the emergency room with Sammy and my bride. "Buzz," I said. "I'm a little too close to this one, Sammy being kin and all. Why don't you take lead? I'll be second fiddle and jump in if necessary."

"Yes, sir!" Buzz answered and smiled. This was the first time I'd given him the lead in a major investigation. Nor was there any reason not to.

Gaylord Smith, as I still think of him, was waiting for us when we got to the Roadhouse. There was a hard-bitten younger man waiting with him whom he introduced as Mario Gatti. I am not sure exactly what niche Gatti filled in the organization, but he had MOB written all over him.

"That was bad news about Sammy," Smith told us. "He was one of my key men. I was lucky to have Mario here to cover for him."

"So you were already here," Buzz responded, looking at Gatti. "How come?"

"We were kicking around new ideas for the place," Smith answered.

Buzz looked at Gaylord. "Sir, it will be better if you let Mr. Gatti speak for himself."

I was proud of my deputy and I saw the ghost of a smile cross Gatti's lips. "What he said is true," Mario told us in a heavy Sicilian accent. "We're thinking about ways we can make the place pay better." He shrugged.

Buzz nodded and looked at Smith. "All right. How did Sammy get shot?"

Smith looked at Gatti before answering but there was no response I could see. "There were these three guys who tried to hold us up late last night," he told us. "Sammy was on duty and tried to stop the robbery. So they shot him. He shot back and hit one of them and they took off."

"I think this will go faster if you talk to Mr. Smith while I talk to Mr. Gatti," I told Buzz. I pointed to a table on the other side of the room. "If you please, Mr. Gatti."

"Of course, Deputy," he answered me. There was nothing in his voice but his eyes challenged me. "That's Sheriff Stone to you, Mario," I corrected him. I saw him flush. Yet he followed me to the table and sat down. "Were you in the room when it happened?" I asked.

"No," he answered. His tone told me all I would get out of him would be curt answers. That was all right. I had all the time I needed to get what I was after and I sat quietly for a long time looking at him. Then I smiled. "Tough guy," I said. "I think we're going to hold you for a while," I said. There was no response to this so I stood up and said, "Stand up, turn around, and put your hands behind your back."

"You busting me?" Gatti asked.

"Yeah," I said, motioning him to turn around. Clear across the room I saw Smith's head snap around toward us and he started to get up. Buzz pushed him back down into his chair but he kept watching. He was clearly worried and I suspected Gatti was his boss.

"How come?" Gatti demanded, ignoring Smith.

I shrugged. "Obstruction of justice. You know what I want to know."

"I ain't no mind reader," Gatti fired back.

"That's too bad," I said. "Maybe some time in the cooler will help you figure it out,"

"My lawyer will have me out before morning," he declared.

"Not in Buford County," I told him. "That's where we send tough guys like you."

"We'll see about that," he told me.

"We certainly will," I said with a smile. "Now turn around or do I have to put you on the floor?" Gatti glared at me but he turned around and I cuffed him. "Carry on," I told Buzz as I took our prisoner out to the cruiser.

When I came back in I used the phone in Smith's office and gave Huck Rawlins a call. I caught him in the office and I think he was surprised to get the call. "I got a live one for you, Huck," I told him. "He's a tough guy from Cowtown – a gangster – and I don't want him corrupting our prisoners."

Huck laughed when I told him this. "I imagine we can get him to see the light," he replied. "How long do you want us to hold him?"

"As long as you can," I told him. "He's a mob hot shot and I imagine he'll have a high priced lawyer showing up pretty quick."

Huck chuckled. "Then we'll put him in the same cage with his client. That will give them lots of time to talk."

I laughed when Rawlins said this. I thought he was joking but I should have known better. That is exactly what he did. Nor did Huck allow either Gatti or his shyster to use the phone. It took a personal call from the Attorney General and a personal visit by a Texas Ranger to get the two released. When he called to let me know, I thanked Rawlins for his trouble and told him to send us the bill. "Not a problem, John," he told me. "You can send birds like that over any time. We had fun playing host."

❧

Buzz told me Smith became a lot more cooperative after seeing me march Gatti out of the Roadhouse. Gaylord kept trying to get away to use the phone, but Buzz kept at him until he was satisfied Smith was telling the full truth. I was there for the last part of it, and Buzz did a good job with Smith.

Smith said that three men armed with sawed-off shotguns had burst into the Roadhouse right after closing and attempted to rob the place. This was a very foolish thing to do, of course. No sooner had the bandits made their demand for money, than all the waiters cleaning the tables had hit the floor and Sammy had opened up with his pistol from behind the bar. Two of the bouncers had started firing, too, and one of the robbers went down. One of the other robbers grabbed him by the arm and pulled him out of the main room while the other tried to cover them. He was outgunned by then and was hit in the arm. Even so, the robber kept firing, hitting Sammy just before he ducked out the door.

By the time the armed bouncers got to the front parking lot, the robbers were in their car, roaring off at high speed. Several shots were fired after them and one took out a tail light. The car was described as an older fastback Chevrolet sedan, one of dozens like it in the county.

As far as we could tell, the whole attempt took less than three minutes. Smith told Buzz that the bouncers were running for a car to make pursuit when he called them back. Nothing had been taken and, aside from Sammy's wounds and those of two of the waiters hit by stray shotgun pellets, the damages were minor. A few of bottles of liquor on the back bar had been broken and there were a number of holes in the walls, but nothing else. Smith told Buzz his main concern was to get Sammy and the waiters to the hospital. Rather than waiting for an ambulance, he had sent the bouncers to take them.

After Smith finished his account, we examined the main room for evidence. Since the robbers had been armed with shotguns, there were no bullets to dig out of the walls but those fired by Sammy and the bouncers. Buzz didn't see much sense in going after those, but I insisted and we found fourteen slugs. We also found a lot of blood on the floor where the robber had bled while being dragged out of the room, and we scraped some of that up for matching blood type in case the robbers were caught. I suspected they never would be, at least not by us. The mob takes attacks like this as a personal affront and I was sure the Civello family would find the robbers and make sure they never did it again.

Once we were done digging out slugs and a few single-ought shotgun pellets, Buzz and I took a look at Sammy's room. I was surprised how neat and orderly it was. There were not many personal possessions aside from Sammy's clothes. Yet there was a framed picture of Milly and I set it apart when we packed Sammy's possessions. I knew Milly would like to have it and I didn't see how we might need it for evidence. There were also some letters from her dated several years before, and I set those aside, too.

The sun was getting high by the time we left the Roadhouse and I asked Buzz to dictate his report to Cheryl before going to work at Charlie's. "I sure wish you could afford a full time deputy," he answered.

"Charlie would never forgive me," I replied and he laughed. "I'll run it by the county commissioners again," I added. "With all this extra work, I could use the help. Can you afford to work for what they'll pay? You probably earn more than I do."

Buzz grimaced and shook his head. "You're right, Sheriff. I can't. Why don't you hold off asking for a while?"

I nodded. What neither of us mentioned was the possibility that I might not win the election coming up that fall. Not that it worried me. The Department of Public Safety had been trying to recruit me as an investigator for years. With a wife and three kids I could use the extra pay. Yet, it would mean being away from home a lot more and I really didn't like that much. I really liked being with my family. How do you put a price on that?

While Buzz was dictating his report to Cheryl, I wrote mine out longhand. Buzz was gone by the time I finished and I asked Cheryl to have both reports ready for us to correct by quitting time. Then I headed for home, taking along the picture and letters I'd found in Sammy's room.

It was clear that Milly had been crying when I got home, but she set aside the letters when I gave them to her. "I'll look at those later, John Paul," she said, holding me tight. "Right now I need you to hold me and make love to me."

Our love was gentle and tender that afternoon. Afterwards we lay quietly, holding one another close. Milly had her head on my chest when my stomach started growling and she laughed. "Poor John," she said. "You had to go to work without breakfast and your wife didn't fix you lunch."

I touched her in a tender place. "I'm not complaining," I said. "As a matter of fact...."

"No, you don't," Milly laughed, slipping out of bed. The sight of her standing there with no clothes was so inspiring I lunged for her, but she danced out of reach. "You've got to let me eat, first," she said, smiling. At the sight of her wonderful walk as she went out the door, I groaned. "Shush," she said, blowing me a kiss. "I'll take care of him later."

❧

I headed for Oliver's place after lunch. As I drove there I thought about where Sammy might have put the set of pictures he took of Lew Tucker and Jeremy. I also thought about bringing murder charges against Gaylord Smith and Mike Simms, but I knew it would be hard to get a conviction with no more than Sammy's deathbed confession. Smith would get the best legal talent available and it would take a confession from Mike to make the case. As far as I could see, there was nothing Mike could gain by confessing but more jail time. That was not much incentive.

Having the pictures Sammy took might make the difference, but bringing them into evidence would blow the lid off the Rutherford County Commission. I wasn't sure this would be a good thing and the judge wasn't there to talk it over. The main reason I wanted to find the pictures was to keep them from falling into the wrong hands.

The question was where Sammy might hide the photos. Had Sammy said one more word it would have narrowed the search, but I decided he wouldn't have put the set where Milly might discover them. That pretty much ruled out the house. So I thought about other places that would be dry enough to keep the prints from spoiling. The first place that came to mind was the barn, but that had been destroyed by the tornado. I didn't think Sammy would want the prints to fall into Oliver's hands, either. So it needed to be some place too inaccessible for Oliver to bother looking if he was searching for something else.

I was still thinking about this when I got to Oliver's farm. As I was getting out of the cruiser, I was struck by an urgent call of nature and headed directly for the outhouse. "Sorry, Oliver," I said, dropping my pants and taking a seat, hoping a black widow spider didn't take my intrusion for an opportunity to attack.

Not having anything better to do, I looked around while I sat there. Like the rest of the buildings on the place, the outhouse was well built. This was not on Oliver's part. The man who had left him the place was a good carpenter and he had made the outhouse to last. The walls were well fitted and showed no gaps, and the roof was, too. The only thing out of place was a single asphalt shingle nailed to part of the roof. This seemed like an odd thing to do, but it was the kind of repair Oliver might make if there was a leak. Yet, the shingle was very carefully nailed square with the walls, and the black side was down. There seemed to be more nails than necessary, and these were quite evenly spaced around the edges of the shingle. In short, this didn't look like Oliver's work and I thought Milly would have had the good sense to put the shingle on top of the roof.

This intrigued me, so I finished up my business and shoveled in some ashes. When I did, I noticed that it looked like no one had shoveled ashes for a good while. This made sense since no one was living at the place, but it also said the outhouse had not had visitors lately. Putting the flap down over the hole, I took out my pocket knife and cut away one corner of the shingle. As I tore the shingle back, the corner of a craft envelope appeared and I cut away the rest of the shingle. The envelope was sealed and I opened it with my pocket knife. Inside was exactly what I thought I'd find, nine eight by ten glossy black and white pictures of Lew Tucker in the buff with a young man. It was clearly Jeremy Barker and he was clearly naked, too.

I looked inside the envelope again and found a smaller business envelope. Opening it, I found several strips of black and white negatives, and when I held them up to the light, I could see they were the negatives to the photos I held. Replacing everything as it was when I found it, I took the photos and the negatives and sat there a while, thinking.

My first inclination was to burn the photos and the negatives. Yet they were evidence of a crime. Homosexual behavior was a felony in Texas back then and the photos left no doubt what the naked men were doing. Then it occurred to me that I could put these photos to use getting Lew's cooperation on the Board of Commissioners. This would involve blackmail, pure and simple, and I didn't know if I wanted to take the first step down that slippery slope to corruption. Even though I intended to use it for good, I wondered if I would later be able to withstand the temptation to use the evidence for my own benefit. From what I have seen in others, power is more addictive than heroin. I have seen it destroy a lot of good men.

Not knowing what else to do, I headed back to the office and locked the envelope in the evidence safe. The next morning I put the evidence in a new craft envelope and sealed and dated it. Then I rented a safe deposit box and locked it away. Only then did I go and have a heart to heart talk with Lew Tucker about our need to exercise integrity on the county board. Once he understood I wasn't out to shake him down or send him to prison, he settled down and agreed to what I proposed. I think he may even have felt a little relieved at being forced to do the right thing.

Down the Years

That's the story of how Milly and I got together and our first year. It's been a lot of years now, good years I never dreamed would happen for me. I'm still the county sheriff, though I don't know if I'll stand for reelection when my term is up next year. I keep saying that, but I always find a reason to stay and the voters seem to think I should, too. The only time an election has been close was the one right after I married Milly. I won by only seventy-three votes, and that was shaved down to fifty-one in the recount. Since then, I discovered that a lot of residents in the local cemeteries voted for my opponent and that the new crowd out at the Roadhouse was behind this. As the judge said on many occasions, knowing it is one thing. Proving it is another, and I didn't waste my time trying to dig up evidence.

The Roadhouse survived the tax audit by going out of business. Even though it folded, the doors were never shut. Another outfit bought the assets at fire sale prices, ten cents on the dollar, and it was business as usual under a different name. The new outfit, of course, was another corporation owned by the Civello family. It went into business as the Live Oak Roadhouse Resort. So when the dust settled, the place was still known as the Roadhouse and very little actually changed. They did add a golf course and a sauna off the locker room, and they expanded the dining room. The place became half way respectable, though everyone knew the same things went on behind the scenes.

One thing that did change was corruption on the Board of County Commissioners. With Lew's help, I was able to get the goods on the dirty commissioners, and most of them saw the light when we confronted them. The one hold-out found himself nailed by the IRS and ended up a guest at one of the federal country clubs designated as "camps." I know a lot of folk might not see this as the right way of doing things, but it worked without their families paying the price of the dad's mistakes. Nor did I ever abuse the power contained in my safety deposit box.

All that is almost twenty years behind us now. Following my footsteps, Louis went into the Coast Guard and became very popular as the mess chief on a destroyer. When his time was up, he went to school on the GI Bill and eventually became a chef *cordon blieu*. These days he lives in Austin with his wife and kids, and they visit Live Oak several times a year.

Mary Alice became a public school teacher when she graduated from college and has worked in Cowtown ever since graduation. She married late to a classical musician who plays with the Ft. Worth symphony and is known as one of the top cellists in the country. After a couple of years they had a daughter who, under the influence of her Uncle Louis, calls her mother mamacita.

Simon is a mystery to me. He is a very quiet, self contained young man who has little to say but who seems to like his Pop. Growing up during the raging 'sixties, he chose to follow a career as a mathematician and became a master hacker when computers came along. I have absolutely no idea what he actually does now, but he tells me he is a cyber cop. He also became a master guitarist and put himself through college with weekend gigs on the metropolitan circuit. I know that when he did a local benefit concert for a family with cancer, the Ft. Worth Telegram wrote about it ahead of time and several hundred fans showed up from all over the state. The writer described his fretwork as "liquid gold" and, like his mother, he has the voice of an angel.

As for my bride, she gets more beautiful each passing day and things between us get even better than I could have imagined. Nor have things always been easy. The rumors that were going around after we married cut Milly to the heart, as did the slim margin by which I won the election that fall. The wonderful pastor we had when we met was transferred to another church by his conference, and the man they sent in his place was a disaster. Within a year of his appointment, had an affair with a young parishioner half his age and precipitated a divorce in the congregation. The woman was the congregational treasurer and about fifty thousand dollars went missing from the building fund. Unfortunately, there was no evidence the city police found that would hold up in court, and even a special investigator from the state came up dry. These days it might be a different story, but back then it was very difficult to follow the paper trail if a thief knew what she was doing. What was surprising is how few people left the church over this.

I know all these things disturbed my bride greatly, but she never faltered. When things got bad, she spent more time in prayer, and when she sang, there was rarely a dry eye in the pews. There was a deep, tragic beauty in her voice that was strangely uplifting. When she was done, there was always a long, still silence before we began to breathe again. Nor was there any mistaking the joy in Milly's face while she sang. Sometimes that joy lasted all day.

Eventually things got better, though one of the great disappointments we lived with was having no more children after Simon. This was not for want of trying or desire. We wanted at least two more but something happened when our youngest son was born. We even went to specialists but the cause was as great a mystery to them as it was to us. Finally, we accepted the situation for what it was and life went on more easily.

Nor did we stop hoping or doing the things that might lead to a child. We just put things into the hands of the Boss and went about being a well married couple deeply in love. "Who knows?" Milly told me one day. "Abraham's wife, Sarah, was an old woman when she had Isaac. Maybe I'll get my miracle then, too."

"We've already had three miracle children," I told her.

"I know," she replied. "I guess I'm just greedy." Then she gave me that wonderful look she knew got me going and said, "Speaking of being greedy...."

Not too long after that we got the news that Travis and Kate were expecting their first child. Milly was as excited as if it was her own and after the baby arrived I flew her out to be with Kate for a couple of weeks. It was the first time my bride had ever been in an airplane and she was as excited as a child at Christmas. The kids went with me to drop her off and again to pick her up, and it took all week for her to tell us about the trip. What really meant a lot to her was that Travis and Kate had named their son Samuel after his late uncle.

❦

There were other changes in town, too. Buzz took the test for highway patrol and scored high enough that the DPS practically dragged him to Austin to attend the academy. His wife didn't like this much and stayed in Live Oak while he was in training. Then, when he got his first assignment she gave him an ultimatum. According to the gossip telegraph, she told him that there was no way in hell she was going to move to Dalhart, Texas, or any other God forsaken place the DPS sent him.

When Buzz came to me to talk about this, I asked him if the highway patrol was what he really wanted to do. "I've always wanted to be a state trooper," he told me. "Ever since I was a little kid, that was what I wanted. Nothing personal, John, but being a part time deputy doesn't pack it. I couldn't ask for better bosses than you and Charlie, but this really is what I want to do. The money is as good as I'm getting now, a little better, in fact, and I hate to pass up this opportunity."

"Then go for it," I told him. "You're the bread winner, so it's got to be your decision. It may be that your wife will come around once she understands how strongly you feel about it. It's got a whole lot better future. This town is dying, Buzz. It has been since the war. DPS offers a greater opportunity for promotion and there's a chance you might make special investigator."

Sadly enough, Buzz's wife didn't see it that way at all, not even when her dad, Charlie, told her Buzz was right. "This town is good for another twenty years at most," he told her. "The handwriting's on the wall, and if I could sell out now, I would. There's nothing here for a sharp guy like Buzz, no future, so to speak."

Fortunately, there were no children yet. When Buzz left for Dalhart for his first assignment, he was alone. Charlie tried to put his daughter to work as the parts manager of his dealership, but he ended up making her the agency go-fer. When he added cleaning the office and show room to her duties, she quit and went to Houston to live with her mother.

Charlie was more accurate about the future of the town than anyone thought. One business after another closed its doors when the owner died or moved away, and little came in to replace them. Live Oak lost population with the 1960 census, and even more with the next two. The only thing that kept the town afloat was being the county seat and the residual business from the oil boom forty years before.

With the decline, some of the local characters began to disappear, too. Neville was killed when an illegal still he had an interest in exploded, spelling the end of the moonshine era in Rutherford County. Thom Jacobs, the administrator of the nursing home, was indicted when one of his patients died of neglect. He barely managed to keep from getting convicted and the civil suit that followed his criminal trail put him out of business. Not only did he lose his business, he lost his license to be in the business and that spelled the end of him in Live Oak. Nobody else offered him a job.

Not long after this Sheriff Huck Rawlins of neighboring Buford County was killed by one of his inmates in the county jail. His history of abuse came out at the trial of his killer, and the jury found the accused legally insane at the time of the homicide. Huck had been torturing the man when the prisoner snapped and went berserk, not only killing Huck but putting two of his deputies in the hospital. Oddly enough, the man surrendered quietly to the jailer and called a good lawyer the next day. The trial was moved to Live Oak, and our good folk talked about the abuse the prisoner had suffered for months after that.

One other odd thing that happened was a letter that came to the office about five years after Milly and I married. There was no return address, but the postmark was from somewhere in South Dakota. When I opened it up, I discovered it was from Nancy Hiller, though her name was different by then. She had ended up in Great Falls, Montana, where she worked as a clerk at the airforce base. It was there she met a dashing young lieutenant who convinced her she needed to be his bride. The delightful irony is that the lieutenant was a Swede and when his time in service was up, they ended up living in Minneapolis. At the time Nancy wrote, they were expecting their second child.

⁂

There was another odd coincidence I've saved for very last. When Oliver died intestate and without children, the land he had inherited went to Milly. She wanted no part of it and I had to talk myself blue in the face to keep her from abandoning any claim to it. She refused to sell it, but what she finally agreed to was to put the place in trust for our children, along with any rent or royalties it produced. While she retained title to the place, I agreed to act as the executive trustee and managed to make the trust a good bit of money from leasing both the surface and mineral rights over the years. At first this money went to pay off the liens against the place, but then it went into the special trust account.

Even so, this took a lot of time I'd rather have spent doing almost anything else. Yet, about five years after Oliver died, I gave up asking Milly if she had changed her mind about selling. Our older kids were getting close to college age and I wanted to set up a financial trust they could draw on for tuition and books, as well as room and board. Fortunately, Mary Alice was able to land an excellent scholarship and Louis went into the Coast Guard. So their schooling wasn't the burden I thought it might be.

Then, about ten years after I found the pictures of Lew Tucker with Jeremy Barker, the bank called one day to remind me my safe deposit box rent was due. I told them to close the account and went down to pick up the evidence I had gathered against the commissioners over the years. I decided it was time to destroy what I had and I decided to burn it.

Not wanting Milly to know what I was doing or why, I went out to Oliver's place to use his old rusty burn barrel. The bottom had rusted out completely, but the sides were good and I used a piece of tin sheeting to catch the burning evidence. I did so mostly to make sure it was completely destroyed.

This worked well and when I was done, I shoveled all the ashes into a tin bucket and mixed them up thoroughly. I was thinking about what to do with the ashes when I remembered what Milly had done with Oliver's remains. It seemed fitting that offal should rest with offal. So I went to the outhouse, which was still standing, and lifted the lid over the toilet hole.

"Hello, Oliver," I said as I poured the ashes over the dusty dry remains at the bottom. "I thought you'd like some company." Then I closed the lid and went home, and it felt like a heavy load had been lifted from my shoulders. Great evil generally begins as a quest for good, and with the evidence gone, I was no longer able to blackmail the commissioners for any good cause. They didn't know that, but what they didn't know would not lead them into temptation.

The coincidence, if you believe in such things, happened after supper that very night. Milly and I were sitting quietly and Simon was busy doing his homework on the kitchen table. I was lost in thought when I heard my bride clear her throat like she does when she wants to talk to me about something important.

"John," she said. "I've been thinking. It's not right for you to have to look after Oliver's farm. You carry a great enough burden with your job."

I shrugged. "I don't mind," I told her, knowing she knew I didn't mean it. "It's for the kids and I don't want to go to the expense of hiring a property manager."

"Yes, that's exactly what I was thinking. I think it's time to let the bank worry about it. Don't you?"

I was confused. "The bank will charge an arm and a leg to manage the farm, sweetheart."

"No, silly man, that's not what I meant. It's time to let the bank manage the money, not the property."

"What money?" I asked. The rents and royalties didn't amount to that much and most of it went to Louis' college fund and Mary Alice's college expenses.

She smiled in that wonderful way she has when I'm being dense. "Silly man, the money we get from selling it."

❧

Coincidence, you say? No, I didn't think so then and I don't think that now. Yet coming to this verdict has raised a lot more questions than it answered. These troubled me until a good friend of mine, a reformed drunk, passed along some wisdom he found in AA. He told me that most people in the fellowship laugh when someone talks about coincidence. To these folk, coincidence is simply a power far greater than ourselves being anonymous.

Unlike Albert Einstein, who coined the expression, these folk aren't joking. To them, the evidence is written boldly across the face of the universe and etched into their souls by the deliverance they have experienced. Most of them consider their recovery a miracle, and most of them will tell you John Newton had it right when he wrote his famous lyrics: "I once was lost, but now am found; was blind but now I see."

OTHER BOOKS BY JOEL B REED

The Jazz Phillips Mystery Series

Murder in the Choir*
Murder by the Board*
Murder in the Kirk*
Murder was a Blast*
Murder by the Queen*
Murder on the Run*
Jazz in the Golden Light*
Jazz in the Cross-hair*
Jazz Plays the Big Easy Blues*
Jazz Draws a Wild Card*

The McKee Clan Intrigue Series

Angels Fight Dirty*
Black Seraph*
Children of Dust*
A Devil on DOS*
Even Angels Cry*

Other Novels

Paul Radford's Private War*
Paul Radford's Alaskan Exile*
Lakota Spring*
Raven Wolf*

* books in print

www.ingramcontent.com/pod-product-compliance
Lightning Source LLC
Chambersburg PA
CBHW071255250626
47159CB00004B/1199